WITHIN YOU, WITHOUT YOU

Sara O'Donovan spent her early years in the UK, brought up in the world of horse racing, but now lives in Ireland with her husband and young family. A former equestrian journalist, horses and writing have been the two constants in her life. This is her first novel.

Within You,
Without You

SARA O'DONOVAN

Valley Press

First published in 2022 by Valley Press
Woodend, The Crescent, Scarborough, YO11 2PW
www.valleypressuk.com

ISBN 978-1-915606-03-7
Cat. no. VP0208

Cover photography by Ben Allan.
Cover and text design by Peter Barnfather.
Edited by Jo Haywood.

Printed and bound in Great Britain
by Clays Ltd, Elcograf S.p.A.

for Steve

'Think… of the world you carry within you.'

– Rainer Maria Rilke

'In the universe,
there are things that are known,
and things that are unknown,
and in between,
there are doors.'

– William Blake

Prologue

Recently, he had come to her in her dreams.

As she slept with the Atlantic waves crashing against the nearby rocks, she met him again. She could not remember what they spoke of or if they had spoken at all. But on waking, she could clutch at the glow of him before it ebbed to that place which lay beyond reach. Until the next time.

And now, although she could hardly make him out on a wet November evening, she knew that he was here again. But this time she was awake and this time he was real. Hunched against the driving rain, hands in pockets, head bowed, walking towards her on a darkening road.

The wipers were no match for the rain streaking down the windscreen so she leant forward, squinting to get a clearer view. She only saw him for a moment before bright lights appeared in her mirror. As the truck bore down, she accelerated past the figure now stepping onto the grass verge. She glanced to the left, glimpsing his face for a few seconds until the truck blasted its horn.

When the truck had rumbled past, leaving a dirty spatter on her windscreen, she pulled over and reversed into a gateway, returning the way she had come. She drove slowly, her heart hammering in her chest, expecting to see him walking towards her.

Nothing.

She stopped the car and jumped out, looking up and down the road. A car appeared, splashing her as it swept past. The red taillights disappearing around the corner.

His name hadn't been on her lips for more than twenty years. But it had been on her mind so often.

'Ed?' she called, timidly at first. 'Ed?' This time louder.

There was nobody there.

But she was certain, more certain than she had ever been, that it had been him. She had recognised his walk, the way he had glanced across at the passing car. She had felt the essence of him.

But a person doesn't just reappear like that.

Not when they died twenty years ago.

Chapter 1

The letter had come a few weeks earlier.

Her mother had never shown any interest in moving over to email, and Kathryn had to admit that she admired her determination to continue writing to virtually everyone she had ever started a correspondence with. She was like that, committed, and expected it of others. Which of course meant she was often disappointed.

Disappointment. Yes, Kathryn understood disappointment.

She opened the small envelope which had been waiting for her on the doormat. The neat handwriting clung to each side of the Basildon Bond paper. Champagne and watermarked – never plain white. Habits that endured.

Putting the letter back into the envelope, she clicked the kettle on. She hadn't seen this coming.

Sitting down at the table with her cup of tea, she looked out of the kitchen window to the garden and beyond to the lighthouse on the peninsula. At night, flashes lit up her bedroom every minute, but over the twenty years she had lived here she had got used to it.

The lighthouse wasn't the only aspect of her life that had become part of her everyday landscape as the years had passed. She looked around her and was once again struck by the thought that this could be someone else's idea of heaven. Living the dream, the newspaper supplements announced whenever they wrote about celebrities who had made their homes in this remote part of Ireland. If it was on a Hollywood actor's wishlist, shouldn't it be enough for an ordinary woman just trying to make her way through life?

This wild promontory where land met sea in the south western corner of County Cork was where Kathryn and Mark had found themselves in their early twenties. It had been Mark's suggestion to load the car up and just drive away from their home town on the Sussex coast, heading to the ferry port at Pembroke and on to a new life across the water. Their families had thought it unusually adventurous of them both and were further staggered to be told a fortnight later that the young couple had not only found jobs but a house to rent. Mark soon found himself in demand as an account-ant in the local town and, before long, Kathryn was pregnant. By the time their landlord decided to sell the house, Mark's salary had grown enough for them to put in an offer and the farmhouse and two acres became theirs.

Those years felt distant now. The enthusiasm with which she had decorated their home in lively shades of rich reds and oranges was now a memory. She had thrown herself into transforming the surrounding wilderness into a lawn and beds of buddleia and rose bushes. Just as the lawn took time to settle, so did she and, by the time the garden was established, the adventure was over and the demands of parenthood had begun.

Maybe everyone feels like this, Kathryn thought as she stirred her tea. Maybe it was normal to live on the edge of dissatisfaction. Maybe the sort of fulfilment that made you gaze out across the sea from your kitchen window with a smile on your face was only for those starting out in life.

The vibration of her phone in her pocket made her jump.

Hi mum, yes all fine. Off to theatre group in a minute. How's dad?

It had taken Alice nearly a day to reply to her mother's text but, still, it was good to hear from her. It wasn't so long since her own university days in the early nineties when having no access to mobile phones meant you could keep your parents at arm's length.

All changed now, she thought, glancing down at her mobile and the letter from her mother.

She tapped out a text to her daughter.

Dad's very well. Have fun tonight and take care.

Words that skated over the surface of meaning. The shorthand of everyday life. She imagined her daughter glancing at the words which said so little yet would give her the reassurance she needed to enjoy her night without giving her parents another thought. What a relief it must be to be able to leave hints of others' unhappiness aside and focus on being young and carefree.

Kathryn knew that domestic life would continue without disruption while she was away. Mark would make sure the dog was fed, the dishwasher filled, the washing hung out to dry. Now that Alice was at college, the chores that came with having a teenage daughter had come to an end – no more driving her to friends' houses or drama lessons, no dirty clothes to pick up off the floor, no mouldy cups to be collected from every surface of her bedroom. Years of endless tasks had stopped abruptly when Alice drove out of the gate at the end of August with her little car loaded up with quilts, clothes and boxes.

Mark had reacted to her mother's letter as expected, with a shrug. As always, he skirted around any possible objections, any complaints that she had to shoulder the burden while her sister moved through life free from responsibility.

'You haven't seen your mum in ages,' he had said with what he probably thought was an encouraging smile. 'It's only for a fortnight. If you can't take care of things while she goes down to help Joyce out, it's a bad job. And besides, it'll be nice to get back to England after all this time.'

Her mother had offered to stay with her sister, Joyce, while she recovered from a hip operation. She had asked Kathryn to come over so she didn't have to ask the neighbours to keep an eye on the house and feed the cat. She wasn't one to be beholden to strangers.

'But why me? I bet she didn't write to Beth.'

'Come on, Kathryn. You're here and Beth's in Boston.'

'And she's got an important job, so she can't leave. Is that it?'

'No, Kathryn, that's not what I'm saying. Although she probably can't. It's easier for you.'

He did what he always did and left the room without making it look as if he were walking away from the early rumblings of an argument.

Kathryn knew she should be glad that he was someone who didn't make a fuss. He never had. When Alice was sick as a toddler, he had been calm and reassuring. When someone had driven into their parked car, he had been reasonable and told her that it was only a car and nobody was hurt.

Yes, life with Mark was calm. Like her parents' marriage had been, it was smooth sailing, without upset. On the surface at least.

Chapter 2

As the plane began its descent into Gatwick airport, the clouds parted to reveal a khaki and brown patchwork of fields. The Irish landscape the plane had risen above just forty-five minutes earlier was richer with greens of every hue. This land was flatter with a busy motorway running east to west like a silver river threading its way between the expansive fields.

As the three lanes of traffic surging along the road came into view, Kathryn wondered how she would ever cope with driving in England again after so many years. The wheels of the plane dropped with a clunk and her ears popped. The ground seemed to be steadily rising to meet her and she closed her eyes and counted. Three, two, one... Kathryn felt the jolt of the plane hitting the tarmac and braced her knees against the seat in front. A screech of tyres and then the rain-lashed land speeding past her window began to slow until finally the plane stopped. People began to unclick their seatbelts, reaching up into the overhead lockers and pulling cases down as she continued to stare out of the window. She was here and would make the best of it. After all, it was only a fortnight.

#

The rain had stopped by the time Kathryn swung the hire car into her mother's driveway. She switched the headlights off and sat for a moment, focusing on the white wall of the bungalow as she braced herself for her homecoming.

She knocked on the front door. Inside the house, a television was quietened.

This didn't feel like home. Indeed it wasn't her home. Her mother Valerie had moved to this secluded housing estate ten years earlier, after the death of Kathryn's father. She hadn't moved far from Kathryn's childhood home but far enough to keep the reminders of what life had been like before they had lost him at a distance.

Kathryn decided not to let her mind wander down that path. Nothing good ever came of it. Losing her dad meant she had lost any chance of their relationship evolving, becoming something different. Somehow, she had always believed there would be time. Time to become close, time to connect as adults rather than as parent and child. Now a parent herself, Kathryn could more easily understand her parents' focus on their children's education. They had only wanted what was best for herself and Beth, even though it hadn't felt like it at the time.

The light came on in the hallway and Kathryn could see the outline of her mother through the frosted glass of the door. A rattle of a chain being unhooked and a key being turned and then the door opened. Her mother, smaller than Kathryn remembered, had the stoop of an elderly woman.

'Hi Mum,' Kathryn said, with a forced smile. She hadn't expected her mother to have aged so visibly.

'Come on in then, Kathryn,' Valerie said, turning back into the house. 'I don't want the cat to get out.'

After dinner, she sat listening to her mother talking about how quiet life was now that she was widowed and living amongst strangers. She was looking forward to staying with Joyce and catching up on old times. Now that Kathryn was here to house- and cat-sit in her absence, Valerie said that she would be on her way tomorrow.

She had mentioned people in her letters and it had been convenient for Kathryn to assume that these were friends. People close by who were somehow able to take the place of daughters who were either busy looking after a young child or looking after a blossoming career on the other side of the world.

'The hospital had Joyce on a waiting list but she'd have to wait a year for her operation. I'm glad I could help her to go private. Your dad had a bit put away in the Post Office. He'd have been happy to help. He always liked Joyce.'

Kathryn gazed at the school photos of herself and Beth that lined the sitting room wall. If she had known, she could have sent money. Beth would have been able to chip in. Surely a high-flying job on Boston's leading newspaper meant she could help the family out when they needed it?

'How is Beth?' Kathryn asked, pushing back her chair and taking her plate to the sink.

'Busy. Well, she's bound to be, with a job like that.'

Kathryn pulled a face, as she had done when she was a teenager. It had always been this way – Beth the achiever, who somehow never had to contribute. Even when their dad died, she could only spare a couple of days before flying back to Boston, to her exciting job and her flat in the salubrious Back Bay area.

Kathryn turned on the hot tap, squirted some bright blue washing up liquid into the bowl and watched the water rise. Her mother had always shunned dishwashers. She said that by the time the machine was filled with crockery, you could have washed, dried and put it all back in the cupboard.

'Beth said she didn't hear from you on her birthday. I

thought you might have rung her,' Valerie said. 'You've only got one sister and one day you might be glad of her.'

Kathryn didn't reply. She and Beth had long since given up any pretence of a close relationship.

As if reading her mind, Valerie continued.

'Why can't you two just get on.'

It wasn't a question but a statement, laced with disapproval.

Kathryn turned the tap off.

'I'm going to ring home. I'll do this afterwards.'

Sitting on the edge of the single bed in her mother's spare room, she stared at her phone. She didn't want to ring home. She wanted to cast back into her memories, for that year with him, bring it up into the light and remember how it had once been. She wanted to feel again.

Chapter 3

She wasn't meant to be there that day. It was unusual for her to be at a racecourse on a Tuesday afternoon in August but one of the lads had called in sick.

While she waited for her university term to start, she worked in the mornings riding out for a local racehorse trainer. Her parents had given her riding lessons for her tenth birthday and she had ridden at the local riding school ever since. When she heard that the racing yard on the edge of town was looking for someone over the summer months, she jumped at the chance.

Her parents hadn't been keen and would have preferred her to get a summer job waitressing in one of the cafes along the seafront. However, when Kathryn pointed out that she would be in the fresh air and getting fit, they had eventually agreed.

She heard him first. Or more accurately, she heard his horse walking towards her. A bright bay gelding, ears pricked, was striding keenly along the tarmac of the parade ring. He tossed his head impatiently and snatched at the lead rein as his stable lad tried to steady him. She was leaning against the rail and, as they drew level, the young man caught her eye and, smiling broadly, winked.

What happened in that moment? In the years that followed, she had never found an answer that encapsulated it completely. She was jolted, struck by a force she couldn't put a name to and would never encounter again. It was certainly a recognition of sorts; a recognition of someone she had never set eyes on before.

Waiting for the horse to complete the circuit of the ring and pass her again, she pulled the race card out of her pocket and pretended to study it. A fluttering deep inside her which had started the moment she saw him, was now growing as the horse swung around the bend and approached her once more.

The clatter of hooves was now steadier and, glancing up, she could see that the horse had settled and the lad had fallen into a slower walk. His stride matched that of the horse; his eyes on the animal, giving her a chance to study him more closely.

He didn't have that hungry, pinched look of the lads who were trying to keep their weight low enough to race ride. Anyone could spot the aspiring jockeys with their pale faces and gaunt frames from sparse diets and daily saunas where they sweated off extra pounds. He was about the same height as her, so not particularly tall, but he was broad-shouldered and strong, with dark brown hair cut short. His faded black suede jacket was zipped up over a navy blue polo shirt, his dark green corduroys were turned up at the bottom and his polished shoes gleamed in the sun as much as the horse's oiled hooves.

He looked up suddenly. Again, that grin that spoke of fun, adventure, mischief.

'All right?' A jaunty, confident voice that immediately told Kathryn he was from the north of England.

Unsure if he had meant that greeting just for her, she smiled shyly.

When he had passed, she felt herself return to her body,

now so electrified, so lit up; her heart racing as it had never raced before.

For the remaining months that summer, Kathryn volunteered to take horses to the races as often as she could and soon became familiar with all of the southern racecourses. Each time, she hoped they would park near his lorry, that the lad leading the horse down the ramp would be him, and that she would finally find out who he was. But just to know he was on the course somewhere would be enough. She hadn't realised that hope could feel like excitement in the pit of her stomach.

One balmy summer's afternoon at Lingfield, she was carrying buckets and her grooming kit through the archway into the racecourse stables. A leather bag containing a set of red and white striped jockey silks was slung over her shoulder. Lazy girl's load, that's what her nan would have said. Too idle to make two trips.

'Here.' His voice from behind her.

As she looked around, the bag slid off her shoulder spilling the jockey's cap onto the gravel.

He was holding up a hoof pick that had bounced out of the kit as she struggled with her load.

Those dancing hazel eyes again. 'You might need this.'

A variety of replies spun through her mind before being discarded as dull, idiotic or too eager. As he leant down to pick up the cap, she noticed his tanned neck, looking away suddenly as he straightened.

'I'm Ed. You're with John O'Sullivan's yard, aren't you?'
She nodded.

'Fancy a cup of tea after the last race?' he asked.

'Um, yes, that would be nice. But we've only got one in the third race so we might have left by then.'

'Okay.' A shrug of the shoulders but still that smile.

And then he was gone. That loping stride, the confident tilt of his chin. She had thought about him so often in her quiet moments that his traits seemed strangely familiar.

Later that afternoon, she took a chair at one of the Formica tables in the brick hut where stable staff clustered, gossiped and swapped tips. A mug of tea in front of her, she pulled her book out of her bag. She might as well have a few minutes to herself before it was time to load the horses for home.

Disappointed that she was too early to bump into him, she took a sip and settled down to read. Fortunately, the canteen was empty except for a woman drying cups in the corner.

She felt a blast of warm air on her back as the door opened. Without turning, she knew it was him. The words on the page started to swim and she read the same sentence over and over again. Her mind was elsewhere. Behind her to be more precise, with him as he crossed the room. A tap of his boots on the flagstones; a murmur at the counter as he ordered. Wiping her clammy palms against her jeans, she hurriedly tugged her hair from its band and pulled it back into a tidier ponytail.

Seconds passed. Maybe he hadn't expected her to be there and wanted a quiet moment to look at the paper. Maybe she should just leave him in peace, giving him a nonchalant nod of acknowledgement as she passes him. Yes, that's what she would do. Act as if she hadn't given him another thought since she'd seen him earlier. Act as if she hadn't been thinking about him every moment since.

'Can I sit down?'

She tried to look casual as she glanced up at him, standing there with a red mug in his hand.

'If you want … yes, of course.'

'Want another cup of something?'

'No, I'm fine thanks.'

She glowed inwardly, noticing that he chose to sit directly opposite her rather than taking a chair further along the table.

'Smoke?'

He pushed a half-finished pack of Benson & Hedges across the gap between them.

She shook her head, wondering if she should close her book or not. What if he wanted to know what it was about? Thought her pretentious?

He shrugged, pulling the packet back to his side of the table.

'What are you reading?' he asked.

'Gaskell,' she said.

He raised his eyebrows.

'*North and South*,' she continued.

'The TV series with Patrick Swayze?'

'No, a different one. Thought I'd make a start getting through my university book list.'

'University?' Now he was smirking.

'What?'

She felt irritated with herself for mentioning university. It wasn't how she wanted the conversation to go.

'Well, I didn't think you'd do anything as boring as that.'

How was it that when she replayed that scene, it wasn't the fact that he thought university could be boring that stuck in her mind. If anyone else had suggested that, she would have been shocked. No, what she held on to was the fact that she was someone he had started to form an opinion about.

'I'm studying English. You know, it's what you do at university when you don't have any other plans.'

She could feel herself becoming someone else in his company, dismissive, irreverent.

He took a cigarette, fished for a lighter in his pocket and lit it.

'Unlike life, which happens when you're busy making other plans.'

Seeing the quizzical look on her face, he said, 'John Lennon.'

His stable pass was under the pack of cigarettes. She tried to make out the date of birth on the crumpled card as he got up to take a glass ashtray from a nearby table. It surprised her to see they were the same age. He struck her as someone who had experienced more life than your average nineteen year old.

'So I've told you my name. What do they call you?' he said, sitting down again and looking at her with a directness that surprised her.

'Kathryn.'

'Kathryn.' He echoed her name, considering it for a moment before tapping the growing ash on the end of his cigarette into the ashtray.

She wanted to ask his full name, where he lived, what his life had been like up to now. All questions which seemed out of place in this moment. She passed each one through her internal filter and dismissed it, leaving a silence to descend.

He broke it by answering a question she hadn't needed to ask, 'I'm at Ron Hyland's in Epsom.'

'Yes, I know.' It was out of her mouth before she could stop herself.

The hint of a smile on his lips. She could kick herself.

'But I'm from Liverpool originally. That's my real home,' he continued, picking at one of his nails, already bitten down short. 'I only came down here a couple of years ago.'

'With your family?'

'Nah. My dad and brother are still up north and my mother walked out.'

'Oh, I'm sorry.'

'Why? I'm not.' He shrugged and lifted the cigarette to his lips again, inhaling deeply. 'I don't remember her anyway. I was only a baby.'

She was at a loss, felt out of her depth and didn't know what to say next.

But it didn't matter; he continued, staring down at his fingers.

'My old man loves racing. So I went into it. He's happy,' he said, tapping the cigarette against the edge of the ashtray.

'And are you?'

'What?'

'Happy.'

'Are you?'

His eyes held hers and she felt herself blushing.

'Yes, I suppose I am. There's lots to look forward to…you know – new places, new people to meet…' She knew it sounded hollow, the sort of cliches you said when you thought they were expected of you, a chasm between what you said and what you meant.

Again, that shrug.

'If that's what you want from life.'

She thought about how she should reply, how to sound more interesting. So far she hadn't done a great job. He probably found her insipid.

'I suppose I don't really know what I want from life yet.'

'Who does?'

His gaze remained fixed on her and she wondered how she could paradoxically feel uncomfortable and thrilled at the same time.

Ed glanced at his watch and quickly drank the last dregs from his mug. Grinding his cigarette into the ashtray and gathering up his stable pass, he pushed his chair back.

'I'd better get my horse ready for the second last. Or get sacked.'

She'd been so wrapped up in him, she had forgotten he had another runner.

'I'm sorry for holding you up and making you late,' she said, jumping up and knocking her book to the floor.

He reached under the table, wiping dust off the cover as he emerged again.

'You didn't hold me up and you haven't made me late.'

He handed the book to her.

'Besides, I've enjoyed having tea with an educated young lady.'

He winked, and she couldn't be sure that he wasn't gently making fun of her.

They walked out into the sunshine together and she noticed how he stood back at the door for her to pass through first. She knew that they would head in different directions at the gateway into the yard. She wondered what she should say, maybe a casual 'bye then' would be best, safest.

Of course, what she really wanted to say was, 'Please ask me for my number, or ask when I'm racing next or...'

She slowed her stride.

'Bye then... Ed.'

He cursed quietly and broke into a jog. Kathryn could see that some of the horses in the second last race were already being led towards the pre-parade ring. He'd be a few minutes late joining them and get into trouble with his trainer, who had a reputation for being a difficult man to please at the best of times.

Feeling guilty, she walked away quickly.

'Kathryn.'

She stopped and looked around. He was calling from the archway.

'See you soon, yeah?'

Chapter 4

Soon wasn't soon enough for Kathryn.

A month had passed since the evening meeting at Lingfield. A virus had swept through the yard so all the horses were under quarantine, unable to travel in case the infection spread to other yards. Kathryn decided to spend her time making preparations for her move to Southampton University. Relatives were visited and the stack of boxes in her bedroom grew steadily. Everything she could possibly need in her halls of residence had been packed.

Throughout all this activity, her mind rarely veered from thoughts of Ed. She had expected to see him a few more times at the local racetracks but with the horses unable to run, her plans had been thwarted. She wondered if he had noticed her absence or whether he had thought little of it. Her stomach tightened at the thought of him and at those wasted chances to see him again. But there was one final meeting left; a prospect that shot a flare of excitement through her.

The last fixture of Brighton Racecourse's flat season was the day before she was due to leave for Southampton. She had checked the *Sporting Life* in the newsagents and had seen that Ron Hyland had two horses entered. One of them was the horse Ed looked after so she knew he would be there. Her mother told her she had plenty to do at home but Kathryn wouldn't be put off.

That morning she made a particular effort, applying a coat of mascara to her lashes. Her best friend Elaine often marvelled at Kathryn's luck in having such striking blue eyes and, while she brushed the compliment aside, she was secretly rather glad and now admired how her make-up accentuated them. She bit the tags off her new Benetton jumper which had been bought for her first days at university, and pulled on her Levi's. Glancing at herself in the mirror, she brushed her fringe straight then pulled her long brown hair into a ponytail.

'Can I take the car, Mum?' she called from the hall as she sat on the bottom stair, hauling on her black Doc Martens.

'You know I'd rather you stay put today. You've enough to do here with such an early start tomorrow,' Valerie said from the kitchen.

'I know but it's the last time I'll get to see Elaine before I go.'

Kathryn kept her eyes on her fingers threading the laces in and out of her boots. If her mother came through and caught her eye, she would know she was lying immediately.

'All right, but don't be all day. You know what you two are like when you get together. We want to have a nice family dinner tonight. Your dad will be home by six so don't be late.'

Kathryn leapt up, grabbed her coat and took the car keys from the hook next to the door. She let the door rattle behind her and, when she got into the small red Austin Metro, she smiled in anticipation and dug out the new Simply Red tape from her bag.

Driving down the road, she turned the music up a few notches and started to sing. This felt like freedom and, for today at least, she could forget any worries about the new life stretching ahead of her.

High up on the edge of the South Downs but just a short

drive from the coast, Brighton Racecourse was unusual. To drive into the car park, visitors had to cross the course and, when a race was underway, gates were pulled across the sand-covered road.

Kathryn sat impatiently, the car's engine running. In front of her was the azure blue of the English Channel stretching away to the horizon. It brought back her sixth form reading of Graham Greene's *Brighton Rock*, which captured the sweltering bustle of August bank holiday in the town so perfectly. Somehow her days at the races here had always been in dazzling sunshine and today was no different.

After leaving the Metro in the car park in the middle of the course, she pulled off her jumper and tied it around her waist. The elderly man on the gate nodded as she held up her stable pass.

'No runners today, Miss?'

She was surprised he recognised her.

'Not for a while. The yard's got the virus. I'm on a day out.'

'Well, it's a fine day for it.' He smiled and turned back to his newspaper.

Usually she was occupied by the race day routine but today her time was her own so she decided to wander down towards the bookmakers' stalls in front of the grandstand.

She hadn't expected to find him so soon.

He was standing with his back to her over by the rail. From such a safe distance she could watch him without fear of being noticed. She enjoyed how her blood began to rush the moment she saw him. It was as if her body had a higher level of awareness, reacting before her brain could register it. It was then that she noticed he was talking to a blonde girl standing next to him. He was leaning in closely and the girl put her hand on his shoulder.

It was odd how a story could be rewritten in a moment and how a body could react accordingly. As she watched him with the girl, Kathryn's stomach clenched. She told herself she had been foolish. She'd spoken to him once and had built a fantasy around him. She knew nothing about him; knew that nothing could come of it. She was heading into a new life of study. The two worlds didn't mix. But she was already mourning the loss of the excitement and anticipation she had been feeling so keenly for the past few weeks.

Watching the couple, who looked locked in their own world amid the bustle of the course, Kathryn felt as if she was shrinking. She scanned the girl, whose curves were accentuated by the extra buttons left undone and the nipped in waist of her tailored trousers. The sort of girl Kathryn gave a wide berth to. The sort of girl who could flatten you with a disparaging glance.

She turned back towards the paddock where the horses for the third race were being paraded. She stared dully as the muscle-bound thoroughbreds jig jogged excitedly. Some of the lads leading the horses nodded at her in recognition. She turned away, burrowing in her bag for her keys. Her fingers brushed the corners of the card she had brought for him. Feeling foolish, she vowed to throw it in the nearest bin as she left the course.

'Hey! What are you doing here?' His voice.

She looked up, her throat tightening.

She had to admit that he seemed pleased to see her. But there was something else. His eyes, usually dancing with life, seemed distant, unfocused. He had been drinking.

'I'm just off actually.'

She turned away.

'Already? Wait a minute. What's wrong?'

He came round to stand in front of her, a puzzled look on his face.

'Look, meet me in the bar in ten minutes, will you?'

The tangy smell of alcohol hit her.

'Okay.'

She looked down, unwilling to catch his eye.

'Nice one. I'll go and find Luke and get him to lead up for me.'

Kathryn had met Luke once before. He worked with Ed and, she suspected, didn't approve of him. She knew the sort of young man Luke was – gaining experience in a yard before going for promotion to assistant trainer, upwardly mobile, a clear trajectory in mind. She found herself feeling protective towards Ed. Luke probably had a supportive family, eagerly encouraging his ambitions. She guessed his mother hadn't walked out when he was small.

During each race, the bar under the stand emptied as its occupants decamped to the rails to shout the horses home. Kathryn found a table in the corner furthest away from the door. This way she wouldn't be surprised. This way she could watch him readjust to the gloom after leaving the glare of the afternoon sunshine.

The barman stood with his back to her, watching the TV high up on the wall announcing runners and riders at race meetings elsewhere that afternoon. She watched how he rubbed the same glass over and over again, mesmerised by the flickering images of horses being loaded into stalls at Newmarket, his back turned to the same images outside.

The door swung open and, as Kathryn expected, Ed faltered for a moment, scanning the bar from left to right. When he saw her, she noticed that his face lit up and she smiled. She couldn't miss how he weaved uncertainly between the small wooden tables though.

He sat down heavily opposite her, jolting the table.

'What'll you have?'

His hand in his pocket, change jingling.

'Diet Coke thanks.'

He frowned in disbelief.

'Come on. That's not a drink.'

'I'm driving though.'

'But one won't hurt.'

'Half a cider?'

'That's more like it.'

This time she didn't watch him as he ordered at the bar. She tipped the ashtray at an angle, tried to catch a glimpse of her reflection in its stainless steel base. She hastily rubbed away the black spot of mascara that had gathered in the corner of her eye and glanced over to the bar to check she hadn't been seen. The barman had reluctantly torn himself away from the TV and was now filling glasses from the taps in front of him.

When Ed turned back to her, he was holding two pint glasses.

He sat down, smiling broadly at her. If it hadn't been for the shadow of the girl at the rail and the fact he had been drinking, she would have been thrilled. But now she felt unsure.

'Cheers, Kathryn.'

He lifted the glass to his lips and, to Kathryn's consternation, drank half of the pint of lager before reaching around to the back pocket of his jeans and producing a crumpled packet of cigarettes.

'So, what's up? First I don't see you around for weeks and now you're here and there's something up. I don't get it.'

He put a cigarette to his lips, struck a match and lit it. A sharp inhale then he blew out a thin stream of smoke through pursed lips.

Kathryn took a sip and felt the cool liquid slip down her throat.

'I've finished at John's. He's had to shut up the yard for a while as he's got a couple coughing. You know, that virus that's going around. And I'm off tomorrow.'

'Off?'

'To Southampton.'

'Oh yes, to become a student.'

He took another drink.

Kathryn watched his bitten nails gripping the glass and noticed a small cut on his jaw, probably from shaving that morning.

'Who were you talking to by the rails?'

It came out more sharply than she had planned.

His eyes gleamed mischievously as he swallowed the lager and placed the glass carefully onto the beer mat.

'Ah,' he grinned at her. 'That was Nicki.'

She tried not to look too interested but her mind was already turning the name over. Nicki – of course, she would be a Nicki.

'You seemed deep in conversation.'

'She works in the yard next to our place. Her horse is in the last race today – should bolt in too. Nicki's all right, just been having some trouble with her landlord.'

He was watching her closely, his eyes laughing.

Kathryn raised her eyebrows in an attempt at indifference.

'She's not a girlfriend, if that's what you're worried about.'

There. He'd said it. Kathryn looked at him, startled. She had tried to hide her jealousy but had clearly failed miserably.

'Nothing to do with me.' She raised her half empty glass to her lips.

Laughing, he winked and turned around to the bar, which was now gradually filling again.

'I was telling her some news about my old man. Nothing I wasn't expecting but still…'

'What news?'

'It's not important.'

'But you were telling that girl?'

'Yeah, she met him once. Look, it's not a big deal. He's just been put away this week.'

She heard herself gasp, sure that being put away could only mean one thing.

'I'm sorry, Ed. It must be hard for…'

He interrupted.

'No sympathy, please. Anyway, you're the one needing sympathy, heading off to join a bunch of college wasters.'

She smiled, the tension broken, and suddenly remembered the card in her bag. She fished it out and pushed it across the table towards him.

'I thought I might meet you today,' she said.

'You didn't, did you?'

He grinned. Kathryn enjoyed the feeling of being gently teased.

'What's this?' he said, opening the envelope with a neatness that surprised her.

'It's my new address. In case you felt like staying in touch.'

She watched him read the lines she had considered for so long, her stomach fluttering nervously.

He smiled at her and put the card carefully back into the envelope.

'I don't get many cards.'

'I don't write many,' she said, glad that he would never know how long she had spent deliberating over which card to pick for him.

'To Someone Special, eh?'

#

When she looked back on that afternoon, she recalled how the half hour journey home had taken twice as long. She had reverted to being a young learner driver, focusing on the road ahead with a concentration that made her head throb. Every gear change felt deliberate, every turning executed precisely.

As she swung the car into the drive, she groaned. Her friend Elaine was on the doorstep talking to Valerie who, on hearing the crunching gravel, looked witheringly into the car at Kathryn.

She knew as she trudged up the stairs, Elaine in tow, that the row would come later. Valerie wasn't the sort of woman who aired family matters in public, even in front of her daughter's best friend.

'So, what did you get up to today?' Elaine asked breathlessly, sitting on Kathryn's bed. 'Your mum was having kittens.'

'I met Ed,' Kathryn replied, hanging her bag on the back of the door.

'What, that lad from Epsom?'

Kathryn nodded, crouching down to unlace her boots.

'And?' Elaine asked, hands on hips.

'And what?'

'Have you been drinking?'

'Maybe.'

'Blimey, Kathryn. That's not like you at all. He must be a

bad influence,' Elaine teased.

'It was only two pints.'

'You'd have been well over the limit if you'd have been caught.'

'Yes, but I wasn't, was I? Everything's okay.'

'No harm done really. It's not like you're going to see him again.'

Kathryn didn't reply.

Chapter 5

She soon realised it would have been simpler to take the train to Liverpool. Her old car was hardly the most reliable transport for a journey which, with countless detours, had taken upwards of five hours.

Yet it had felt like an adventure. She hadn't been that far north before and with each passing signpost bearing names of towns and cities she had heard of but never visited, she had felt she was venturing further into a land of dark satanic mills. The reality, of course, was somewhat different. A service station on the outskirts of Walsall was much like one near Stafford.

She had been surprised how quickly he had replied to her letters. In his first letter, he had explained that he hadn't written to anyone before but, within a fortnight of starting university, Kathryn regularly found the familiar pale blue envelope sitting in the pile of post on the desk in the porter's office at her halls of residence. He wrote his phone number in one of his early letters and from that moment on, they spoke each Sunday evening. It was during one of these conversations that he hesitantly asked her to visit him.

'I know it's a long way,' he had said hurriedly. 'If it's too far, I understand.'

But Kathryn, with the novelty of tutorials and lectures now wearing off, jumped at the chance and circled the first Friday in December with a red marker on the calendar beside her bed.

She knew she wouldn't reach Liverpool until the afternoon but, still, by the time she swung the car off the motorway and followed the signs for the city centre, she felt as if she had been driving for days.

The idea of seeing him after nearly three months filled her with excitement, but it was tinged with nervousness. She hadn't seen him since that day at Brighton Races and had impatiently looked forward to this moment. Yet now the day was here, she was gripped with dread at the prospect of seeing him in his home environment. What if they had nothing to say to each other?

The crisp sunshine of Southampton had gradually given way to duller, damper weather and when she finally caught sight of the city's famous Liver Birds on top of the stately Royal Liver Building, one looking across the Mersey to Birkenhead, the other casting its eyes inland, a fine mist had descended and Liverpool was cloaked in grey.

The meeting place was the statue of Queen Victoria in Derby Square. She hurried along a wide, sweeping street with terraces of three storey Georgian townhouses each side. The houses were red brick and had the same six steps up from the street, railed on each side, to a grand pillared entrance. The wrought iron balconies over the brightly painted front doors spoke of affluence and couldn't have been more different from the image of Liverpool she had constructed in her mind. That image, mainly courtesy of news reports, was of riots and burning cars, poll tax marches and raging unemployment. She had the sense of Liverpool as a city that demanded respect, that had seen life and took no prisoners.

Ed had told her to look out for the imposing white building with the words Rigby's Building carved in stone at the very top. She could see it at the end of the street. Just one more turn, one more street and she was sure the statue would be there.

And so it was. In a paved area off the main thoroughfare, the black iron figure of Queen Victoria stood on a raised limestone platform. People were sitting on the steps around the base of the statue, teenagers in huddles, older couples surrounded by shopping bags.

Spotting him, she felt a surge of exhilaration deep inside. He was sitting apart, hunched over, his chin resting on his clasped hands. She would have known him anywhere. She had never taken any notice of how others filled the space around them but his physicality had been etched into her consciousness from the first moment she saw him. The way he tilted his head as he watched people passing by, the bend of his back beneath his faded suede jacket, the way his hair was cut short into the broad nape of his neck.

He checked his watch and took a packet of cigarettes out of his pocket. Standing up, he patted his jean pockets as if in search of a lighter.

'You probably thought I'd never get here,' she said, breathlessly.

He turned round quickly and, grinning, seemed to forget his search.

'Two hours late – you could have walked here quicker.'

'I've been driving since ten o'clock.'

'Yeah, sorry,' he said, abashed. 'It's a long way.'

For a moment, she thought he was going to lean over and kiss her but he hesitated, as if unsure, and hugged her quickly instead. She noticed the blush creeping across his cheeks as he stepped back from her and felt like she might burst with happiness.

He lived on one of the estates that had been built at the end of the war, stretching the city boundaries into surrounding farm land. As Kathryn drove them through streets of red brick houses facing each other, she noticed they were all almost identical except for their small, square front gardens, some of which were hedged, some fenced with metal railings and others filled with mattresses, old bikes and piles of sand, half covered by sheets of plastic. This, she thought, was the other side of Liverpool.

'This one here,' Ed said, gesturing to her to pull over.

As he was about to get out of the car, he hesitated, his hand on the door handle, and glanced across at her.

'It's a bit of a mess. Not the sort of place you're used to.'

'You haven't seen my room at uni,' she replied, reaching into the back seat for her bag. It didn't look like the type of street where bags could be left in cars.

As he turned the key in the lock of the pale blue door, Kathryn glanced around. The front garden, while not quite as chaotic as those filled with discarded mattresses, was still unkempt and the narrow flower bed running alongside the path was choked with weeds. A grubby plastic tub next to the front door, its plant long gone, now contained cigarette butts floating on waterlogged soil.

'Come on in,' he said, over his shoulder.

As he shrugged off his jacket and threw it over the banister, she was hit by an unfamiliar smell, a fug of stale cigarettes, fried food and musty dampness. It hung heavy in the air. Dance music throbbed from an upstairs room and she shivered in the chill air of the house, which felt as if it hadn't been heated for days. She decided to leave her coat on for now.

Brown linoleum, ripped in places, exposing the grey concrete beneath, led the way through the narrow hall and into the small kitchen beyond.

Ed was already at the sink, filling a kettle.

'Sit down. Tea okay?' he asked.

She pulled out a chair and sat at the table in the corner of the kitchen. Under a window misted with condensation, the sink was full of plates smeared with the leftovers of several meals.

He threw open the fridge door to reveal little more than a pint of milk, a plate of leftover sausages and enough cans of lager to fill the bottom shelf. After giving the milk a sniff, he took two cups from an assortment on the draining board and swilled them under the tap.

As he poured the water from the kettle into the mugs, the music suddenly became louder, as if a door had opened, then quietened again as the soft thud of footsteps could be heard coming down the stairs.

The young man who came into the room was clearly Ed's brother. His hair was closely shaved at the sides and longer on top. He wore a long red football shirt, hanging loose over tracksuit bottoms. A thick silver chain glinted around his neck. Kathryn wondered how he didn't seem to feel the cold.

He went straight to the fridge, pulled out a can and came over to where Kathryn was sitting.

'You must be Ed's bird,' he said with a smile that was Ed and yet not.

His mouth turned up at the same angle but the smile didn't quite reach his eyes, which darted over her, taking in everything from her long knitted cardigan to her Doc Marten boots.

Ed spoke up before she could reply.

'This is Kathryn, Paul. She's come all the way from Southampton.' He sounded proud.

Paul opened his can, keeping his eyes on her.

'What... to see him? Are you mad or summat?'

She did what she usually did when she was unsure, she smiled.

He took a swig and continued to look at her.

'You've come all this way? Why?'

Ed was now putting their cups of tea down on the table.

'Because she's a friend of mine and I said I'd show her around.'

Paul shrugged. 'It's a dive.'

Kathryn glanced at Ed, who was searching for biscuits in cupboards almost as empty as the fridge. As Paul left the room, grabbing a pack of cigarettes from the worktop, the way he said 'See you later' sounded very much like his brother.

As they drank their tea, Kathryn said, 'Your brother doesn't seem too keen on Liverpool.'

Ed took a rich tea biscuit and dipped it in his tea.

'Don't mind him,' he said, shaking his head 'There's not much he is keen on. Except drink and... anyway, forget him. I'm made up you're here.'

#

Opening her eyes gradually in the thin grey light threading through the grubby net curtains, she wondered why there was a nagging ache at the back of her head. Her eyes felt heavy-lidded, her mouth dry.

Last night. The memory inched into her consciousness as she pulled the damp blankets to her chin, shivering and trying to piece things together. She turned over and then recoiled as her bare arm brushed against the iciness of the radiator next to the bed. It had been painted the same cream as the rest of the room but that had clearly been some years ago. The paint, chipped and smudged with dirt, had seen better days. Orange and brown floral curtains hung limply either side of the nets and, while paper-thin, pulling them last night might have taken the chill off the room.

A small table by the bed held an ashtray with a couple of discarded butts and wires reached up to a stereo on a shelf, high above her. At the other side of the table was another bed, strewn with clothes.

She leant back against the pink draylon headboard and tried to remember what had happened last night.

She hadn't intended drinking and had offered to drive but Ed had persuaded her otherwise. She didn't mind if she drank or not but she was glad she didn't take the car – where they had ended up had been so rough it would probably have ended up on bricks by the end of the night.

And it had been fun to have a drink. It had made her fit in more easily, knocking the edge off her shyness so that, by midnight, she was laughing along with everyone else when Paul was thrown out and yet reappeared through another door without the barman noticing. It felt nice to be inside a circle rather than on the outside peering in. And despite their initial wariness, she had felt accepted by Paul and Ed's friends.

Every now and then, she had glanced around to find Ed. Sometimes he was there and would give her a wink, at other times he would be missing. As the evening wore on, she wondered why he was going to the toilet so often. When she mentioned it to the girls next to her, they had exchanged glances and laughed.

Kathryn, her head light and her senses dulled, could remember little of their journey home. She had been too preoccupied with making sure she didn't stumble up a kerb or bump into any of the bins left out on the pavement. She remembered him coming into the bedroom with a cup of tea for her, looking pale in the glare of the single bulb hanging from the ceiling, and that he had taken the blankets and cheap thin quilt from the other bed downstairs.

There was nothing for it but to get up and see what the day had to offer. After pulling on her clothes, she tiptoed along the corridor to the bathroom to clean her teeth and wash her face before hastily applying some foundation to cover up her blotchy complexion.

There was a sound coming from the kitchen below and she guessed, from the state of both of them last night, that Ed would be up before his brother. But as she entered the kitchen, she saw Paul in boxer shorts and a t-shirt rifling through the drawers.

'Kettle's boiled,' he grunted.

'What are you looking for?' Kathryn asked, from the doorway.

'A lighter. There's a spare here somewhere.'

Noticing a box of matches amongst a jumble of plates, newspapers and videos on the worktop, she handed it to him.

Ungraciously, he took it from her and hastily lit the cigarette between his lips. A few inhalations seemed to improve his mood.

'Last night was a bit hectic,' he offered.

It sounded like a statement so Kathryn didn't reply but looked around instead, wondering where Ed might be.

Standing at the sink, Paul peered out at the garden.

'It's still pissing down.' He turned back to her. 'Is he getting up today?'

'Ed? I don't know, I haven't seen him since last night.'

Filling a mug from the tap, he said, 'Blimey. So he didn't sleep…'

She interrupted him. ' I don't know where he slept.'

He shrugged and looked at her with a puzzled expression.

'Doesn't sound like our Ed. Must be summat up with him.'

Putting the cigarette back between his lips to free up his hands, he grabbed a box of own brand cornflakes and a bowl and spoon from the draining board and put them in front of her with a clatter. The milk was still on the table from last night and she didn't like the look of it, but in the absence of an alternative, helped herself.

'He's a dark horse our kid,' Paul went on as he sat down opposite her. 'He's probably not told you the half of it. Wouldn't want to shock you.'

She noticed a bowl of clumped sugar on the window sill next to her and sprinkled some over her cereal.

'No, he's told me everything, I think,' she said, with more conviction than she felt.

'And you still hang about with him?' he asked, raising an eyebrow before descending into a fit of coughing, sounding like a man three times his age. 'He's better now he's working with the horses. But before,' he whistled. 'Hit the skids proper. Did time and all. Was in Feltham for six months when he wasn't more than a bit of a kid.'

She stared at him.

'Feltham?'

He spotted the change in her expression.

'Ah, so he didn't tell you that much. Thought not.' He continued. 'You've heard of Feltham? For young offenders.

46

But it was only assault. And the bloke had it coming to him.'

'Who had it coming to him?' Ed was behind them at the door. He was in jeans and a thin sweatshirt; his feet still bare.

Kathryn wondered how nobody felt the cold in this house. Maybe northerners really were tougher than those from south of Watford.

Ed glanced between his brother and Kathryn and then to the paltry breakfast she was picking at.

'Come on, let's go into town and have something. You'll starve in this house.'

#

Driving in cities had always filled Kathryn with dread. She could cope with the outskirts of Southampton but Liverpool on a busy Saturday lunchtime was a different matter and by the time they reached the city centre, her nerves felt frayed. It didn't help that her head was pounding and she was still trying to process what she had been told by Paul.

They had breakfast at the Berni Inn, looking out across the Mersey from upstairs in the Pier Head terminal. As a waiter brought heaped plates of bacon and eggs to their table, Kathryn began to cheer up. Beyond Ed's head, bowed as he scraped butter across his toast, she looked across the stretch of churning grey water to the distant chimneys on the far side of the river. Smoke billowed skywards and while she recognised that the scene was bleak, industrial, harsh and about as far away from the aesthetic as it was possible to get, she still felt drawn to its sense of workmanlike continuity, the toil and labour of generations.

'I like this place,' she said, picking up her knife and fork.

'You do?' He seemed surprised.

'Yes, it seems…honest. Does that sound daft?'

'A bit.'

He laughed, stabbing a piece of greasy bacon with his fork. As he chewed, he looked at her thoughtfully.

'How are you feeling now?'

'Better, thanks. All that drink was a bit of a shock to the system.'

'He was a bit rough last night. Paul. Now that the old man's away, he's gone off the rails proper. He's been barred from a couple of our locals and he's got a court case coming up soon for nicking from an offie in Garston.'

The life he described was so alien to Kathryn, like something from one of the gritty soap operas Elaine watched. She had never met anyone before who had been to prison, who didn't have food in the cupboards, who didn't have parents watching their every move. It felt exciting to be here, far from her dull suburban home and the disappointing routine of university life. She felt glad to be here with him, having breakfast with the rest of the day ahead of them, full of promise.

'It's not what you're used to, is it?' he said, mopping his plate with a piece of white bread. 'Court cases, robbing, getting stoned every weekend – most of the week too.'

'I suppose not. But it doesn't matter. I'm just enjoying being here,' she said, adding shyly, 'with you.'

He furrowed his brow as if he didn't believe her. 'Yeah?'

She nodded and watched him as he drained his cup and stood up.

'You done? Come on, I'm going to give you the grand tour.'

Money being short meant the tour was a walking one and didn't involve museums or anything involving an entrance fee. He led her along the Mersey and down to the recently rejuvenated Albert Dock, its red brick warehouses now restored to their past glory and standing resplendent around the inner waterway, on which bobbed a couple of boats. The Beatles Story museum looked tempting but he convinced her it wasn't worth the money, so they crossed back over the main road and climbed the steep hill towards the vast outline of Liverpool Cathedral. Ed proudly told her that it was not only the largest church in Britain, it was the largest Protestant cathedral in the world.

'Are we going in?' Kathryn said as they reached the entrance to the cathedral grounds.

Ed shook his head and carried on walking. 'I've a better idea,' he said.

They turned off along Hope Street with the pale, futuristic shape of the city's Catholic cathedral ahead of them. Suddenly, Ed took Kathryn's hand and pulled her through an ornate iron and gold doorway. She found herself in the lavish interior of the Philharmonic pub.

Kathryn decided that this was the most opulent pub she had ever seen. Letting the heat from the glowing coals in the fireplace warm her legs, she found herself looking into a vast circular mirror. It was framed in the same dark mahogany as the wood panels on every wall, which would have made the bar too dark had it not been for a line of elegant tiffany lamps throwing out gleams of golden light.

In the mirror, she watched Ed order their drinks at the bar. As he gathered two pints and two packets of crisps to his chest and turned around, he caught her eye and grinned. She looked away, embarrassed.

'What an amazing place,' Kathryn said.

'That's why I brought you here,' he replied, setting the drinks down. 'If it's good enough for John, it's good enough for us, eh?'

She looked at him blankly.

Sighing and rolling his eyes in mock frustration, he explained, 'John Lennon. He said one of the worst things about fame was that he couldn't go to the Phil for a pint.'

He drank thirstily before looking around the room in admiration. 'It feels like you're in another world, doesn't it?' He put his pint down again, 'Away from what's outside that door. Who's outside that door.'

The afternoon passed quickly and, by the time they left their seats by the fire, it was dusk. Kathryn didn't relish the walk back to the riverfront car park.

'We'll get the night bus rather than walk all that way,' Ed said as they waited to be served in a fish and chip shop near the pub. They wandered through the darkening streets, glancing in through the glowing windows of a casino and a bar, where a crowd jostled. A blackboard outside announced '70's Disco Tonite' and, as the door swung open, ABBA blasted out onto the pavement along with a giggling trio of women, clutching their bags and each other. At the doorway of the shop next door, an elderly man dragged newspaper racks inside before pulling down the grey metal shutter with a clatter.

At the bottom of the hill, Ed suddenly said, 'I know where we'll go,' before turning off the pavement and climbing steps that seemed to disappear into the gloom. Leaving the lights, traffic and people behind, Kathryn followed him. At the top of the stone steps, she found herself standing in front of a church, its shape silhouetted in the twilight.

Just feet away from the liveliness of the city, it felt deserted, out of place. Along the side walls were tall, arched windows, but it was only when she turned the corner of the church and looked through a broad stone archway that she saw it had no roof. And there, within the walls of this great, abandoned ruin, she saw Ed watching her.

He was sitting on a bench where once worshippers sat in pews in prayer. She picked her way across the grass, still wet from the earlier rain. Patting the wooden slats beside him, he said, 'What do you think?'

She shivered as she sat down and looked up at the open stretch of sky above. 'It's a bit creepy, isn't it?'

'You think so?' he said, reaching his arm around her, as if to protect her. She wasn't scared but was happy to let him think she was if it meant he left his arm there.

'What happened to it?'

'It was bombed in the war and they never rebuilt it. Everyone calls it the Bombed Out Church but its real name is St Luke's. I come here sometimes. You know, to get away from everyone. Have a think. Even have a read sometimes.'

'Do you?'

Detecting approval in her voice, he laughed, 'Yeah, I have been known to pick up a book. You must be a good influence.'

The idea filled her with pride.

'What are you reading?' she asked.

He reached into the inside pocket of his jacket, pulling out a curled paperback and handing it to her.

She peered in the half-light at the cover. '*Sons and Lovers*,' she said, surprised. 'Do you like D H Lawrence?'

'First one of his I've read. I found it in a charity shop in town.'

She looked at the dated orange cover showing a black and white photograph of an early film adaptation of the story.

'Yeah, I know – the cover's a bit naff but I like the story.

And the father in it reminds me of my old man.'

'In what way?' she asked, keen to draw him out.

'Angry, frustrated. Pissed off with how life's worked out for him.' He took the book from her and, in a quieter voice, said, 'Feeling like he's never good enough. Like they all treat him like he's nothing.'

'Well, they're standing up for their mother, I suppose.' Kathryn replied, not sure where the conversation was heading.

He snorted, thrust the book back into his pocket and started to fumble for his cigarettes.

She continued carefully. 'You've never told me anything about your mum, Ed.'

The lighter flame flickered and the end of the cigarette glowed as he inhaled deeply, paused and then let a thin stream of smoke escape from his lips.

'Sorry for prying,' she said, irritated with herself for causing the conversation to drift into silence.

He stared at his fingernails for a few moments before muttering, 'Nah, you weren't prying. But what's there to say?' He was looking through the empty space above them to the darkening evening sky. 'She couldn't put up with the old man and did a flit one day. Ran off with some bloke, by all accounts. We never saw her again.'

'But he must have tried to find her? You must have heard from her on your birthday? Christmas?'

He shook his head and shrugged. 'Nothing.'

'How does Paul feel about it?'

'He's always hated her. Blames her for everything that's ever gone wrong in our family. Which is quite a lot.'

'And do you blame her?

'No. I just don't think about her.'

Silence descended.

Kathryn was wondering how to change the subject without being too obvious when Ed did it for her, 'What was Paul talking to you about in the kitchen?'

'This morning? Just the weather.'

'There was something else. Tell me.'

'Well, he mentioned that you were in some place for young offenders when you were younger.'

Ed cursed. 'I warned him not to say anything.'

Turning to look at him, she replied, 'Why? It's nothing to be ashamed of.'

He smiled that smile that made her heart feel as if it was filling her chest.

'What are you like? I bet you've never even met anyone with a criminal record before. But things like that don't seem to bother you'

She blushed. 'I know you wouldn't do anything without a good reason.'

Years later, she would remember this moment. When it had been just the two of them alone in the ruins of this old church and she had silently vowed that she would never let him down as he had been let down in his first nineteen years.

By the time they caught the last bus back it was late and they found Paul slumped on the sofa, a sea of cans and empty bottles on the coffee table in front of him.

'Christ sake, not again,' Ed said, turning the light on.

Paul opened his eyes, blinking at the brightness.

'What the…' he started.

'You've got to get yourself sorted out, mate,' Ed said, picking up a carrier bag from beside the sofa.

Paul was now sullenly staring at Ed as he threw the cans into the bag. As they clattered in, one after another, Paul leant forward to put his head in his hands. Kathryn watched as his elbows slipped from his knees and he toppled forward onto the carpet.

'God, I'm sorry about this,' Ed muttered, going to the sprawling figure jammed between the sofa and the coffee table. 'He's not normally this wasted.'

Between them, they managed to get him up and, taking an arm each, dragged him up the stairs and into his bedroom. Without turning the light on, they hauled him across to his unmade bed and rolled him onto the mattress. Ed pulled the blankets up to his brother's chin and tucked them around him.

Backing out of the room, like the parents of a sleeping child, they closed the door quietly. 'Sorry about all this,' Ed muttered again, avoiding her eyes. 'Bet you can't wait to get back down that road tomorrow.'

'Of course not,' she said, wondering what she could say to lift his mood.

'I should never have asked you to come up here. Dunno what I was thinking. A girl like you. Here,' he said, casting a glance around the bare landing.

'I've loved every minute,' she said, pulling the sleeves of her cardigan over her cold hands.

Ed's expression indicated he knew she wasn't telling the truth. As he turned towards the stairs, Kathryn felt the crush of disappointment. Retreating into Ed's freezing room alone wasn't how she had expected the night to end.

'Can I ask you something?'

'Yeah, course. Do you want something to eat? Drink? An extra blanket?'

'Can I come back again? I honestly have enjoyed being here… with you.'

He broke into a smile for the first time since they had come into the house.

'You sure?'

She smiled back and nodded before adding, 'One thing though.'

He raised his eyebrows.

'It's freezing up here. Can I have that extra blanket?'

Chapter 6

That winter was a time of firsts for Kathryn, crucially her first Christmas without her parents. She had told them a tale about a girl on her course who had lost her mother that summer and who had invited her home to Cornwall for Christmas. They had initially refused to allow her to go but then Beth had announced that her office could struggle on for three days so she could pay her parents a flying visit from Christmas Eve to Boxing Day. With all their attention on the return of the daughter they hadn't seen in so long, they immediately lost all interest in Kathryn's plans.

Eager to be gone, Kathryn left on the day before Christmas Eve. Without the return of the prodigal daughter, she would have been unable to leave and so gave silent thanks, probably for the first time, for her sister. Guilt flickered briefly at the thought of not being part of the welcoming committee when Beth arrived home, but it lasted only as long as it took to drive to the motorway, where she turned, not towards Cornwall, but northwards.

As the hours passed behind the wheel, Kathryn thought about the weeks since her last visit. She had spoken to Ed often, either on the payphone in her halls of residence or, for more privacy, in the phone box a couple of streets away. But in the days that stretched between their calls and letters, she wondered what he was doing, whether he was thinking of her and when she would see him again. Her university work had slipped into the background and, from morning to night, her attention was elsewhere.

Three months ago, Liverpool had been just a place on a map, but now, as she drove past the cathedral and down the hill towards the River Mersey, it was verging on the familiar; a place she could claim as her own. And Ed's.

She was beginning to understand the draw of this city and wasn't surprised that he hadn't returned to his work digs in Epsom. He had told her he was needed at home – someone had to keep Paul on the straight and narrow – but she could also tell that he had missed Liverpool. Although life here was tough with no money, it was still home.

She suspected that he wasn't missed in Epsom. That's how it was in the racing world. A merry-go-round of the young and not so young, staying months or years with a racehorse trainer before seeking better conditions or just a new start with another yard. Sometimes people dropped out of the racing world altogether, migrating to the factories where a five-day week out of the wet and cold was more palatable. Easily replaced, they were rarely spoken of again.

Again, they were to meet in the shadow of Queen Victoria and, again, her heart leapt at the sight of him. This feeling that flooded through her when she saw him was becoming addictive. She had wished away every day of the last month so she could be one day nearer to meeting him, one day nearer to this feeling, this exhilaration.

He spotted her and waved. When she reached him, he jumped up from where he had been sitting on the steps. He seemed pleased to see her and this time when he hugged her, his arms stayed clasped around her a little longer.

'I bet you're starving,' he said, grinning. 'Let's get something to eat. I've something to tell you, Kat.'

It made her glow inside to hear him shorten her name. He'd done it suddenly on the phone one day and hadn't used her full name since. Nobody had called her Kat before and she didn't think anybody else ever would. It was his name for her and that's what made it so special.

They found a cafe down a side street and settled at a corner table. Ed seemed impatient as he waited for the waitress to take their order.

'My old man's getting out tomorrow.' The words came out as soon as the woman turned away from them, as if they had been sitting in his throat waiting to escape.

'Your dad?' Kathryn asked.

'Yeah, temporary release. Happens sometimes if you keep your nose clean.'

'How long is he out for?'

'For good, if he behaves himself.'

'But I thought he had another six months to go?'

'He does, but if someone's not a risk they sometimes let them out early. Only trouble is we didn't have much notice. I'd have liked to clean the place up, you know, and have a bit of a party for him.'

'How do you feel about him coming out?'

He stopped fiddling with his fork and looked up with a puzzled expression.

'I'm made up, of course.'

But he didn't look made up. Not like someone happy at the prospect of their father coming home after an absence of four months. And she didn't like to admit it to herself, because she should want what was best for Ed, but she felt uneasy about meeting the man who cast such a shadow over his sons.

As the waitress put their plates in front of them, Ed continued. 'Paul's acting all hard about it but I know he's glad too. And just in time for Christmas.'

He started to eat ravenously and Kathryn guessed there was as little in the cupboards at home as before.

'I can help you make it nice for him. And we can pop into a supermarket on the way back and get some food in.'

He stopped chewing for a moment. 'You're the best, Kat. The old man'll be mad about you, I know he will.'

#

Christmas clearly hadn't yet reached their house. All along the street, neighbouring houses had been transformed with colour and lights. Bright red, blue and yellow bulbs were strung outside one house while lights glinted on the silhouette of a small Christmas tree through the frosted glass door of another. Net curtains had been pulled aside in the window next door, so that a tower of red and silver tinsel stood resplendent for the whole street to notice.

Their house was still as cold as ever. It was, however, a little tidier. As they hauled the supermarket carrier bags in through the hallway, it was clear that some sort of effort had been made. Piles had been sorted, coats had been moved from the banister and hung on hooks, trainers tidied. But still that damp, musty odour lingered and, as Kathryn deposited the bags on the kitchen table, she wondered how they could get rid of it.

As the cupboards were nearly empty, it was straightforward enough to find space to store the provisions. As Kathryn stacked packets of custard creams and a Jamaican ginger cake – his dad's favourites – on an upper shelf, she suddenly sensed there was someone behind her.

Turning, she saw a young woman watching her.

'Hi,' Kathryn said.

'The door was open,' the girl replied, pushing a blonde curl behind her ear.

At that moment, Ed came through from the lounge.

'Didn't take long for the news to travel then. Who told you he was out today?' he said.

Crossing to the sink, he filled the kettle.

Ignoring his question, the girl said to his back, 'Didn't know you had a girlfriend installed.'

'That's because I don't have one installed,' he replied, without turning around.

Kathryn left the kitchen and hovered a moment in the hall. She heard the girl remark, 'not your usual type, Ed.'

'Yeah, whatever.'

Not wishing to hear any more, Kathryn went out to the car for the last bag of shopping. As she slammed the boot shut, she saw Paul walking down the street towards her.

The last time she had seen him, he had been drunk and snoring under a heap of blankets. He spotted her and, to her surprise, his face seemed to light up.

'I was wondering when you'd be back,' he said. 'Ed wouldn't tell me so I thought you might have given him the flick. Here, let me take that.'

He grabbed the carrier bag from her.

'You've heard the news then?' He glanced into the bag and rolled his eyes. 'I see our kid wants to lay the red carpet out for him.'

'He wanted to get some food in for him, yes,' Kathryn said defensively.

'Oi, while I've got you on your own. I heard I was a bit out of it last time you were here. Can't remember it but...' he tailed off, with a rueful glance at the ground.

'I don't remember,' Kathryn lied, appreciating his attempt at an apology.

Paul shrugged and glanced towards the house, narrowing his eyes as if he had spotted something of interest.

Linda was wandering down the path towards them.

'What's she doing here?'

'She just popped in a moment ago. Who is she anyway?'

He lowered his voice. 'That's Linda. The old man's bird.'

Kathryn raised her eyebrows. Linda couldn't be much older than she was.

'He met her when he was signing on,' Paul said, obviously feeling the need to explain the relationship. 'It turned out he used to be mates with her old fella.'

'There's a bit of an age difference,' Kathryn remarked, finding herself pulled into the story despite her better judgement.

'You could say that,' Paul said. 'Nothing like an old fool, I s'pose, but...'

He switched his gaze to Linda as she reached them, 'All right, Linda?'

'I was on my way over to the precinct to pick up some milk for me mam. Came to see if you needed a hand with anything, what with Terry coming out.'

She turned the full wattage of her smile on him, leaving Kathryn in no doubt which brother she most favoured. She had turned her back on Kathryn, who watched her slide her manicured hands into the back pockets of the marble wash jeans that hugged every curve as she pointed the toe of her stiletto towards Paul.

Ignoring her offer, he said, 'Why didn't you go and see him? He was gutted.'

Tossing her bleached curls, she whimpered, 'You know how I hate those places. He wouldn't have wanted me upset now, would he?'

'No, s'pose not,' he said, leaning down to pick up the carrier bag. 'Couldn't have you upset, could we?'

Unsure how to take his comment, she smiled weakly before throwing a scathing look in Kathryn's direction and turning on her impossibly high heels to sashay away down the street, leaving the scent of cheap body spray in her wake.

Later, Kathryn, Ed and Paul shared a frozen pizza in front of the television. Paul slid a tape into the video recorder and settled down to watch it.

'How many times have you watched this?' Ed asked, picking up the plates from the floor in front of the sofa and taking them through to the kitchen.

'You can't watch *Top Gun* too many times,' Paul shouted after him.

A minute later, Paul came wandering into the kitchen, blinking under the bright fluorescent light. He went to the fridge and took out two cans of beer.

'You having one?' he asked.

'Nah, we'll call it a night,' Ed said.

Paul smirked at his brother before pushing the fridge door closed with his shoulder. He looked as if he was about to say something but a glare from Ed made him think better of it and he disappeared back into the darkness of the sitting room.

When Ed opened the door to his room, Kathryn saw there was a bottle of wine and two tumblers on the small table between the beds.

'Just to say thanks,' he said. 'You've been ace. I'm made up you're back here. Really.'

She glowed. At that moment, life felt as if it couldn't get any better.

He poured the wine and handed her a glass.

'We'll have to make do with these. You might be surprised to hear that we're not usually wine drinkers in this house,' he said, grinning.

She took it and sat down on one of the beds. The room was so small that there was hardly space for Ed to squeeze between the two beds to reach the stereo.

'What shall we have on?' he asked, looking down at her. 'I know you're not into rave stuff. What do you like? I'll see if I have it.'

'I don't know... The Cure? Morrissey?'

He frowned. 'You're joking. Bloody hell, Kat. Life's tough enough without listening to that miserable crowd.' Laughing, he turned back to the pile of tapes.

She heard him flicking through his collection and then a click. He grabbed the other glass and sat on the bed with his back against the wall, looking at her. The music started.

'Simply Red?' she said.

'Yeah, but don't go broadcasting it. I've got my reputation to keep up.'

He clicked on the bedside lamp. Kathryn was glad of the softer light as well as the softening effect of the warm Lieb-fraumilch. The music was low and the wine so sweet that she had finished the glass before she knew it. Ed leant across and refilled her glass before leaning back and closing his eyes.

'I don't know what tomorrow will bring, Kat,' he said, cradling the glass between his knees.

'You'll be together again, and in time for Christmas too. That's what you want, isn't it?'

'I guess so. It's just hard to know how it'll go. Last time he came out, it was difficult, you know?'

'Last time?' She hadn't meant to sound surprised.

He opened his eyes and she saw a hint of shame there.

'Yeah, it's not the first time he's been inside. I wasn't here the last time he got out so I didn't have to be around him those first few weeks.'

'You were down in Epsom then?'

He nodded. 'Yeah, it was mental down there, you know? But at least I didn't have to see him get completely wasted every night.'

'It sounds like it was hard on Paul.'

'But what could I do about it? He was in a mess, not eating, not washing. I mean, I knew what he could get like. We'd had him like that when we were kids. Now and then, not all the time, but enough that I'd have to stay off school and make sure he didn't do anything daft.'

'Like what?'

'One night I woke up and there was smoke coming from his room. He'd only fallen asleep with a fag in his hand and set fire to the blankets. I remember going in, room looked like a squat, cans everywhere. We were able to keep it quiet that time. Didn't want social services around again.'

'How did you manage to…?'

'What?'

'Well, turn into someone so, you know, sorted out. It's like there's nothing that fazes you.'

'You're joking, aren't you?' he said, looking around the room and shaking his head. 'I live in a dive with no job, no money, no prospects. How can you call that sorted?'

Kathryn wanted him to know that she didn't care about material success. The measure of someone couldn't be found in their wallet. That's what her nan had said and Kathryn agreed.

'I couldn't care less what you have or where you live,' she

said, once again feeling her words fall short. 'I think you're just really…'

'Really?'

She wanted so much to say what she had rehearsed when alone, that he was the best thing that had ever happened to her, that he was colour and life in a world that felt grey and numb without him.

'I think you're… great.'

He laughed. 'I don't feel great. More like well out of my depth. It's like I'm just waiting for the next time something kicks off. Because it always does. Sooner or later.'

'And Paul?'

'Paul's Paul. There's no harm in him but not much else either, if you know what I mean.' He tapped the side of his head and rolled his eyes.

'I'd never have guessed when we met first that you were going through all of that. You seemed, well, upbeat; happy with life.'

'Maybe I'm good at acting.' He winked. 'Or maybe I was just trying to impress you.'

She was glad the room was dim enough to cover the blush she could feel on her cheeks.

'Before I forget, and because tomorrow might not be the right time with everything that's going on…'

She shuffled off the bed and started to dig inside her hold-all on the floor. Her fingers closed around a small package that she held it out to him.

'Happy Christmas.'

'You haven't, have you?' he said, but he was already picking at the tape which bound the gift so tightly.

It wasn't her habit to stare into jewellery shop windows but she had spotted it when wandering through a precinct in Southampton. Almost hidden within the endless rows of sparkling diamond rings and silver bracelets, there it was – a perfect choice.

'Yes!' he said, gazing at the silver lighter in his hand. 'This is wicked. I've always wanted a Zippo.' He looked across at her and beamed. 'How did you know?'

She shrugged, thrilled at his reaction, then told him to turn it over.

The light from the lamp glinted on the lighter as he squinted, trying to make out the words engraved on the other side.

Ed

Love

Kat x

1992

She had deliberated whether to have it engraved. Finally deciding that this message was perfect – as light as the way they signed off their letters. She was careful never to hint at the feelings that had overcome her since they met. As far as she could tell, he didn't see her as a girlfriend as such. There had been nothing beyond a hug, shared confidences on the phone and a kiss under his name at the bottom of his letters. But, still, she didn't want to ruin it.

He emptied what was left of the wine into their glasses, careful to make them equal. He handed one to her and then, kneeling beside her, pulled the curtain aside and retrieved something from the window sill.

'We can christen it, if you like,' he said.

She took another mouthful of the syrupy white wine, not quite sure what he meant.

'Okay,' she said uncertainly.

He slid off the bed and, crouching at the table, expertly rolled a joint. Handing it to her, he said, 'You've smoked before?' and she nodded, unwilling to reveal just how sheltered her life had been up to now.

With a quick flick of the wrist, he swept the Zippo upwards against his jeans. A flame flickered into life and he held it towards her. Inclining her head, she let the tip of the joint touch the flame and watched it catch light.

She closed her eyes and inhaled deeply, intent on acting as if this wasn't the first time she had ever sat on someone's bed with a joint in her mouth. She knew he was watching her and, to her intense embarrassment, as the smoke tickled along her throat, she lurched into a fit of coughing.

She grabbed the glass, gulping down what remained of the warm wine.

'Here,' he said, 'I'll show you. You only need to take small hits when it's your first time.'

Blushing, her cover blown, she watched his demonstration and then tried it herself, relieved that her body didn't react as violently to this new, not unpleasant, substance reaching her lungs.

They sat in silence, passing the joint between them, listening to the songs emanating from the stereo above them. In the darkness, she felt the warmth of his hand on hers.

'Anything happening yet?' he asked.

Was anything happening? She couldn't quite tell. She was a little light-headed for sure, but that could have been the wine.

'Don't think so,' she whispered.

'Maybe next time, babe,' he said, lifting the joint to his lips.

And then, gradually, her heart felt as if was growing in her chest and the music seemed to get louder.

'Did you turn the music up?' she asked, confused because she hadn't noticed him move.

He laughed. 'Ah, now we're getting somewhere.'

She looked down at his hand, now clasping hers firmly, and was aware of a wave surrounding them, pressing in on her and then receding in tune with something that seemed to be rising in her, a sense that touched the edges of euphoria before shrinking back again. It was as if she was being pulled out on the tide towards something so vast that she dare not reach out to claim it before the wave brought her back to herself.

The very idea of something so limitless in such a tiny space suddenly seemed so ludicrous that she laughed. His voice, as if far away at the end of a long tunnel, said, 'What's so funny?' And she laughed again before turning to where his voice had come from and saying, 'I don't know. Nothing. Everything?'

All the while, her body felt soft and dormant, disconnected from the peaks she was reaching in her mind. Or was it in her heart? She felt unable to distinguish between the two.

He was saying something but there seemed to be a delay between his mouth moving and the sound reaching her.

'Sorry, Ed. I just feel a bit…' she mumbled.

He laughed. 'You're lovely.'

And the next thing she knew, the rush of elation had fallen away to leave in its wake an odd sense of melancholy. Tears started to well and then suddenly she was weeping without knowing why.

'That can happen too. Come here,' he said, pulling her close. Any other time she would have delighted in feeling him holding her tight. Wasn't it what she had so often rehearsed in her mind? But now, she felt distracted, fragmented, wondering how she could be helplessly traversing such peaks and troughs. Usually in complete control of herself, she now felt pulled in all directions by something outside of herself. But gradually she let these thoughts ebb away and contented herself with the sensation of his hand stroking her hair.

'What did you say a minute ago?' she asked quietly.

'Can't remember,' he said, pausing before adding. 'But I expect I meant it.' That tease was never far from his voice but she didn't care. She could read between the lines.

However altered she felt tonight, she still felt the chill of the room. Deciding it would be warmer in bed, she got under the covers.

It felt necessary for him to do the same, his body heat making up for the lack of central heating.

'Budge over,' he said, as he climbed into the single bed beside her, 'I need the ashtray, unless you want to risk setting fire to the place.'

And so, as they lay side by side with the orange quilt pulled tightly around them, her mind became fixated on the parts of their bodies that were touching. Her ankle brushed against his calf before edging away again and she felt his hip against hers for a moment as he leant over to tap the ash off into the stained John Player ashtray. It felt good to be close like this and, as he switched the light out, she smiled into the darkness.

She lay for some time, listening to his breath; the occasional draw on the joint before the leisurely exhale that sent smoke wafting into the air above them.

'Do you ever think about the future?' His voice came as a surprise.

'What, like next month, next year? Sometimes.' The future was actually in her mind far more frequently. When she'd hear from him next, see him next.

'No, I mean way off into the future. Like when we're in our thirties, forties.'

She hadn't thought that far ahead.

'I wonder what we'll be like then? Will we still be… us? Like, will we have forgotten everything about now, you know, this quilt cover, that jumper of yours, our mates? Will they just be faces we can't put names to?'

He took another drag of the joint, blew the smoke out of the corner of his mouth. 'I mean, will you even remember smoking your first joint with some bloke in Liverpool?'

'You'll never be just some bloke, Ed.' Her words shot out, determined, sure.

That laugh again. 'You'll have lived more life by then. Everything from now will just be pushed further away while the conveyor belt keeps moving on.'

She stared into the dark. What if her future didn't offer up too much excitement? What if the time she was sharing with him now was the defining moment of her life? She put this to him, more confidently than she would usually have felt able to.

'Blimey Kat. This place, this life isn't for you. You're different to the rest of us.'

Crossly, she replied, 'Okay, I know I'm different to other girls you … know. Or so Linda said.'

'Don't mind her. She's only jealous. She'd love to have the future you have waiting for you.'

Kathryn snorted.' What future? It's not like I'm at Cambridge heading for a first. I'm only at university because my grades were just about good enough. That's all. It's only because my parents pushed me so hard. I could just as easily have not got in.'

'Yeah, but that's not what I'm saying. University or not, you've always had opportunities. Not like us, scratching around from one week to the next, getting high to get through the day.' He shifted slightly, so there was more room between them. 'There's more on offer for people like you.'

'But you always complain about students. Wasters you call them.'

He didn't reply.

She didn't see it. Would never see it. Why didn't he want her in his world?

'What if I don't want that life, Ed? What if I want something else.'

'Then you're daft. Don't you think I want what you have? A family who are normal and boring?' He sniggered as she nudged him. 'In a good way. I don't think your old man is going in the nick anytime soon.'

She felt the weight of the person he was not mentioning, the mother he hadn't known. In the silence, she felt a tear rolling down her cheek. Then another. She didn't know if she was crying for herself, for Ed, or for a future that looked blank and empty without him in it.

He stubbed the joint out before turning back to her. She felt his fingers on her cheeks, stemming the course of her tears, and then the softness of his t-shirt as he lifted it to dry her eyes. It smelt of sweat, weed, tobacco and this house.

And then, huddled under the blankets in that dark bedroom, he kissed her for the first time with a gentleness that she hadn't expected. Not that she had expected him to be rough, but she had imagined lips that were well-practiced and assured. But he seemed surprisingly tentative. She closed her eyes and felt his lips soft on hers, leading the way, but only just, so that it felt like a conversation, his lips suggesting, her lips responding, at first hesitantly, then more eagerly. Her thoughts dissolved into nothingness, so that all that existed was the feel of his mouth on hers, his fingers stroking the nape of her neck. When he finally lifted his head, she opened her eyes slowly to see him looking at her intently.

'I've wanted to do that for a while,' he said, pushing a strand of hair behind her ear.

'I'm glad,' she whispered, emboldened by the joint. 'But why did you wait until now?'

'Didn't want to push my luck I suppose.'

'Do you always wait this long before kissing a girl?'

'What sort of question is that?' he muttered, and she heard the embarrassment in his voice.

She left it to Ed to break the ensuing silence.

'Maybe I couldn't believe that someone like you would bother with someone like me. Maybe I didn't want to ruin things by going too fast.'

She moved onto her side and felt his body inch close behind her. His arm encircled her waist and his hand clasped hers.

'Night, Kat.'

She felt his words against her neck and, closing her eyes, grinned into the darkness.

\#

In the morning, before she'd even opened her eyes, she felt a nagging ache stretching from the top of her ribs to her hip. It was the sort of cramp caused by sleeping awkwardly in a shared single bed. Easing herself straight, she felt him next to her.

She looked at his dark head, his face buried in the pillow, his arm hanging over the side of the mattress. It was no wonder she had slept so awkwardly; he had taken more than half of the bed, leaving her with the width of a plank.

She heard the sound of the toilet flushing and the bathroom door opening. She waited for Paul to pass along the landing to his own room and was horrified when the door swung open, without even a knock of warning.

Paul was already dressed in his usual football shirt and tracksuit bottoms, his hair still damp from an early shower. Kathryn found herself pulling at the quilt, as if to cover her modesty, even though there was no need. She still had her jumper and jeans on.

'Bloody hell, it's not that cold, is it?' he asked, a puzzled look on his face.

She didn't know how to answer because if he didn't feel the iciness of their house, she was wasting her breath.

'I don't get you two,' he said, shaking his head as he backed out the door and went downstairs.

Kathryn went to the bathroom, returning to find Ed sitting up in bed and rubbing his eyes, clearly hovering in that dim space between sleep and wakefulness.

'What time is it?' he asked, drowsily.

'Half ten,' she said, putting her toiletry bag back in her holdall.

He swore under his breath. 'The old man's meant to be here by lunchtime.'

He staggered out of bed, grabbed some boxer shorts and socks from his chest of drawers and headed towards the bathroom.

Pulling the bed straight, Kathryn lay her hand on his side of the mattress, feeling his warmth against her palm. The remnants of the joint they'd shared still lay in the ashtray and she picked it up, a souvenir, and slid it into her back pocket.

#

Ed's father arrived by taxi in the early afternoon.

Kathryn watched them from the kitchen door. Ed's hands were balled into tight fists while Paul glanced into the mirror at the bottom of the stairs and, seeing that the hood of his sweatshirt was tucked into his collar, pulled it straight. Ed turned the stiff latch and yanked the door open, revealing a small wiry man, his hand raised as if to knock.

'No red carpet, I see. Not even a bloody welcome mat,' he said, stepping purposefully over the threshold. Ed stood back to let him in.

Their father's eyes darted around the hallway, taking everything in. He looked past his sons to Kathryn, his gaze lingering for a few seconds longer than felt comfortable. When he looked back at Ed and Paul, his face finally relaxed. Hardly a smile, more of a softening of the muscles of his jawline.

Ed wrapped his arms around his father's thin shoulders and said, 'You're back then, Dad.'

For a moment, he stood rigid in his son's embrace before shrugging off the younger man's arms.

'All right, soft lad,' he said.

Ed thrust his hands in the pockets of his jeans as his father stepped towards his other son.

'Okay, mate?' he asked, aiming a playful punch at Paul's shoulder. They both grinned, almost conspiratorially, and Kathryn noticed for the first time the strong resemblance between them. Smiles that didn't quite reach their dark, watchful eyes. Eyes that flitted and took the measure of things.

'I heard there was a girl staying with you.' He was looking at Kathryn again but his words were directed elsewhere.

She hadn't been prepared for the discomfort she felt when his eyes settled on her. He seemed to take in every detail from her hair down to her boots.

'Dad, this is my girlfriend Kathryn,' Ed said.

The casually-added word made her stomach twist with pleasure but she maintained her composure under the scrutiny of his father. It was enough to have heard how certain he sounded.

'I'm Terry.'

As she took his outstretched hand, she noticed how soft it was. She also noticed the almost imperceptible rub of his baby finger against her palm. He kept her hand in his, only letting it drop when Paul said, 'Have you heard from Linda?'

'Yeah, she's coming round later.'

Neither brother responded.

Terry turned to his sons. 'What's a fella got to do to get a drink around here? Go on Paul, do the honours.'

The honours turned out to last well into the evening, as they set about drinking the house dry. Kathryn had assumed the booze they'd bought yesterday was at least a few months' supply. But as the hours wore on and the pile of discarded cans and bottles grew, she realised her mistake.

There was a knock on the door at eight o'clock that only Kathryn heard. Terry and his sons were talking about people she didn't know so she was glad of the excuse to leave them for a moment. As she pulled the door open, she saw Linda on the doorstep holding a Threshers' bag.

Linda had clearly made an effort, her curves once again packed into tight jeans but now with a black lace top, cut low, under a short, close fitting leather jacket. Her blonde curls, loose around her shoulders, looked expertly blow-dried and her features, accentuated with heavy make-up, made her look years older.

'All right? Are they through there?' She pushed past, the bag clinking as it caught the door.

Linda squeezed herself between Ed and his father on the sofa. 'I splashed out. Got a bottle of Bacardi and some vodka too... what'll you have?'

Paul had zoned out from the conversation and was slumped in the armchair, flicking through the TV channels, a can at his feet. Terry's attention was fixed completely on Linda, and Ed, confronted with her back, got up and went to the kitchen.

Kathryn followed him.

'Are you all right?' she asked, as he tugged the fridge door open.

He said nothing, slammed it closed again, and shot a frustrated look towards the lounge, where they could hear Terry's low voice say something undecipherable followed by Linda's high-pitched squeal of laughter. Through the open door, Kathryn could see them wrapped around each other, Terry's fingers gripping a tangle of blonde curls and their heads locked together, oblivious to anyone else.

'He promised he wouldn't take her back,' Ed muttered, his jaw clenched. 'Didn't take him long to go back on his word.' A vein pulsed at his temple. 'She's nothing but a ...'

'Shh,' Kathryn said, conscious that they could hear him. 'Not tonight, Ed. Let's talk about it tomorrow when you're sober. You don't want to say something you'll regret.'

His face softened a fraction. 'Okay. Only because I don't want there to be a scrap. Not tonight.'

Paul came wandering in.

'Leaving 'em to it,' he said. 'Got a light, mate?'

Ed dug his new lighter out of his pocket and handed it to his brother, who turned it over in his hand and whistled appreciatively.

'Where did you get this?' he asked. 'Did you rob it?'

'Have a look and you'll see,' Ed said, his eyes gleaming 'It's a present.'

Having drunk more than she was used to, drinking tea not being an option tonight, Kathryn was suddenly struck by a need for fresh air. She ventured out of the back door into the darkness, where she found a plastic garden chair and sat down. Lifting her head, she closed her eyes, relishing the cold night air on her cheeks and brow. After a few minutes, just as she was wondering if she should go back in, she heard the door open.

'You out here somewhere?' It was Terry.

Her stomach lurched. Ed's father made her nervous, a fact not diminished by the amount of drink she had consumed.

'I'm just coming in,' she called back, hurrying to her feet.

In her haste to stand, she felt dizzy and staggered. She would have fallen if he hadn't reached her in time to catch her by the arm.

'Steady on. No need to jump up.'

'I was just coming in,' she said, his hand still clasping her arm.

'Yeah, you said. But you're not leaving me out here on my own, are you? Not when it's my special night.'

She didn't reply but wished one of his sons would come looking for them. There wasn't any reason for him to be out here. The garden, she guessed, was just where the bins were kept.

'So, you're Ed's girl then.' It was a statement rather than a question.

In the garden next door, a security light flicked on, making them both look up in surprise.

'Probably a cat.'

The beam illuminated his face as he spoke. Lines spread across his forehead and crinkled the corners of his eyes, and an aquiline nose gave him a hawkish appearance. Cheekbones, most likely attractively defined in youth, now jutted in his gaunt face and she could see that, while he might have been striking once, the years had left him worn, a shadow of his youthful self.

'So what's a girl like you doing with someone like my son?' He leant so close to her she could smell the beer on his breath.

'Ed's great,' she said, the drink making her more assertive than usual.

'Is he?' He raised his eyebrows mockingly. 'I hadn't noticed.'

The light extinguished as suddenly as it had turned on and they found themselves in near darkness again. He loosened his grip on her arm slightly, but rather than letting go, he slid his hand down towards hers.

'And what has he told you about me?' She felt his fingers moving in a circular motion on the inside of her wrist.

Then a voice from the door.

'Hey, you'll catch your death out there. Come in and have another drink.'

It was Paul. Terry dropped her arm discreetly and walked sharply back to the door, where he passed his son without so much as a word.

She felt shaky, unsure if it was the drink or because she didn't know what would have happened if Paul hadn't come out of the house at that moment. She thought it had simply been a lucky break but as he held the door for her to come inside, Paul said in a low voice, 'Try not to be on your own with the old man.'

She left them soon afterwards and went to bed. There didn't seem to be anything worth staying up for. But she couldn't sleep and lay there trying to catch the words spoken, to detect whether a voice was raised in temper or in good spirits. Every now and then, she thought she heard footsteps on the stairs and hoped it was Ed, but midnight came and went, and the next time she checked her watch it was ten past one.

Finally, she heard his voice on the landing. Blinking at the light cast by the opening door, she watched him tiptoe in, trying to make as little noise as possible. Closing the door behind him, he bumped into the end of her bed and cursed quietly.

As he was trying to find his bearings in the pitch black, she leant across and clicked the bedside light on.

He looked surprised. 'Thought you were asleep,' he mumbled.

She shook her head and, sitting up, hugged her knees to her chest in an attempt to get warm.

He dropped his jumper on the floor and clicked the light off. She guessed he was pulling his jeans off as he stumbled between the two beds and then fell back, landing awkwardly on her legs.

'Sorry,' he whispered, climbing in beside her.

It wasn't long before he was asleep and snoring softly. She moved closer and fitted herself around him, feeling the rise and fall of his chest, and wondered what her parents would say if they knew where she really was.

She might have been asleep minutes or hours when she was jolted awake by the sound of footsteps. Someone passed along the landing to the bathroom. When they came back out of the bathroom, they went downstairs.

The next sound she heard was a giggle and hushed voices, followed by a series of sounds that made her put her head under the covers, wishing for sleep.

#

It was unlike any Christmas she had ever experienced. Her family never missed the morning service at their local church and, while she usually complained about the consequently delayed Christmas dinner, she had to grudgingly admit that it was a ritual that made the day that bit more... well, Christmassy. But here, nobody suggested going to church and clearly it was drink rather than food that was going to be the focus of the day.

It flowed from late morning with Terry's mood veering from a bonhomie clearly fuelled by drink rather than natural inclination to a moroseness that Kathryn guessed was caused by Linda's absence. She had left earlier to spend the day with her mother and younger sisters, causing Terry's mood to change immediately.

Paul, on the other hand, seemed more buoyant than usual, perhaps, Kathryn pondered, because of what she had heard last night. She knew she wasn't mistaken and that Linda had crept downstairs in the middle of the night to the sitting room where Paul was sleeping. It had shocked her. Not because she judged the way he was double-crossing his father – Terry didn't deserve any better – but because she had assumed that Paul was as unimpressed with Linda as Ed.

What she soon discovered about being sober in a house where everyone else was drinking was that the day dragged. She passed a bit of time by gathering up the debris from the kitchen and taking it out into the garden. As she lifted the metal lid of the dustbin and dropped the empty bottles in with a clang, she let her mind drift to how her parents and Beth would be spending the day. By now, everything would be washed up and her dad would be having a nap in the front room. The presents would have been opened and stacked neatly beside the sofa and her mother and Beth would be sitting at the kitchen table, with Beth talking incessantly and her mother hanging on her every word.

'What are you doing out here, babe?' Ed was in the doorway, a can in his hand.

'Just tidying up a bit,' she said, looking away so he couldn't see her face.

'You're not hear to clean up after us,' he said, beckoning her to come in.

She didn't want to tell him that it gave her something to do, that if she couldn't have him to herself today then what she really wanted to do was to sneak up to his room and read the book she had thrown into her holdall. Bringing it had been an afterthought – reading her course books was not a priority when she was with Ed. But things were different now that Terry was home.

She sat on the plastic garden chair, as she had last night. She didn't want to be anywhere near Terry, who was so drunk it was surely only a matter of time before he picked a fight with one of his sons or turned his attention towards her.

'You're pissed off, aren't you?' Ed said, crouching in front of her. She could smell the lager on his breath. 'I know you are. But he's only just out of the nick and I can hardly ignore him, can I?'

She said nothing. He was right. It wasn't every day your father returned to the family home after being away for so long, but what was she meant to do while they drank the house dry and caught up on yesterdays that were clearly better in the remembering than they ever could have been at the time?

'Tell you what, you probably want to ring home. We can go down to the phone box now if you like.'

At least it was a way of breaking up the day. And she did actually feel better as she listened to her mother describe Beth's arrival in a taxi – 'she wouldn't hear of your dad collecting her from the airport' – and how she had hardly recognised her because she looked so slim and well-groomed and, well, American. However disappointing Christmas Day was turning out to be, at least she had avoided the Beth fan club at home.

Ed squeezed into the phone box alongside her.

'I doubt I'll be back in time to see her. Yes, I'll be home tomorrow but I don't know what time.' She pulled an exasperated face. 'It's a long way from Cornwall.'

Ed spluttered with repressed laughter.

'Who? Oh, it's just... her brother. No, don't worry, I'm in the same room as the girls.'

It was when he started to tickle her and she discovered she couldn't escape his hands in such a tight space, just as her mother was suggesting she have a quick word with her sister, that she breathlessly explained she had to go and ended the call with a hurried Happy Christmas.

As they walked back to the house, Ed said, 'Your mum treats you like a kid, doesn't she? Why didn't you just tell her where you are?'

Kathryn didn't know how to reply. She could never tell them where she'd been. They would never trust her again.

'Well?' He kicked irritably at a can on the pavement. 'Don't you think it's better to be honest?'

'They wouldn't see it like that,' she said, quietly.

'You're nearly twenty, Kat.'

'So?'

'It just seems weird that you have to lie about where you're going.'

'If I told them… they wouldn't like it,' she said, wishing she could think of something more persuasive.

'Now we're getting somewhere,' he said, stopping suddenly. 'What you really mean is that they wouldn't want you wasting your Christmas with some scally off a council estate.'

They were at the house now.

'It's not that,' she said.

'So what is it then?' There was a quiver in his voice.

When she didn't reply, he bit his lip angrily and shook his head before storming up the garden path. The door slammed shut behind him.

She couldn't believe their conversation had descended to this in less than a minute. It was the first time they had quarrelled and her stomach twisted and knotted with dread. She wished she had said something – anything – so that he hadn't jumped to the conclusion that her parents wouldn't approve of him.

Relieved to find that the door wasn't locked, she went in and, as she passed the sitting room door, saw Terry in the armchair in front of the television. Without looking up, he said, 'If you're looking for boy wonder, he's upstairs.'

She knocked quietly on the bedroom door and pushed it open without waiting for a reply. He was sitting on the bed, his head in his hands with a white paper bag beside him.

Looking up, he took the bag and held it towards her.

'What's this?' she asked.

'For you. For Christmas,' he said.

She could feel herself blushing.

'Open it then,' he said, pushing it into her hands.

It was wrapped carefully with just enough tape to secure the red and green paper.

She pulled off the paper and smiled.

'*A Christmas Carol*?' It was a beautiful hardback edition bound in a burgundy tartan fabric. 'It's gorgeous. Thank you.'

He smiled. 'I thought it would remind you of your Christmas in Liverpool. I got it in one of the shops on Bold Street.'

'Ed, I never said you were a…' she said.

'Scally?'

'I mean, I don't even know what a scally is.'

'Really? It's like a loser, a wrong 'un.'

Kathryn frowned and said, 'I would never call you that.'

'Look at my family, where I live. Look at what Christmas Day is like in this place,' he said.

'You aren't your family, Ed.'

He interrupted, 'Is it okay? The book. I mean, you haven't read it or anything?'

She shook her head, smiling. Hugging the book to her, she vowed to keep it with her forever.

Chapter 7

It was three months since Kathryn had seen Ed so nothing could stop her on that cold Thursday afternoon in March, not the threat of snow or a quiet warning from her course tutor about her falling marks.

This time she drove straight to his house.

As Ed led her through to the kitchen, she had the sense that the house was empty.

'Your dad not around?' she asked.

'He's gone to Blackpool for a couple of days. Paul's out too.'

She felt a change in him. She had picked something up on the phone but had pushed it to the back of her mind. A sense of distraction, as if his mind was elsewhere. He looked the same, still smiled that smile she had looked forward to seeing, but there was something altered.

'Everything all right?' she asked.

'Course. Come here.' He wrapped his arms tightly around her, kissing her with a sureness that pushed any concerns from her mind.

'Shall we head into town later?' he asked. 'Go to a club?'

#

The taxi dropped them in the city centre. She would have preferred to stay in and make the most of the empty house, but she knew Ed had been stuck in the house all week and if clubbing could lift his mood, then it wasn't such a hardship for her to show willing.

They hurried through the shopping precinct against a biting wind. Usually swarming with a seething mass of shoppers during the day, it had taken on another identity by night. One of its dark doorways was the chosen shelter of someone down on their luck, huddled in a sleeping bag and settled in for the night ahead. Carrier bags filled with a life's worth of possessions were piled between the sleeping bag and the street beyond.

A little further on, a group of youths clustered. Some kicked at the ground, while a couple wheeled around on bikes. As they murmured in low voices, their words became condensation in the chill, dark night. They looked unsure of what to do next but clearly aimlessness was preferable to turning for home.

Mannequins stared sightlessly from dimly lit window displays waiting for shop managers to unlock the doors for eager customers to part with their money. There seemed to be only space for the cheap and discounted in this city, which, like so many others, was in the grip of recession. At least the stores here were open; along the side streets, every other shop was boarded up. Pasted onto the plywood nailed across their windows were lurid posters for upcoming gigs and protest marches. Junk mail was rammed into letterboxes of doors that hadn't been opened in months.

'Are you sure it's along here?' Kathryn asked.

'Course I'm sure,' he replied.

Just when she was beginning to think he must be wrong and should admit defeat, she spotted light, and life, at the end of the dark street. People were milling around the door of a single storey building and every time the door opened, a blast of pulsing music was released onto the street.

'This queue is ridiculous,' groaned Kathryn as they reached

the back of a line that stretched far down the street from the door.

Stamping his feet to keep warm, Ed said, 'Anything worth having is worth waiting for.'

Kathryn had always felt nervous in a crowd. She felt trapped, cornered. It wasn't so bad waiting to go into the lecture hall. Students tended to just chat quietly or sit alone on the wall outside, pulling out a book. But here, people were jostling and bumping each other as they edged forward impatiently. The energy felt restless, agitated.

And then she heard a voice she recognised. It was raised and arguing with someone. Ed had clearly heard it too.

'What the...?' he said, stepping out of the queue and looking up the line.

And then they saw Paul, shoved out of the line and into the street. He stumbled for a second and then launched himself back into the group of bodies that had filled the space he had just been occupying.

Ejected again, he came swaggering towards them. Kathryn prayed that he hadn't spotted them and would just keep going. But then Linda emerged from the queue and followed him, shouting at him to stop.

Ed swore quietly and turned his back to them. At the last moment, Linda caught a glimpse of Kathryn and stopped.

'Hey Paul, it's Ed's girl,' she called.

Paul zig-zagged back towards her.

Ed turned to face them.

'Mate! Didn't think you were out tonight,' Paul said.

Ed looked from Paul to Linda and back again before hissing, 'What are you doing with her?'

'I can explain,' Paul said, his eyes lowered. 'Ain't what you think.'

Linda stepped towards them, as someone tried to squeeze past on the pavement.

'I suppose you thought you'd make the most of the old man being away?' Ed said.

Linda just shrugged.

'I just bumped into her in town earlier. Thought it was too early to go home, you know?' Paul said.

'Yeah, whatever,' Ed said, turning away from them.

Paul winked at Linda and she bit her lip, smirking.

The people in front began to move as the club doors were opened.

'What we doing then?' Paul's words didn't seem to be addressed to anybody in particular.

Ed shrugged. 'We're going in. Up to you what you do.'

Paul grinned and squeezed into the line in front of them. Linda edged in beside him and Kathryn noticed him reach across and slide his hand into the back pocket of her skirt.

The music had been growing louder the closer they got to the club and, when they stepped inside, it pounded so that the floor felt like it was shuddering. Kathryn could feel it reverberating to her fingertips.

Inside, it seemed far larger than the entrance on the street suggested. It was like a huge warehouse, the dark only pierced by flashing strobe lights that picked out the mass of dancers jamming every inch of the floor. Kathryn had only been to a club like this once and had vowed never to go again. She didn't understand the appeal of this incessant, repetitive din. Maybe it was the music of her generation but she remained puzzled by the enthusiasm of those around her whose faces lit up in anticipation of getting onto the floor. Was she the only person here who wanted to be elsewhere? The music was her idea of torture and yet the dance floor was crammed.

With nowhere to sit and hardly enough room to stand, Kathryn knew she was going to hate every moment. Even being near Ed couldn't make up for this feeling she had that this would be a night which would never end. Not that there was any point in being near him. Words were impossible.

Ed shouted something undecipherable in her ear and, with no hope of understanding, she just shrugged. He winked and was gone, joining the throng under the flashing strobes.

Every now and then, he tried to lead her into the crowd but when she shook her head, he disappeared again. When he hadn't returned for half an hour, she thought about leaving, but that seemed a bit dramatic so she pushed it out of her mind. Why had he brought her here if he was just going to leave her standing here like a fool? He could have come out clubbing any night but to decide on tonight when she had driven all that way to be with him. Tears pricked her eyes and, as she stood gripping a plastic cup of flat Coke from a soda gun, she told herself to pull herself together. Just get through tonight and never come to a place like this again.

To break the monotony of staring at strangers, she decided to go to the ladies. The scene inside was pretty much like the bathroom of every nightclub. The queue stretched around every wall and when the door opened to let in another girl, it would knock into whoever was jammed against it.

As Kathryn waited, one of the cubicle doors opened and Linda tottered out. She pushed her way through so she could get to the washbasin and reapply her makeup, oblivious to the looks of those who had to shuffle out of her way.

Linda leant towards the mirror brandishing her mascara wand. Her tight pink cardigan, with as many buttons undone as she could get away with, crept up so that her lower back was exposed above the gold link belt of her black mini skirt. Her heels – the same ones she had worn the day Kathryn met her – added two inches to her height so that she towered over most of the other girls.

Kathryn knew what her friend Elaine would think of Linda. Common as muck. But, she had to hand that to her, she did dazzle. In comparison, Kathryn felt even drabber than usual, flinching at her jeans and jumper reflected back at her in the bathroom mirror while all those around her were dressed up for the night with bare arms and barely-there outfits.

As Linda wound her lipstick back into its case, she caught Kathryn's eye in the mirror.

'All right, Kathryn?' Linda smiled, putting her makeup back into her tiny bag. She jerked her head towards the cubicles. 'Go 'ed. I'll wait for ya.'

She was there when Kathryn came back out.

'Here, I'm going for a smoke. Coming?' Linda said.

As Kathryn trailed behind her, she could see how lads' eyes followed Linda. Pints were held suspended, conversations paused momentarily. When she passed them, their stares switched to disinterest. Some primal instinct in these strangers was triggered by Linda; the sight of a body so perfectly proportioned and on show. Maybe they believed Linda was parading past just for them, to tempt them to approach, to try their luck. Maybe she was.

Linda found a corner of a corridor that wasn't occupied and delved into her bag for her cigarettes. She lit one between her vermillion lips.

The music was a little less deafening here.

'Smoke?' She turned the packet towards Kathryn who

found a spot against the opposite wall.

Kathryn shook her head.

'You don't think much of me, do ya?' Linda said.

'Sorry?' Kathryn said, unused to someone cutting to the chase so quickly.

'Come off it. You think we're all trash. All but lover boy,' Linda said, matter-of-factly, as if it was to be expected.

'No, I don't. How could you even think that?'

'Paul says you're sound but from what I can make out, you don't say a word and just look down your nose at us.'

Kathryn looked at the black bricks behind Linda's blonde hair.

'I don't say much because I don't know what to say.'

Linda seemed to consider this for a moment before softening a little.

'Okay, maybe I got it wrong.'

They stood for a moment in silence.

'You two going okay?' Linda asked.

'I think so,' Kathryn said. ' We don't see each other that much, what with the distance.'

'Bet you make up for it though,' Linda said, winking. 'You know, when you get together.'

As Kathryn reddened and looked away, Linda came closer and asked, 'You do sleep together, don't you?' Kathryn's expression told her everything she needed to know. 'What, not even once?'

When Kathryn didn't reply, Linda let out a low whistle. 'Bloody hell. So, you're just mates. Is that it?'

Kathryn shrugged. 'No, it's just not happened yet.'

Linda looked mystified, 'Do you want it to happen?' She watched Kathryn through narrowed eyes.

'I suppose so.'

'So give him a nudge. Not that Ed usually needs one.' Linda seemed to be turning something over in her mind. 'You're pretty innocent, aren't you? Maybe that's the problem. Maybe it kinda... puts him off.'

It wasn't said unkindly but the words wounded Kathryn and she felt the need to hit back.

'Does Terry know you're here?'

Linda's gaze hardened. 'Terry doesn't own me. Last time I looked, I was a single girl having some fun.'

Kathryn looked away, chastised.

'Judge me all you want but I'm not doing anyone any harm. Terry's crazy about me but, you know, he's old enough to be me da.'

'And Paul?'

Linda shrugged. 'I just met him down town tonight. By accident. He's just Terry's lad.'

She must have spotted something like disbelief in Kathryn's expression because she said, 'What?'

Kathryn stammered, ' Last time I was here, the first night Terry was back, I heard something in the night. Downstairs.'

Linda coloured and bit her lip. 'Did you tell Ed?'

'No, why would I?'

'That's right sound of you.'

'None of my business.' Kathryn glanced back towards the dance floor.

At that moment, Paul edged out of the crowd, looking around as if searching for someone.

Linda waved and when he saw her, his eyes lit up and he headed over.

'All right, girls?' he said, putting his arms around them both. 'Thought you'd cleared off and left us.'

Linda laughed at him. 'Got anything for us?'

'Might have.' He smiled before leaning his cheek on Kathryn's head. 'Hey, girl, it's ace to see you again.'

'All right soft lad, hand 'em over,' Linda said, nudging him affectionately as he started rummaging around in his pockets.

Kathryn wondered how much he'd had to drink. But was this just drink? There was no hint of the aggression she had witnessed in the past.

His eyes widened as he discovered what he was searching for – a small square of paper folded like an envelope. He opened it carefully and dropped something into Linda's outstretched palm.

'Come on, Paul. Don't be tight. Anything for Kathryn?' she said, before turning away and popping whatever was in her hand into her mouth.

'Nah, you don't want anything, do you? Just a drink maybe?' he said, turning to her.

'Have you seen Ed anywhere?' Kathryn asked.

'Haven't seen him in a bit. Has he left you alone all night? Hear that, Linda? She comes all this way and then he just pisses off and leaves her.' He shook his head.

Kathryn recognised the truth of what he was saying and, to her shame, felt the warning tingle of tears welling up once again. He was right. She hadn't wanted to come to the club but he'd brought her anyway and then just deserted her in this dark, sweaty din. She was on the outside looking in, watching other people having fun while her own sense of adventure was limited to putting a tank of petrol in her car and driving to Liverpool.

Good old reliable Kathryn. Never been in trouble in her life, never taken an illegal substance... well, just that spliff at Christmas... but apart from that, nothing. Always abiding by the rules, doing the right thing. Behaving as she had been taught to behave when, inside, she felt like exploding. That was the trouble with politeness, it stifled and smothered her words, even her thoughts, so that the truth of what she wanted, who she was, stayed buried.

Rubbing her sleeve across her face as if to wipe the sweat from her brow, she dried her eyes. The idea forming in her mind was making her stomach twist with something that felt like nerves. Or excitement. How about if, just for tonight, she became someone else?

She turned to Paul.

'Can I have one?'

He frowned and looked at Linda, who nodded enthusiastically.

'I dunno… if you've never…'

'Go on Paul, she's not a baby. Let her take one or else she'll be bored off her head.'

He shrugged. 'Okay, but keep an eye on her, yeah?'

He produced the square of paper again and tipped out a small round pill. It sat in Kathryn's palm, looking as innocent as something she might take for a headache. How dangerous could it be? Most people in the club had probably taken something similar. A voice inside her head urged her on, to be like everyone else for a change, to have the sort of fun she found so elusive. This little pill was her gateway into a new version of herself for a few hours.

She slipped it onto her tongue and swallowed.

It seemed like an obvious next step to follow Linda into the mass of bodies under the lights. As they queued at the bar for exorbitantly priced bottles of water – Linda insisted that the only rule was that they must have water – Kathryn felt the drug steadily assert itself, pushing her racing thoughts aside. Any negative thoughts about where Ed had disappeared to or her frumpy appearance drifted away, leaving space for a contentment that was swelling into something bigger. As they threaded their way through the swaying mass to a spot that was less packed, Kathryn started to grin.

Before long, she forgot any concerns she'd had about how to dance or how she looked and just let herself move with the others around her. She understood now what it was about the music that pulled them onto the floor, its beat hypnotic and magnetic so that whatever she did with her body, it was in time with its throbbing pulse.

Now and then, Linda nudged her, reminding her to drink. Kathryn felt warm with gratitude. Here was this glamorous girl, staying close, keeping an eye on her, making sure she drank enough to stay well. She thought how harshly she'd judged her, just because she dressed differently, spoke differently. So what if she was sleeping with father and son? What's so wrong with showing love?

That was it. How could it be wrong to show love in a physical way? Everyone had the right to do as they wished with their bodies. Who was she to judge? Imagine if she hadn't taken that tiny tablet; she'd be over on the sidelines, miserable and resentful.

Linda moved aside to let Paul in to the space with them. He was grinning inanely, throwing some daft moves. He winked at Kathryn, making her feel as if she'd got them all wrong. The flicker of guilt soon evaporated, leaving her with the thrill of feeling like she belonged.

It was getting hotter. Linda mimed something to her that she couldn't fathom. Then she shouted in her ear, 'Take your top off. You mustn't get too hot.'

She pulled off her jumper and tied it around her waist so

she could continue dancing in her crop top and jeans. Immediately, she felt the air on her shoulders and back as her body starting to cool.

She felt her arms move and her body sway as if they belonged to someone else. Why had she left it so long to become like everyone else? To drop her guard, to embrace this freedom.

She felt a hand on her arm.

'Ed!' her mouth formed the word but the sound was drowned by the music.

His hand tightly clasped hers as he pulled her roughly out through the crowd. Meanwhile, the music continued to throb and people continued to dance, hardly aware of him forcing his way past them, dragging her behind.

It wasn't until he pulled her into a small alcove, some- where where the music was less deafening, that he dropped her hand and faced her, his eyes flashing.

His jaw was tightly clenched.

'What's wrong?' she asked, staring at him.

She couldn't understand his anger. She'd only been dancing.

'Where did you get it? Who gave it to you?' he asked, as he began unknotting the jumper at her waist.

'What?' she stared at his hands pulling impatiently at the fabric.

A muscle twitched in his temple as he looked back at her.

'You know what I'm talking about,' he said, pulling the jumper from her waist and pushing it into her hands. 'Now, put that on.'

'No, it's too hot,' she said, feeling like a surly school kid and letting the jumper drop onto the floor.

He glanced down to where it lay in a heap and then started to shrug his denim shirt off, leaving just a white t-shirt beneath.

'Here then,' he put it across her shoulders, more gently this time.

'Why are you so keen to cover me up?' she asked, hearing the uncharacteristic coquettish tone in her voice. She was glad that one little tablet had allowed this more confident Kathryn to step forward.

'I'm not, it's just … this isn't like you.'

She looked at him with a directness that was also unlike her. She barely recognised herself. The dynamics were shifting. No longer meek and unsure, she now felt equal to him.

It was as if he didn't know how to respond to her as she continued to hold his gaze, feeling powerful, in control, euphoric. And if he didn't know how to respond, then she would have to lead the way.

She closed the gap between them, her body just millimetres from his. He gave a knowing smile as if he had just read her mind and she knew, with a glow deep down inside, that he was going to respond.

'Here you are,' It was Paul, chewing gum faster than anyone Kathryn had ever seen.

Cursing, Ed stepped back and leant down to pick up Kathryn's jumper.

'Sorry, did I interrupt something?' Paul said, winking at Kathryn. His eyes seemed to be flickering as he nodded his head to the music.

'Why don't you do one and go back to the old man's girlfriend before she finds another loser to cop off with. Come on, Kat, we're off.'

'I'll ignore that cos we're rolling and you're pissed off,' Paul said, still beaming.

Kathryn didn't want to leave. She was going to make the most of how she was feeling. She had no idea how long it would last. For all she knew, her old self might return at any moment, like Cinderella's coach turning back into a pumpkin.

It felt like she was watching herself with a mixture of shock and delight as she draped her arms around Ed's neck.

'Come on, we're having fun,' she said. 'Let's go and dance.'

'You're not having fun, you're just high, that's all,' he replied, unpeeling her arms and stepping back.

She shook her head, annoyed. 'You know what, Ed? For the first time in ages, I'm actually enjoying myself and I can't believe you want to sabotage that. Why shouldn't I let myself go for once in my life?'

'You don't need drugs for that,' he shot back.

'Well, I was having a pretty miserable night until then. Being left on my own all night like that.' She snatched the jumper from his hands and knotted it around her waist again. 'Do what you want but you're not ruining my night more than you have already.'

Ed took her arm and steered her away from Paul, who was absorbed by their exchange.

'I'm sorry, okay?' he said. 'I lost track of time and then when I came back you were gone. Look, it's just that, you don't need to become like the rest of us. You're different.'

Kathryn snorted. If he said that one more time, she'd scream. She knew she was different. She didn't need him to point it out. It was why she had felt so out of place here, why she felt out of place almost all the time except when it was just the two of them.

'So, why do you bother with me then if I'm such a bore?' she snapped.

Ed frowned, confused, 'What? I mean, you're different to the rest of us because you don't need to score drugs or get off your face to be yourself. You're better than that.'

Kathryn had been staring crossly at the swirling pattern of the red carpet but now looked up and smiled.

'Really?'

'Yeah. I shouldn't have brought you here tonight. I should have known you'd hate it. I thought I needed to go to a club because it's pretty shit being stuck at home right now. But I was wrong. I don't need any of this when you're around.'

'What difference does it make if I'm around or not?' She knew she was fishing for compliments but didn't care.

'I dunno, maybe being around you makes me feel safe, stronger.'

'Can I tell you something?' she said. 'Sometimes I get tired of being different to you all. Just for tonight, I'd like to have fun. But only if you do too.'

'So, it's you who's the bad influence now, is it,' he laughed. 'Leading me astray. Who'd have thought it.'

'Just for tonight.'

Ed jerked his head at Paul, who hurried over and slipped something into Ed's outstretched hand with the swiftness of a relay runner.

Ed moved it equally swiftly to his mouth and then led Kathryn by the hand back into the crowd.

Although they seemed to dance for hours, she still felt more energised than ever before and, all the while, she also felt unbelievably happy. Happy to be here, with this person who she loved more than her own family. Whenever she looked at Ed, she wondered why she had waited so long to act on her feelings. She'd taken the lead, shown him what she wanted. And it had been so easy.

When they spilled out onto the street, with Paul trying to convince her to put her jumper back on as it was March in Liverpool not July in Ibiza, Kathryn was surprised to see that the sky was now streaked with purple and the darkness had retreated.

As they sat on a wall with other revellers waiting for a taxi, it felt natural to have Ed's arm tightly around her. She lay her head on his shoulder, smiling at how wonderful the night had been.

She looked along the wall to see Paul and Linda entwined, their attention firmly fixed on each other.

She waited for Ed to spot them, for a row to erupt, but he just sighed.

'You knew?' she asked.

'Had my suspicions, yeah.'

'I suppose there's no harm in it. Just single people having some fun.' A few hours earlier, who would have imagined she'd be quoting Linda by the end of the night.

'Don't think the old man would see it that way, but maybe he deserves it.'

'She's all right though, Ed.'

'Kat, you're just seeing the best in everyone because you've had your first E.' And he laughed, leaning in to kiss her hair.

When a taxi finally arrived, the sky had lightened still more, prompting Kathryn to muse on whether it was already time to get up even though they hadn't been to bed yet. She was still pondering this conundrum as she piled into the back with Paul and Linda.

Ed asked Linda where she wanted to be dropped off.

'I was thinking of coming back with you lot,' she said, hopefully.

It turned out that Terry was out of town for another couple of days, so why break up the party now? Ed just shook his head and sighed while Paul smirked. The taxi driver glanced across at Ed, 'So, the one drop off in Speke then?' and was answered with a curt nod.

A lot can happen in a few hours, thought Kathryn as she watched Ed turn the key in the lock and switch the lights on. Paul and Linda had stopped off halfway along the path to pick up where they left off in the back of the taxi.

The house seemed to have taken on a brighter prospect. Cosy and crammed with the minutiae of Ed and his brother's lives, she decided she had been wrong about their home. So different from the neatness of her parents' house where life was comfortable, tidy, lacklustre. This was where life happened.

'So?' Ed said, his hands around her waist. 'It's ten to six. You realise you can't drive home today?'

She looked at him, mystified. 'I'll be okay with a few hours' sleep.'

He pulled a face and laughed. 'You'll soon see.'

'See what?' Paul was pushing past them, still chewing, still full of energy.

'See what a div you are, for a start,' Ed said. 'Pushing pills on her like that.'

'Yeah? And remind me why you're complaining exactly?' Paul said, bending down to turn on the stereo.

Ed filled two mugs with water. 'Ready to turn in? Or do you want to stay down here with that pair?'

Paul was now jumping around the dim sitting room to a dance track while Linda, perched on the edge of the sofa, was easing her stilettoes from her feet.

As Kathryn followed Ed upstairs, the music was turned up louder and she wondered vaguely if the neighbours would be able to hear. Usually, this would have bothered her and she would have pleaded with them to turn the volume down, but now she let the thought drift away.

Ed put the cups carefully on the bedside table and it was all she could do to stifle a grin as she let her mind wander to what lay ahead. As if reading her mind, he caught her eye and gave her the same smile that had captivated her the first time she had laid eyes on him.

'So,' he said, 'what happens now?'

'What are the choices?' she asked.

'Well, we could try and get some sleep but that's usually difficult on E. Or we could have a smoke. Or we could play music, but we probably couldn't hear it with that racket down there,' he said, raising his voice at the floorboards.

'Sounds like we're running out of options then,' she said.

'Or,' he said, his eyes fixed on hers.

'Or?' She held his gaze.

As she remembered Linda's words from earlier in the evening about Ed not usually needing a nudge, jealousy flickered deep inside her. She turned the key in the lock.

He was watching her intently.

'You're sure?' he asked quietly.

'Of course,' she said. Because she was sure. There was nothing she wanted more.

And then he was in front of her, his arm stretching around her to the wall behind. He clicked off the light, leaving the room shadowy with just the early morning light finding its way through a gap in the curtains. She felt his fingertips on the back of her neck and then his lips on hers for a brief, tantalising moment.

'It has to be because you want to…'

He bent to her mouth again before pulling away once more.

'And not because you've taken something or feel you should or…'

She hadn't realised how wonderful his lips would feel on her neck, and how much more insistently they would move when she slipped her hands under his shirt and ran her fingers over the smooth skin of his back.

The music downstairs suddenly stopped and, hearing footsteps on the stairs, Kathryn stiffened, pulling her hands away.

'No one can come in,' Ed whispered, before taking a step back. 'But we can stop if you want to.'

But she didn't want it to end here, so she eased her jumper over her head and dropped it on the floor. She shivered in the chill of the room as she turned her attention to the buttons on his shirt. Her fingers struggled clumsily with the first two before he took over, tugging the shirt and then his t-shirt over his head and throwing them onto the carpet.

As he gently took her face in his hands and began to kiss her again, she felt the warmth of his chest against her, his fingers lost in her hair. She wondered if he knew this was her first time, whether it mattered to him. But the thought was lost as he lifted his mouth from hers and with raised eyebrows, nodded towards the bed.

\#

Afterwards, when morning had flowed seamlessly into afternoon, one of her first thoughts when she woke was that she couldn't wait to tell Elaine about what had happened. Even though she would inevitably jump to the wrong conclusion and assume that Kathryn had been coerced into taking drugs. And the rest. No, it would have to remain her secret.

When she tried to move, she discovered that every muscle

in her body was cramping in protest. Her legs felt like they were weighed down with bricks while her back ached miserably when she tried to sit up. A wave of nausea swept through her so ferociously that she had to drag herself from under the covers and rush to the bathroom.

As she was clinging on to the toilet, waiting for the queasiness to end, she heard Ed coming up the stairs. She was aware of him beside her as she expelled most of the water she had diligently consumed last night but it was only when she knew her stomach was empty that she glimpsed him through the tangle of her hair.

She closed her eyes and groaned. 'Why didn't you tell me?'

He put a face cloth under the tap, squeezed it out and handed it to her.

'I did, a few times. Sometimes the comedown can be quite hard.'

The cloth gave her the cooling jolt she needed to straighten up. After dragging some clothes on and pulling a brush through her hair, she crept downstairs.

Glancing in the lounge, she saw a heap of blankets on the sofa, a tattooed arm with a silver watch hanging over the edge at one end and glossy red painted toenails poking out the other.

Ed had made her some toast and tea but she could hardly face them and, instead, filled a cup at the tap.

'It's best to eat, Kat, or you'll feel like shit all day.'

Staring at the weak afternoon sun, reflected in rainwater collected in a dustbin lid in the garden, she vowed that aspirin would be the only pill she would take in future. She gulped the water and refilled the cup.

The house now seemed so small that it felt as if the walls were pressing in on her. When Ed switched on the light, she flinched at the sharp glow from the harsh fluorescent bulb.

'Is it always like this?' she asked, easing a chair out from the table and sitting down.

'Not always. But when it's your first time...'

She felt herself blushing.

'I didn't mean...' he said.

She busied herself buttering the toast.

Mustering the final traces of last night's confidence, she said, 'So, how do you know it was?'

'What?' he said.

'My first time.' She put the knife down but didn't look at him.

'Doing drugs? Or...' His voice was uncertain.

She looked at him. 'What happened afterwards.'

'I dunno, I suppose I just guessed.'

He stared at the ashtray in front of him, pushing it from side to side without lifting his eyes.

'You don't regret it or anything?' he mumbled.

She lifted the cup. 'Course not. It was... lovely.'

He grinned, still staring at the ashtray.

'More than that, babe. It was blinding.'

\#

Later that afternoon, Ed suggested that the only way to shake off the malaise that had set in was to take a walk. With heavy, aching legs, Kathryn agreed, if only to get away from the atmosphere in the house. Linda was still asleep and Paul's high spirits had crashed, leaving a sourness that was best avoided.

As they walked, the houses of the estate eventually gave way to a landscape of factories and industrial units and, just as Kathryn decided this was probably as good as it got, the road ended abruptly, narrowing into a path that led into thick woodland.

It seemed odd that it was the woodland that seemed out of place, like it had been dropped into this industrial setting, when, in reality, the urban sprawl had begun as a small cluster of buildings that had spread relentlessly like ink on blotting paper, obliterating everything natural in its way.

Yet once they'd entered the woods and were sealed off within the hush of the trees, the mechanised world felt like a memory. Only the sound of planes coming in to land on the nearby runway reminded them that they were still in the 20th century.

Despite her dragging tiredness and lingering sense of being completely out of sorts, Kathryn felt her spirits lift.

With his hands thrust into the pockets of his coat, Ed strode on beside her. She wondered how he had so much energy after so little sleep. When she asked him, he laughed and reminded her that he was used to it; the surge of energy then the sudden decline of a typical night out.

'Well, not exactly typical,' he added, with a wink.

They continued to walk as she blushed.

As the path began to curve to the right, he stopped and sat on a bench beneath an ancient-looking oak tree at the edge of a sea of snowdrops. Kathryn was a little disappointed to realise that this oasis wasn't a secret; that other people sat here and enjoyed the peace. But, for now, it was theirs and she sat beside him, gazing at the spectacle before them.

He was leaning forward, his elbows on his knees, chin in hands. She had noticed him sitting like this often. It made him look deep in thought. Deciding to wait for him to speak first, she leant back against the tree, feeling the solidness of its trunk, which must have endured much over the centuries. As she heard the distant roar of another plane taking off, it struck her that this tree, and its neighbours, had escaped much too.

'We came here when we were little,' he said, staring ahead.

'You and Paul?'

'Yeah. I don't really remember but he does. He says we'd be right here, me in the pushchair, him playing.'

Ed straightened up, picking at his finger nails distractedly.

'She probably sat where you're sitting now.'

They sat in silence, broken only by the sound of a black-bird high in the branches above them.

'I don't even know what she was like. Can't picture her. The old man got rid of her photos so it's like she never existed.'

He cleared his throat and she watched his hands, clenched into fists on his knees. She wanted to say something that might help, something that might make him feel less alone. But she knew better than to talk as if she knew how it felt to have a blank space where a parent should be.

She wanted to press his hand into hers but couldn't bear it if he snatched it away. Last night's version of herself wouldn't think twice, she told herself. She'd do what felt natural, what felt right. Pull him tightly to her, press the sadness from him. For now anyway. But that sureness had retreated now and she'd walked back into herself as she always was, reserved and uncertain. And with the sense that her body had been wrung out, leaving it raw and exposed.

'You never asked your dad?' she asked.

'You know when there's things you can't bring up?' he said, a brittleness in his voice. 'Like if you say it, there will be this big scene and you'll regret opening your mouth? It's like that with him. Everything's okay as long as you're going along with him. Just don't veer off the script, you know.'

'You think a lot of him though,' she ventured. It had been clear from the first time they had spoken that he had a regard for his father that she now realised was wholly undeserved.

'Well, yeah, he's my old man, isn't he?'

She couldn't see the logic in this. From what she'd seen, Terry had scant regard for his son. Surely Ed had to have picked up on this over the years?

As he dug the toe of his trainer into the soft earth, he said, 'Anyway, what choice do I have? He's all I've got.'

She laid her hand over his fist and felt his hand relax then turn so his fingers could clasp hers tightly. He looked at her. When he had mentioned his mother before, he had affected indifference, but now she could see that the mask had slipped enough for her to see hurt, a lifetime of it.

'Maybe there's a way of tracking her down somehow? Is she still…'

He shrugged. 'Dunno. If she is, she's not come near us in twenty years. And if she's dead… it's like it's a lose-lose, you know?'

'I can see how you'd think that. But maybe there's someone else who knew her. Surely, finding out more about her would be better than this?

'Maybe.'

Silence descended.

'You know what I did once?' he looked at her as if considering whether to continue then shook his head. 'Nah, forget I said anything.'

'Go on.'

'You'll only laugh. Think I'm mad.'

'I bet I won't.'

He shrugged. 'Okay, I went to someone once to find out if she was still alive.'

Kathryn looked mystified.

'A few of us were down in Brighton for the weekend and the others were sleeping off the night before. So I went down to the pier and there was a woman there. I don't know what you'd call her. A psychic? Fortune teller? Anyway, I went in for a reading and I asked her about my mother.'

'And what did she say?'

'Not much. Just that she couldn't connect with her,' he shrugged.

'But that's good news surely? It means your mum's alive somewhere.'

'Or the woman on the pier was a fake, more like,' he snorted. 'She told me other stuff that sounded mad, like apparently I'm really lucky because one day I'll be able to put something right when most people don't get the chance. I mean, that could mean anything. Complete waste of time. And of a fiver.'

'Do you believe in that sort of thing?' Kathryn asked. 'You know, that we go somewhere when we die?'

'Yeah, I think I do. Life would be pretty pointless otherwise, wouldn't it? You know, when life's shit, maybe it's because we're paying for something we've done in another life or something.'

'Like karma, you mean?'

Silence descended once again.

'I like it that you listen to me. I mean, really listen.' The observation was unexpected.

'Why wouldn't I?' What she didn't say in that moment was that her happiest times were when she was listening to him, when she had a part to play but all eyes were not on her, when there was no expectation for her to shine. Shining wasn't her way.

'It's rare, you know? Most people are only waiting for the other person to shut up so they can start talking again,' he said, continuing to dig into the soil with his foot. 'My other friends just want to talk about doing drugs, who they're shagg– sorry, sleeping with and…'

'So why do you bother with them?'

He paused as if considering the question.

'They're a laugh, I suppose. They're mates, you know. We like doing the same things.'

She didn't say anything.

He glanced across at her.

'Yeah, doesn't sound too convincing, I suppose. I mean I couldn't go telling them about asking a psychic about my mother or anything like that. But I can tell you.'

'You can. You know that.'

'Enough about me though. How about you? You never say much about home. You know, your family, your mates.'

'There's not much to say about them. Mum stays at home, Dad works in an office, and I've got an older sister. Other than that, there's just my best friend Elaine who I've known since I was little.'

'I bet they're all proud of you. Getting to university and that,' he said.

She didn't think her family was proud of her. Elaine maybe, but her parents had taken it for granted that their daughters would be the first in the family to go to university. After all, they had worked hard to send the girls to the town's private school to give them the best possible start. And it wasn't like Kathryn had got into Oxford like Beth. Kathryn didn't know how to tell him that growing up under a looming pressure to succeed had left its mark on her. It would sound ridiculously privileged to someone whose mother had left and who had a father like Terry. But her parents had been so determined that their daughters should succeed in life, they had corralled them into a narrow world of school and home with the usual stuff of teenage lives decidedly off limits. School discos, hanging out with friends in the precinct; Kathryn knew better than to even suggest what her parents would view as a waste of time. Besides, both girls had their Saturdays filled – piano lessons for Beth, riding for Kathryn. Beth was a high flyer at school who thrived under the pressure, but Kathryn just felt as if her wings had been clipped.

'What about your sister? You never say much about her. Are you alike?'

'Not particularly. She's the star of the family. Going places.'

He laughed. 'The way you say it, she can't go far enough. Is that it?'

And then she laughed too, knowing how obvious she made her feelings towards her older sister.

'Sometimes I think life would have been different if she hadn't been so talented. There wouldn't be this standard that's too high for me to reach all the time. You know, it's not great to feel that you're never quite good enough. Sometimes I hate her for it. Because there's this shadow – her shadow – that I never seem to be able to escape.'

'Not good enough? Bloody hell, how can you think that?'

She shrugged. 'It's just the way it is at home.'

'Yeah, well, that's not how it is up here. You're a Derby winner in a house of selling platers.'

Kathryn laughed at the racing analogy, picturing her family

running in a selling race, the lowest grade race on the card.

'Anyway, you're not likely to ever meet Beth.'

'Why?'

She didn't want to tell him that she feared her sister would captivate him as she did most men. Possessiveness and jealousy were not attractive traits. So, instead she said, 'Because she's in Boston.'

The look he gave her suggested that he had already picked up more about the relationship she had with her sister than she would have guessed.

'We'll leave her where she is then,' he said, leaning across to kiss her.

When they were retracing their footsteps out of the wood and back into the industrial estate, Ed brought up what had happened last night.

They were picking their way around puddles on the track when he said, 'You know you didn't have to do what the rest of them were doing last night.'

'I know,' she said. 'But I wanted to try it.'

'It's not all fun though,' he said, stopping to rub the mud from the side of his trainer. 'Sometimes, when you're in it, it can be hard to get out of, you know? Fun at first, yeah, but then you can get to the point where you can't go out without taking something and then you're...' he stopped, seeming to pick his words carefully, 'in trouble.'

'But you're not in trouble, are you?' she asked. 'I mean, you hadn't taken anything until...' her voice trailed off.

'Until you threw yourself at me and insisted?' he laughed.

They were on the pavement now, outside the Dunlop factory.

She felt her cheeks glow as her mind wandered to the night

before and then on to the early hours of the morning.

'What's up? You've gone all red,' he said gently.

'I suppose you think it's a bit strange that last night was my first time,' she said, unable to catch his eye.

'Why would I?' he asked. 'You've waited until it was with someone who meant something. That's something to be proud of, isn't it?'

She smiled as they continued to walk.

'I mean, I'm assuming it was with someone who meant something?' he asked, a hint of laughter in his voice.

Putting her hand in his, she smiled.

'Definitely.'

They walked on in silence for a while.

'How about you?'

'Huh?' he asked, as if pulled from his thoughts.

'Your first time. I mean, was it with someone who…?'

'Who meant something?'

She nodded, suddenly wishing she hadn't asked. What did she want him to say? That it meant nothing? Everything? Either way, she'd feel disappointed.

'I don't know,' he said, shrugging. But his cheeks coloured as he stared at the ground. 'Maybe I thought so at the time.'

As they walked around the corner into his street, they could see a car parked outside the house, its engine still running.

'Shit. What's he doing back?' Ed muttered, quickening his stride.

Kathryn hurried to catch up, watching Terry straighten from where he had been leaning in through the passenger window, talking to the driver.

As the taxi drove away, he started to walk towards the front door.

'Hey, Dad, you're back already?' Ed had broken into a jog to catch up with him.

His father stopped. 'Nothing much doing in Blackpool. A couple of days with your nan's enough for me. She asked after you both, said she hasn't seen you in years.'

Ed nodded. 'Yeah, we should get up to see her some time. All right is she?'

He was speaking louder than usual and Kathryn realised he was trying to keep his father talking rather than let him continue into the house.

Terry said, 'She's good enough. But yeah, she'd like to see you. The days are long when you're old.'

Ed nodded sympathetically and moved around his father, nudging the door ajar with his shoulder.

'Here, I'll take that,' he said, reaching down for his father's cracked Adidas holdall.

Terry looked confused and grasped the handle tighter. ' I can take…'

He stopped talking when he spotted Kathryn hanging back on the pavement. He dropped the bag, breaking into a wide smile.

'Hey, girl. I didn't see you there. The lad been treating you okay?'

She nodded. 'Yes thanks, Terry.'

He had turned his full attention onto her, as was his way, allowing Ed to slip into the house and raise the alarm. Kathryn played her part by keeping Terry talking for a few more seconds.

'Have you been visiting relations?' she asked, aware of how polite she always sounded when talking to him, as if he was a respectable retired bank manager spending his days tending his garden rather than an ex-con who drank from morning to night and was sleeping with a woman young enough to be his daughter.

'Only my old mum,' he replied, his smile fixed but his eyes trailing up and down her body. His gaze seemed to linger on her mud-covered boots. 'Where's he dragged you today?'

'We went down to the woods on the other side of the estate,' she said.

'Yeah? What for?'

'To see the snowdrops,' she said.

'Likely story,' he sniggered. 'Snowdrops!' With that, he picked up his bag and went into the house.

Hasty efforts had been made to put the house straight so that no signs remained of what had been going on in the hours earlier. Luckily, Paul had heard his father's voice in time to stuff blankets into the cupboard under the stairs, toss cushions back onto the sofa and yank the curtains open.

As Terry stepped through the door, his oldest son was wriggling into his t-shirt with the flustered look of someone who had nearly been caught redhanded.

'Late one?' his father asked with a knowing look.

Linda was sitting at the kitchen table, a cup of coffee in front of her. As Terry walked in, she was applying her lipstick carefully, only glancing up when she had closed her compact mirror with a click.

'Linda,' Terry said, shrugging off his brown suede jacket and throwing it over the back of a chair. 'What you doing here?'

'I thought you might be back home around now so thought I'd surprise you. I got here about ...' She casually glanced at the clock, 'five minutes ago.' She pushed her chair back and flounced towards him. 'But I can go if you want?'

Kathryn watched how Linda pulled an expression of

feigned hurt. And how when Terry pulled her into a hug, she caught Kathryn's eye and winked. She was good at this, moving through life with enough guile to get her what she needed, or thought she needed. Curves and just enough flesh on show to attract the gaze of those whose attention she depended on. For what, Kathryn had no idea. She couldn't imagine what Linda gained from these exchanges with father and son. Knowing that their interest rested purely on her fleshly attributes seemed to empower Linda, but Kathryn wondered what would happen when her body was no longer her currency.

She liked her though and couldn't help acknowledging her wink with a fond smile and shake of the head. By the time Linda had disentangled herself from Terry's arms, her expression had returned to one of eyelash-fluttering coquetry.

Taking her by the shoulders, he murmured, 'I'm going for a lie down in a minute. Why don't you go up first and warm up the bed?'

He gently pushed her into the hallway. With an artfully concealed eye roll as she passed Kathryn, she went upstairs.

At the sound of his bedroom door closing, Terry grinned and picked up Linda's abandoned coffee cup. Rubbing red lipstick from the rim, he lifted it to his lips and drank, his eyes on Kathryn.

Paul came into the kitchen, his manner and tone deliberately casual, 'Linda gone?'

'Not yet,' Terry said, gesturing towards the ceiling with his cup.

Paul shrugged nonchalantly but as he turned away, Kathryn saw his angry scowl.

'Well, no rest for the wicked,' Terry dropped the cup into the sink with a clatter. Kathryn smelt the tang of his aftershave as he brushed against her before running up the stairs two at a time.

'Is Ed upstairs?' Kathryn asked.

Paul looked round distractedly. 'Think he went out the back. Want something to eat?'

She shook her head.

Armed with a bag of crisps and the remnants of a packet of digestives, Paul made his way back towards the lounge. In the doorway, he looked back at her.

'Bit close for comfort,' he said, putting his hand to his heart and shaking his head.

'I know,' Kathryn said in a low voice. 'Imagine if you hadn't heard the car.'

'Don't even go there,' he said, shuddering before disappearing into the lounge.

Kathryn found Ed leaning against the garden shed, smoking. As she joined him, she glanced up at his father's bedroom window and saw the curtains being tugged closed.

He followed her gaze and shook his head before throwing his cigarette on the ground.

'Half the time, I don't know which way is up with him,' he said, crushing the glowing butt under the toe of his trainer.

'Your dad, you mean?' she asked, her eyes taking in the garden. She wondered if it had been different once, whether there had been a swing, a paddling pool, if children's bikes had been propped against the wall or whether it had always been this neglected square of ground, its only use as an escape when the confines of the house became too pressured.

'They're playing with fire. At some point, he's going to find out and there will be hell to pay.'

'Will he go mad?' she asked.

'Too right. I don't know why Paul risks it. Plenty of other

women out there to mess around with.'

'Maybe he's not interested in the others?'

'If it's female and it moves, he's interested. I dunno... maybe he's punishing the old man. In his own way.'

Kathryn considered this. 'Maybe. He might not even realise he's doing it.'

Ed snorted. 'He'll realise when they get caught and the old man pulverises him.'

#

Later, after Linda had left, Ed and Kathryn lay listening to tapes in his bedroom while Terry and Paul finished off a six pack in front of a film downstairs. They'd treated themselves to fish and chips from the takeaway a couple of streets away and the papers were now stuffed in the bin. The room smelt of vinegar and batter.

'Don't have any air freshener,' Ed said with a grin as he retrieved his box of weed from the window sill. 'We'll have to use this to get rid of the smell.'

They shared a joint and this time she didn't cough or cry but, inhaling it deep into her lungs, felt its magic work more swiftly so that before she knew it, she felt like she was floating outside of herself.

'I can see why you do this,' she said, staring at the ceiling shifting and kinking above them.

'Yep,' he replied, his arms folded beneath his head. 'Takes it all away, doesn't it?'

'And replaces it with...' She hesitated, searching for words to describe this sensation of formlessness.

'No idea. I wouldn't know where to begin. But maybe I don't have to; maybe I don't need to say how it makes me feel. I just need to feel it.'

She was trying to follow him in her clouded mind, 'But how can we express to others how we feel, you know, without words?'

'But why do we have to?'

'What?'

'Tell other people? I mean, it doesn't alter the fact one way or another. It won't change a thing for them to hear what we feel or don't feel.'

'But I like to know what someone is thinking, how they're feeling.'

'Do you? I mean, really? Or do you just want them to say what you want to hear? Because I doubt any of us wants to hear the truth all the time.'

She felt the conversation slip away from her, slinking from her grasp. She was not sure if this was Ed being philosophical or trying to make a more personal point.

'I mean, take my old man. Could he deal with the truth? Would he want to know that we don't think he's dead hard for beating a bloke to within an inch of his life and doing time for it? That we're ashamed of him?'

'But you love him?'

'What's love though? It means different things to different people. What does it mean to you?'

Afterwards, she wished she had told him she knew exactly what love was. Because she had fallen in love for the first time in her life. But she couldn't risk a lukewarm reaction, she couldn't risk ruining what they had. So she took the safe option.

'A step up from liking someone a lot, I suppose,' she said quietly.

'Okay, so tell me, how could I like my dad a lot?'

'I don't know, Ed.'

'I mean I used to. When I was little. But now that I see what his life is really like? Nah.'

'But you went into racing because you thought it would please him.'

'Yeah, somehow I thought I could fix him. But that didn't work, did it? So, what's the point?'

'You have to do what's right for you, Ed.'

'I know. That's why I'm thinking of moving away.'

Chapter 8

Moving away. The idea absorbed most of her waking thoughts. In lectures, she would try to concentrate on the words floating across the hall and attempt to keep up with her notes but suddenly her thoughts would stray off Chaucer and return to Ed's plans to leave Liverpool and forge a new life elsewhere.

He hadn't elaborated on his plans when they had spoken on the phone a few days later and she hadn't probed. Maybe if she didn't bring it up, he would forget it. It could just have been a spur-of-the-moment pipe dream prompted by anger.

It wasn't so much the location that worried her, it was more about what a new start could lead to. To leave was easier than to be left. And she didn't want to be left on the sidelines watching him live a new life. Sometimes as she walked to lectures along the edge of Southampton Common, she dared to hope that his moving away might actually bring him nearer to her. But then the promise of the day, with its bright sunshine and backdrop of birdsong, would be clouded over with thoughts of him taking a new path to fresh experiences and a new world that she had no part in.

He had been her focal point for seven months and, because of him, everything had taken on a brighter hue. University life was bearable because she eagerly anticipated speaking to him or finding a letter in her pigeon hole in the porter's office.

She knew these were supposed to be the days to make firm friends, maybe even ones to last a lifetime, but the other students didn't particularly interest her. And besides, she didn't have time for anyone else. Not that the other students weren't welcoming. They often asked her to join them in the student bar after an afternoon tutorial or to come along to a party in someone's room, but while she occasionally went along, her mind was elsewhere.

It was the same when she visited home. She went through the motions, pining to be spending the weekend in his room rather than around the dinner table trying to answer her parents' barrage of questions about her course.

'And you're keeping up with the work? Getting good marks?' her dad would ask. 'We know Beth found it plain sailing but you'll need to get stuck in and go the extra mile to get the grades you need.'

She couldn't tell them that she was behind with her reading list and that her latest essay had been returned with the margins full of disappointed comments in red pen. The extra miles she was travelling were not what her dad had in mind. But if she didn't have Ed and her escapes to Liverpool, life would be so monotonous and she resented her parents for thinking that the routine of lectures and writing essays every evening was enough for her. Ed had rescued her from that.

Elaine told her she was obsessed. Sitting in Kathryn's bedroom one Saturday night, listening patiently to her friend, she had a puzzled expression on her face.

'But I don't get why you're worried,' Elaine said, flicking through the pages of an old Just Seventeen magazine. 'Who's to say he won't move down south and then you won't have to drive so far.'

'It's not the distance though. It's that everything will be different. He'll meet new people.'

'New girls, you mean,' Elaine said, shaking her head. 'So you want him stuck with his alcoholic family because you know where he is and who he's talking to? Even though his life sounds pretty depressing.'

Kathryn knew how it sounded. She also knew that a new start was exactly what he needed. And she wanted the best for him. Or, at least, she told herself she did. But if he left Liverpool, an exciting new world would open up for him and where would that leave her? He'd meet someone else – she just knew it. She would no longer be enough for him.

She tried to untangle her thoughts.

'I'm different to his family, his mates. I don't know why but I think he finds me interesting. But if he leaves, he'll be able to find someone like me anywhere.'

'So what you're saying is that your relationship depends on his life being at a standstill? You're being a bit selfish there, Kathryn.'

Kathryn bit her lip. Elaine had a knack of getting straight to the heart of the matter . She also had a knack for sounding middle-aged.

'Look, it might be the best thing all round if he does move on,' she continued, bluntly. 'You can't keep going on as you are. I mean, if you don't watch out, you'll come out of three years of study with a big fat fail. All because you're messing about with him.'

Kathryn bristled. 'Actually Elaine, it's almost unheard of to fail. I think you mean a third.'

'Yes, whatever they call leaving university with little more than you went there with. You know, I thought when you told me you were off to university that you'd surround yourself with all these intellectual types and wouldn't want to know anyone from your old life.'

'You know that would never happen. You're my best friend.'

Elaine closed the magazine and put it back on Kathryn's

bedside table.

'Maybe it wouldn't have been so bad – at least you'd have been moving up in life. Yes, I'd have felt hurt at being left behind but I'd have been pleased that you were making your way in the world. As it is, you're stuck with the sort of boy you find propping up the bar on any Saturday night in any town.'

Not that Elaine had actually met Ed. But Kathryn had written long and enthusiastic letters to her friend, detailing her trips to Merseyside with hardly a mention of university life. The only clue that she was actually in higher education was the Southampton postmark on the envelope.

Kathryn knew her friend had her best interests at heart. Elaine had never been academically gifted, had taken her A levels grudgingly and, when she came out with disappointing grades, she hadn't been surprised. Now in her first year at catering college, Elaine was happy to be able to apply herself to what she called a trade, something she could soon make a living from. And besides, Kathryn told herself, when she did meet Ed, she'd soon change her mind.

#

She had nearly finished the essay she was working on when she heard a voice outside her door shouting, 'Phone for you, Kathryn.'

Running to the end of the corridor, she snatched up the receiver.

'Hello?'

'All right?'

'I thought it was my turn to ring you, Ed. Everything okay?' she said, trying to smother the pleasure in her voice.

'Yeah, course. I was just thinking about you. And how it's your birthday on Saturday.'

His words, lifting her out of the jumble of thoughts and worries that consumed her, made her grin at the grubby cream wall in front of her. Hearing from him, she felt as if her life had once again come out from behind the clouds.

'How about I come down to see you at the weekend? I mean, you're always coming up here.'

She made noises about enjoying the drive and enjoying the change of scene, but he insisted and she was secretly glad.

'Shall I collect you from the coach station?' she asked.

'I thought you were going home this weekend to see your folks? How about I see you there?'

As she replaced the receiver, conflicting thoughts raced through her mind. She felt wildly excited that she was going to be seeing him sooner than expected, but the idea of introducing him to her parents felt like a bucket of cold water had just been thrown over her. Maybe she didn't need to introduce them though, maybe she could just meet him in town and they could book somewhere for the night. But then he'd wonder why she was keeping him hidden. And her parents would be disappointed that she was coming home for her birthday and then disappearing. Her joy had fallen into a sea of nagging doubts so she turned to the person who usually set her straight.

After retrieving a handful of change from her room, she dialled the familiar number.

'Elaine?'

'Hey, to what do I owe the honour?' Her friend sounded surprised. 'I didn't expect to hear from you till you get back on Friday night.'

'Ed's coming to visit on Saturday night. What should I do?'

'He's your boyfriend. That's between you two.'

'Very funny. No, I mean, I don't want to introduce him to Mum and Dad.'

'Come on, Kathryn. They're not that bad. Anyone would think they're the Addams Family, the way you go on about them. And if he's as brilliant as you make out, I'd have thought you'd want to show him off.'

'I know, I know. They're not, and he definitely is. But you know what I mean. I can't imagine it working out, that's all.'

'Oh, Kathryn, you're mad about him and it's your birthday. Don't worry about the details. Just enjoy it.'

#

Waking in her bed at home, she stared at the posters on her wall. She'd meant to take them down but hadn't got round to it and now, locking eyes with a pensive-looking Kurt Cobain, she thought she might as well leave them up as some sort of commemoration of her teenage years as she left them behind.

Looking around with a critical eye, she saw the bedroom of a school girl. A huddle of teddies was peering down at her from the top of the wardrobe. Her desk was still cluttered with the debris of her long hours of A level revision. Inside the folders piled on top of each other, she knew she would find her work, colour-coded and divided into topics. A study timetable was still pinned to the wall above her desk. Pins wouldn't damage the wallpaper like Blu Tack, her mother had said.

Elaine had always been envious of the sink in the corner of Kathryn's room. It lent a touch of maturity, she had said, so it was less a teenager's bedroom and more a college bedsit.

Alongside her toothbrush mug on the glass shelf above was a bottle of cheap perfume and a nail varnish bottle, long forgotten and unscrewed, so the sludgy purple contents were solidified and useless.

Should she change things up a bit? No, she dismissed the thought before it had even completely formed. Her posters could stay where they were. He wouldn't be stepping across the threshold, not tonight or any night, not with her parents downstairs. Shuddering at the thought, she jumped out of bed.

Her mother announced over breakfast that they had booked a table at a new restaurant in town. She asked Kathryn if she might like to ask Elaine to join them.

With her spoon suspended midway between her mouth and her bowl of cornflakes, Kathryn frowned. She should have guessed that her parents would want to mark her birthday in some way, but she was meeting Ed tonight. She had booked a room in one of the seafront hotels – it was all arranged. Her plans would horrify her parents so she was all set to tell them she was staying at Elaine's.

'What time?'

'Seven. Why?' Her mother looked at her sharply.

It wasn't what she wanted. Why couldn't they see that? Did they honestly think she wanted to spend her twentieth birthday in the same way she spent her childhood birthdays? Could they seriously not remember what it was like to be young? And yet, she couldn't say anything because Valerie would be so visibly hurt, and George so disappointed in her. She knew better than to rock the boat. You fell in line with what was expected. That's how it was in her family.

And that's why some things – some people – had to be kept secret.

She calculated how long dinner would take and how quickly they could be out of the restaurant and on their way to the next part of her birthday night, the part without parents.

'I expect we'll be finished by nine?' she said.

'We'll be finished when we're finished. We've got all evening if needs be. It's not every day you're twenty,' her mother said, turning the tap on to fill the washing up bowl.

Her dad came into the kitchen.

'Happy birthday, Kathryn. I thought you'd be having a lie in today, giving yourself a well-earned break from all that studying you're doing,' he said.

He put the bottle of milk he'd just picked up from the doorstep in the fridge, where it clinked next to yesterday's delivery. Her mother dried her hands before opening a drawer and retrieving some envelopes.

'Be sure to remember who's given you what so you can thank them,' she said, putting them on the table in front of her daughter. It was what she said every year.

'Oh, to be young again,' said George. 'What do you think Val?'

'Only if I could know what I know now,' Valerie replied, watching her daughter with her hands on her hips.

It was what they always said when anyone under the age of thirty had a birthday and not a year went by without it being repeated for Kathryn's benefit.

Her parents were united in their expectations of their daughters; each as determined as the other to bring them up to have successful, well-paid careers. George went out to work and Valerie stayed at home but they couldn't have been more similar in the way they saw the world. Beth was fulfilling their dreams, but Kathryn was, frankly, proving to be not quite up to par.

At that moment, the doorbell rang out.

For a split second, and even before the thought appeared in her mind, her stomach lurched. What if it was Ed? He said he'd ring later in the afternoon, but he could have decided to surprise her. But, wait, it couldn't be him. He didn't know where she lived. Or did he? She tried to remember if he'd ever written to her at her home address.

Her mother bustled through to the hall before she had a chance to get up, so she looked through the envelopes while she waited. The writing was familiar, all family members. She knew she should muster some sort of enthusiasm, because they had been good enough to think of her, but she couldn't face opening them.

When her mother returned to the kitchen, she was carrying a bouquet of yellow roses.

George raised his eyebrows. 'Looks like you have an admirer, Kathryn. Anyone we know?'

Thrilled yet embarrassed by the lavish arrangement, Kathryn jumped up and took them from her mother.

There was a small envelope attached to the cellophane wrapping and she opened it impatiently. The only words on the card were 'Happy 20th Birthday!' But it was enough. She knew she was grinning inanely but couldn't help it. She must have given him her address at some point and he had gone to the effort of sending her an expensive bouquet of flowers on her birthday. Suddenly everything seemed bright and wonderful.

Stealing glances at the flowers now arranged in one of her mother's vases by the kitchen window, she returned to the cards with more enthusiasm. They turned out, as expected, to be from her three aunts and uncles as well as an old babysitter who still kept in touch. There were five pound notes folded carefully inside each.

Her parents gave her a new CD player to replace the old one in her room in Southampton that had started to skip. When Elaine called round at midday, Kathryn was in a buoyant mood. Opening the door, she could hardly contain herself.

'He sent me flowers. A gorgeous bouquet.'

Elaine followed her into the kitchen and then stood, wide-eyed.

'Blimey, Kathryn, that's some display.'

The volume of the television was turned down in the sitting room next door and George called through, 'Hello, Elaine. Kathryn won't tell us who the admirer is.'

'I don't know either, George. Probably one of many though,' Elaine called back as she took her coat off and hung it on the back of her chair.

Kathryn rolled her eyes but was secretly enjoying the attention. It was a rare enough pleasure in this house, after all. She popped the kettle on, threw teabags into two cups and put a tin of biscuits on the table.

Elaine took a chocolate digestive. 'You always have such nice biscuits at your house. We only ever have rich teas.'

'Would you like to come out for dinner with us tonight?' Kathryn asked, taking a digestive for herself.

'You sure? I mean, isn't it a family occasion?' Elaine wiped the crumbs from her chin.

'You'd be doing me a favour. I don't think I can cope with another grilling about this term's syllabus. And then we can go into town afterwards.'

'Sure I won't be a gooseberry?' Elaine said.

'Course not. And I want my two favourite people to meet at last.'

'Go on then,' Elaine said, with mock weariness. 'Now, let's get shopping before the day's gone on us.'

#

Throwing their bags onto the bed later that afternoon, Kathryn and Elaine chatted breathlessly the way good friends do even when they have chatted all afternoon and will continue doing so all evening.

Holding up first one option and then another, they were still no nearer to deciding what Kathryn would wear for her birthday when the phone rang downstairs.

Kathryn stopped talking and put her finger to her lips. Elaine raised her eyebrows.

Her mother called up from the hall. 'There's a boy on the phone for you, Kathryn.'

She dropped the blouse she was holding and ran down the stairs two at a time.

'Who shall I say's calling?' her mother said, hesitating a moment before handing it to her daughter with a shrug.

She lingered, pretending to wipe dust from a picture frame, but Kathryn held her hand over the phone and waited for her mother to get the hint and to return to the kitchen.

'Ed?'

'Yeah, I've got to be quick because my money's running out. You said to ring when I got down.' His voice was faint against a background hum of noise.

She was about to thank him for the flowers but he carried on, obviously keen to get the arrangements sorted before his money ran out, 'I'll be at the station by eight. Do you want to meet us there?' The line was bad but it wasn't so bad that she didn't hear the plural in what he had just said.

'I'll be out with my parents having dinner then,' she said hurriedly, in case he was cut off. 'We'll get away as soon as we can and meet you in Chapman's, the hotel opposite the station.'

'Okay, see you…' The beep of the phone told her the call had been disconnected.

As she climbed the stairs, she felt perplexed. It definitely sounded as if he wasn't going to be alone and she wondered if Paul was with him, maybe Linda too. Her heart sank a little because it wasn't what she had expected and now she would have to make an excuse and leave her parents early rather than keep Ed waiting after such a long train journey.

Elaine had tidied the clothes and hung everything in the wardrobe.

'What's up?' she asked, studying her friend's face.

'I don't know. It's probably nothing,' Kathryn replied, trying to shake off the niggling doubts that had now worked their way into her mind, 'So, what's it to be? The blue dress or the jeans?'

#

It felt as if the waiter would never clear the plates. He darted around the busy restaurant taking food to some tables, scooping unused wine glasses and cutlery from others.

George pushed his chair back a little to stretch his legs. 'I must say, that was worth the wait.'

Kathryn had been regularly checking the clock on the wall behind him and knew exactly how long they had had to wait to order, and then how long it had taken for their main course to arrive. She was now expecting a similarly lengthy period before the waiter returned again. She knew her mother would want the Black Forest Gateau, her father the sherry trifle and yet would still insist on seeing the sweet trolley. Dinner wouldn't be finished until after nine o'clock.

She would happily have avoided the family meal. Feeling ungrateful, she reflected on how it had once been such a treat. Dressing up in her smartest clothes, graduating from the kids' menu to choosing something she regarded as sophisticated like scampi and crème brulee. It had marked the point in her life when she started to leave childhood behind to join her parents in the world of grown-ups. It had now lost its lustre though and she was itching to grab her coat and leave her parents to admire the maritime-themed décor while debating whether or not to have a calypso coffee.

Without Elaine, the same ground would have been covered, the same topics side-stepped. But her presence was enough to steer the conversation in new directions.

She saved the day when, spotting Kathryn checking the clock yet again, she said, 'It's been lovely, George, but I'm not feeling too great. Sorry to break up the party, but could you give me a lift home, Kathryn?'

It was fortunate that they had arrived in separate cars. Her parents' ailing car had needed a jump start from a neighbour, so Kathryn had suggested collecting Elaine herself so they could make it to the restaurant on time. After reassuring George and Valerie that it was only a stomach ache and really nothing to do with the wonderful dinner, Elaine now thanked them profusely for inviting her and then, almost as an afterthought, asked Kathryn if she fancied staying at her house.

Kathryn said nothing and looked at her parents.

Elaine added, 'Of course, say no if you'd rather not. You

know, if you'd prefer to stay at home tonight.'

But Kathryn's parents wouldn't hear of it, sending the girls on their way with instructions to go to bed before the witching hour and not to stay up all night chatting.

Out on the street, Kathryn and Elaine waited until they had turned the corner before collapsing into giggles.

'You're such a good liar, Elaine,' Kathryn said, shaking her head. 'But I thought you were never going to say it. You let it drag on long enough. And what was that about the witching hour? What am I? Ten?'

'Your poor parents. If they only knew what we were up to. I tell you, if you looked at that clock one more time, I was going to burst,' Elaine replied, grabbing her arm. 'Now, come on, where's this man of yours?'

It was only a five minute drive to the station but that was time enough for Kathryn's doubts to resurface. As she looked for a parking space near the illuminated exterior of the hotel, she wondered what Elaine would think of Paul and Linda. Kathryn couldn't picture them here, in her home town, so far from their own environment.

In the quiet street, they could hear the distant roar of the sea. A sharp breeze gusted in from the seafront and Elaine hopped from foot to foot as Kathryn locked the car.

'When you want to go home, we'll just put you in a cab,' said Kathryn.

'You make me sound like a kid,' Elaine replied, rolling her eyes. 'Have you got your overnight bag with you?'

Kathryn grinned guiltily and tapped the boot of the car.

The hotel wasn't a usual Saturday night haunt for the town's youth. They tended to congregate in the pubs around the shopping precinct and down the side streets leading to the seafront. And so, as Kathryn pulled open the heavy door, she was surprised to see quite a crowd.

It only took seconds to spot that this was a hen party, still relatively sober, with L plates and bridal veils still in place. Kathryn and Elaine headed straight for the toilets for a quick mirror check.

Watching her friend brush her hair, Elaine said, 'You look great, Kathryn. That dress was definitely the right choice.'

Kathryn blushed as she admired the plunging neckline in the mirror. The material flattered her without clinging too obviously and she had to agree that by finding the dress in Miss Selfridge's and buying it for her as a birthday present, Elaine had done her a favour.

'Shall I leave my hair down?' she asked. 'Or tie it back?'

'Here, I've some pins in my bag, I'll put it up for you. Won't take a minute and you'll knock him out,' Elaine replied, digging in her handbag.

She could hardly contain her excitement as she watched Elaine, with pins between her teeth and a look of intense concentration on her face, expertly twist her hair and secure it in place so she looked older and far more glamorous than she had ever felt in her life.

'You should do more with your hair,' said Elaine, admiring her handiwork. 'It's such a lovely colour. Look at all those glints of gold running through it.'

Kathryn pulled a face. 'Come off it, Elaine. It's brown and boring. People dye their hair all the time to be a blonde like you. And what is it they say about blondes?'

Elaine laughed, pushing her hair behind her ears. 'Give over. There's no danger of your fella preferring –'

She stopped talking as the door swung open and a young woman passed them on her way to a cubicle. There was something about her that looked familiar to Kathryn. Her blonde hair was pulled back tightly into a uncomfortable-looking ponytail revealing a face made all the more striking by expertly applied make-up. Her cool eyes swept over them with little interest.

'Come on, let's go and find him,' Kathryn said, holding the door open for her friend.

She spotted him before he had a chance to notice her and that sensation she craved when they were apart rippled through her. It only lasted seconds but the warmth that flooded her veins, so that her skin tingled, felt addictive. He was talking to someone hidden from view. Paul, she assumed. She would prefer to be alone with Ed, obviously, but she could cope with Paul too. And anyway, a handbag hanging from the back of another chair indicated that Linda was there too, so there was a good chance they would disappear together.

But it wasn't Paul who sat across from Ed. It was someone she had not met before. He looked a little older than them and was leaning across the table, deep in conversation.

Ed was sitting with his chair turned away from her so it was only when she reached the table and touched his arm, giving him a small jump, that he saw her.

'Hey, birthday girl, I'd nearly given up on you,' he said, smiling before jumping up and kissing her.

He turned and nodded across the table. 'This is Roland.'

Roland put his cigarette between his lips to free his hand. She shook it before turning her attention back to Ed who was trying to peer around her.

'This is Elaine,' Kathryn said, stepping aside.

Ed smiled, 'I've heard a lot about you.'

Elaine, who had been studying him closely, replied, 'Nice to meet you,' before looking across at Roland and adding politely, 'And you too, Roland.'

Kathryn noticed how Roland's eyes flicked over her friend disinterestedly before he nodded and stubbed his cigarette out in the ashtray.

In that moment, she wished it was Paul sitting there. He would have jumped up, offered them a drink, said something inappropriate about her dress and made her laugh. But Roland was sullen, as if their arrival was an inconvenience. She studied him as he fingered a fat gold chain that glistened around his neck. Ruddy and plain-featured, he had the indistinct look of someone you could walk past in the street without recognising. Kathryn disliked – and distrusted – him on sight.

'Budge over,' Kathryn turned to see the blonde from the bathroom, pushing past Elaine with three glasses and bottles balanced on a tray.

'This is Nicki,' Ed said, standing to make room for her to pass.

Kathryn watched as the girl, holding the tray aloft, squeezed past him so closely that her hip brushed against him.

'I remember,' she said, tight-lipped.

Ed caught her eye and grinned. 'Oh yeah, you saw each other at Brighton.'

Nicki shrugged. 'Nah, don't think so.'

'No, we didn't meet. I just saw you from a distance,' Kathryn said.

Ed, grinning at the other girl, said. 'Kat thought you were my bird, Nick.'

The girl sniggered as she poured Coke into the clear liquid in her glass. As she leant across the table to fill Ed's glass, one of the straps of her tight black top slid off a tanned, defined shoulder.

Roland pushed his cigarettes along the table towards Nicki. She pulled one out, slipped it between her lips and again leant towards Ed, who fished his lighter from his jeans, struck one and held it out towards her.

A flash of anger jolted through Kathryn at this easy familiarity and she felt her world begin to fold in on itself.

Elaine touched her arm. 'What do you want to drink, Kathryn?' Ed jumped up, 'You stay there, Elaine. I'll get them in.'

Standing at the bar beside him, Kathryn waited for the barman to turn away to get their drinks before speaking. But it was Ed who spoke first, staring along the bar and drumming his fingers on the wooden counter.

'You're wondering what they're doing here, aren't you?'

'I thought you were coming down on your own,' she said, shortly.

'Yeah, I was but it seemed daft not to stop off at Epsom and meet up with my mates.' He picked up a beer mat and tapped it on the counter.

She said nothing but pulled at the hem of her dress, which now felt too short, the colour too eye-catching. She felt overdressed and foolish.

'You're looking mega, by the way.' He caught her eye and winked, making her feel as if the night was not beyond rescue.

The barman put two glasses of Southern Comfort and lemonade on the bar in front of them, before turning back to the till.

'I've booked us into one of the hotels on the seafront for tonight. Elaine's going to get a taxi home and....' She broke off as the barman returned.

'That's three pounds eighty,' he said.

Ed handed the barman a crumpled fiver before turning to Kathryn. 'Yeah, we can do that. But later though, eh? The others want to go to that club on the hill. They've been before – said it's banging – that's why they're here. There's different rooms with techno, garage, jungle and all the top London DJs.'

'Sounds like it's all arranged,' she said.

'Well, yeah, kind of. But we've got to go, haven't we? I mean, they had The Prodigy there last year. I can't believe that place is on your doorstep and you never said.'

She watched the excited gleam in his eyes and wondered why he couldn't understand that she felt utterly let down.

'Come on babe, don't go all quiet on me,' he said, touching her cheek. 'You'll see, this'll be a birthday you won't forget. Trust me.'

When they reached the table, it was clear that nobody had said a word since they had left. Nicki was picking at a gold tassel holding the heavy burgundy curtains back from the window, idly watching the train passengers who'd just got off the 9.30 from Bristol move as one towards the car park. Roland was reading the label on the mixer bottle, and Elaine, clearly being ignored by the other two, was perched awkwardly on the edge of her seat, looking plaintively at Kathryn.

'You can stop talking about us now,' Ed joked as he put the glasses down.

Roland, now peeling the label from the bottle, looked up.

'We'll be off in a minute, yeah? There's always massive queues up there and we don't want to be waiting all night,' he said, before continuing in a lower voice. 'I mean, we've been waiting all night as it is.'

'Yeah, all right, mate,' Ed said, in a conciliatory tone. 'It's Kathryn's birthday so…'

She felt his hand around her waist, guiding her into the seat beside him.

Turning back from what had been absorbing her on the street, Nicki looked at Kathryn. 'It's your birthday, is it? Get anything nice?' Her voice couldn't have sounded less interested.

Elaine chipped in. 'She got some beautiful flowers,' she added, to Ed. 'We were all admiring them.'

'Yeah?'

Despite the disappointment of the evening, Kathryn couldn't help but feel lifted. There was always the flowers.

'Who were they from?' Ed asked.

Elaine glanced at Kathryn and rolled her eyes extravagantly.

'You'd better play along,' she whispered.

Kathryn, enjoying the banter, said, 'Um, well, let me see…'

But seeing Ed's quizzical expression made her smile fade.

Nicki sat up straighter, as if the evening had suddenly become more interesting.

She looked from Ed to Kathryn and then to Roland before laughing.

'Classic. Not the knight in shining armour after all, is he? I mean, he didn't even remember to get flowers,' she said, mockingly.

In that moment, Kathryn hated her as she had never hated anyone in her life. Not just because of the way her lips, so full and generous, twisted into a sneer or how her violet eyes, sultry and fringed with false lashes, danced in a way that was cruel yet bewitching. She hated her because she felt plain and colourless beside her, stripped of any interest, a sparrow in the shadow of a goldfinch.

And she hated her because she knew that if he wasn't

sleeping with her now, he had in the past, and might even do so again.

It was Elaine who spoke next.

'I'm sorry, Kathryn, but I'm still not feeling too good. Certainly not up for dancing the night away,' she laughed gently and pushed her half empty glass along the table to Kathryn. 'I just need to get something out of the car.'

As soon as the doors swung closed behind them, Elaine turned to Kathryn. Her joviality had disappeared and her face was now pinched with anger.

Ushering Kathryn out of sight of the window, she hissed, 'I can't tell you how angry I am, Kathryn. How you were treated in there. If I were you, I'd leave him to it.'

Kathryn faltered, tempted by the thought that if she left now, he might come running after her.

As if reading her mind, Elaine shook her head. 'He won't come after you. You know it. Not when he's with that pair.'

'He's never like that normally. If he was on his own, you'd see what he's really like,' Kathryn said, wondering what she could say to redeem him.

'So tell me, what is he like?' Elaine said, her arms folded. 'Because from where I'm standing, he looks like he's not fit to clean your boots.'

Kathryn would usually have been amused by her friend's quaint turn of phrase, the result of parents who had celebrated a late pregnancy, but now her voice quavered. 'He's clever. Fun. And I love being with him. He's not like anyone I've ever met.'

'You can say that again,' Elaine said sharply. 'Kathryn, he's a shit and you're throwing yourself away on him. I'd guessed as much but now I know for sure.'

The doors of the hotel opened, throwing light out on to

the street. She didn't have to turn around to know it was Ed and his friends. The look on Elaine's face told her everything.

'I really think you should come with me,' she said.

'You ready, babe?' Ed called from the doorway.

She knew she was at a fork in the road. As she took in Elaine's raised eyebrows and firmly set mouth, she knew that going with her was the sensible option. Her friend was right and she felt crushed. But Elaine, protective and loyal to the last, couldn't compete with the pull of being with him, if only because she couldn't bear to think of Ed, annoyed at her for deserting him, turning his attention to Nicki, who would be only too glad to see her leave.

Kathryn unzipped her bag and pulled out her purse, 'You're right in everything you say but, look, let me pay for your taxi.'

Shaking her head, Elaine said in a low voice, 'I've never seen you do anything as stupid. You do know that you'll regret this?'

Turning on her heel, leaving Kathryn holding out a five pound note, Elaine strode across the road to where a taxi was parked. Moments later, she was gone.

Turning around to where Ed, Nicki and Roland were standing, Kathryn was suddenly gripped by a sense that she should have gone with Elaine; who was always in her corner, who had never let her down, and who had been willing to put her reservations aside tonight and give Ed a chance. She also wondered who had sent the flowers. It clearly wasn't her boyfriend. Her thoughts were interrupted by his hand on her shoulder.

'Look, sorry your friend went off in a huff.'

He was on his own and, for a moment, she dared to hope that Roland and Nicki might have left.

He inclined his head towards the back of the pub.

'They'll be back in a minute; they've just gone for the car. I know I should have stopped them coming down but when Nicki's got something in her head, she always gets what she wants. I'll make it up to you later, honest.'

There was no time to respond. A silver car came speeding around the corner and mounted the pavement with its engine revving.

'Wicked motor,' Ed said admiringly. 'Roly's only just got it off his old man.'

Nicki had to climb out to let them into the cramped confines of the back seat. Then they were off, roaring along the seafront with the stereo cranked up to max. As they sped under the streetlights, the interior of the car was washed bright before being plunged back into darkness again. As Roland put his foot down, the flashes of light quickened.

The level crossing gates were down outside Kathryn's old secondary school and as they waited alongside the white pillars, she realised she had been standing on that spot waiting for the bus less than two years ago. She had memorised the graffiti scrawled across the back of the metal sign with the name of the school, its head teacher and deputy head on it after gazing at it every day at half three. The names of the students damned and shamed in marker pen would be strangers to those waiting there now. She could still picture herself though in her navy school skirt of a sensible length and robust shoes. In short, the uniform exactly as stipulated.

She couldn't imagine that Nicki had ever worn a sensible school skirt. She watched her blonde ponytail swing as she moved her head in time to the pounding beat coming from the stereo. Kathryn willed the flashing lights to stop and the gates to lift so they could move on. At school, they had always been warned not to make noise outside the gates as it was a residential area. Now, she sank into the soft seat of the Renault, wishing that Nicki hadn't opened the window and allowed the thump of the music to invade the houses on Goring Avenue.

And then they were away again, tearing along the main road. Roland cursed impatiently as they roared up to the car in front, turning the small steering wheel so they swept past leaving an oncoming car to swerve and flash its lights.

Nicki and Ed whooped gleefully but Kathryn gripped the handle above the door, helplessly. This, she thought, was what it must be like in speeding cars moments before they hurtle into a crash barrier and end up in a twisted heap of metal in the middle of the road.

But now they were slowing and turning up a driveway lined with cars on both sides. People were climbing the steep incline in couples and groups while the odd car continued on, hopeful of finding a space further along.

'Why don't you drop us off and then come back and park?' Nicki said, chewing gum as she glanced across at Roland.

'Yeah, no point in us all being late in,' Ed said, leaning eagerly between the front seats.

Nicki turned and held out her pack of chewing gum to him. As he slid a stick out, she winked.

Scowling, Roland drove on past the shuffling pilgrims in their baggy t-shirts and jeans, arriving at the top of the hill where he swung the car round and let them out.

'Nice one, mate. See you later,' Ed said.

As Kathryn watched the car's tail lights disappear back down the hill, she once again felt as if she'd made a mistake and wished she was sitting in Elaine's kitchen crying into her tea rather than here amongst strangers. But she reminded herself that she'd felt this way before when they had been clubbing in Liverpool and how that had turned into one of the best nights of her life. No, she'd push through her doubts and try the new Kathryn on for size again. It had gone well before.

The queue snaked along a canvas-roofed alleyway before swelling into a crowd stretching further and further back under ancient oaks. Kathryn wondered what all the fuss was about. She knew kids from school used to come here and there had been local newspaper reports about late night police raids and drugs busts. She had no idea it was so fashionable that it drew people all the way from London.

She had always thought that people spent their time trying to get away from this dull seaside town where nothing ever happened and was surprised to learn that it was secretly a mecca for ravers from all over the country.

These were the thoughts which occupied her mind as they inched forward in a sea of expectant youth. Few spoke, keeping their eyes on the gravel as they waited to finally make their way through the doors to an underground world of throbbing music.

Although she had lived in the town all her life, she had never actually seen the house as it was hidden by trees and couldn't be seen from the main road. It was an imposing Georgian manor with ivy-covered flint walls. It had a tall tower with a flat roof and strobe lights flashing from its mullioned windows, illuminating the surrounding lawns like flares. Kathryn tried to imagine what the house had been like a hundred years ago. Peaceful and calm with gardeners and housemaids and grooms tending to horses in a cobbled stable yard. So much had changed. Music its past inhabitants couldn't have even imagined now reverberated through its rooms and corridors.

By the time they reached the entrance, Kathryn's feet tingled with tiredness and from the feel of the gravel through the thin soles of her shoes. She stifled a yawn, wondering aloud how much time they'd actually get in the place as it was already so late. But Ed just laughed.

'Hey, Nic, what time do you think we'll be getting out of here?' he asked, tapping the other girl on the shoulder.

'Dunno, sixish?' she replied, impatiently edging forward.

Not for the first time that night, Kathryn wished that Paul and Linda were with them. Despite her first impressions of them – wayward, chaotic – she now knew that they were fundamentally decent when it came to sticking by their friends. If she had said she wanted to go home, they'd grumble but grab their coats. She could see that tonight, however, it would be Nicki who was calling the shots.

At the top of the stairs, she was reminded of her one visit to London when her parents had taken her to the Natural History Museum. Descending the steps to the Tube, leaving the cool city breeze for the airless heat of the underground, her twelve year old self had thought she would suffocate. Or at least faint.

Nicki grabbed Ed by the hand and pulled him down into the crowd.

'Wait a minute, can't you?' he said, shaking free of her grasp and turning to Kathryn.

Nicki rolled her eyes and descended halfway down the staircase before turning expectantly.

'Come on, Kathryn, we're gonna make a real night of it,' Ed said, grinning and tapping his pocket.

'But you said you didn't want to do that anymore' she said, disappointed and relieved at once. Disappointed because he'd told her that being with her meant he had left his drug taking behind, and relieved because she didn't know if she could get through the night ahead without something to help her along.

'I have, most of the time, but you can't be out with these two without dropping an E. Tonight's my last time, honest. And it'll be a laugh, I promise,' he said before taking her hand and tugging her behind him down into the pit of bodies.

When Ed went to the bar for water, she found a space on one of the sofas in a corner where the music seemed to be slightly less deafening. In the gloom, only broken by the rhythmic flashes of the strobes, she could hardly make out individuals in the heaving mass on the floor, so when someone suddenly sat beside her, she jumped.

It was Roland, moving his head to the music so energetically that she wondered why he didn't go and dance.

'Ed's getting the drinks,' she said, needing three attempts before he nodded.

'I knew it would be packed by now,' she felt his breath on her ear.

There was no point in futile attempts at conversation so, conserving her voice, she just nodded.

'Not your thing.' It was more of a statement than a question.

She shrugged, unsure if it was a challenge or if he was commiserating.

They had given up on further exchange when she spotted Ed weaving his way back from the bar. He was looking around him, trying to find her. When he spotted her, his eyes lit up and he made his way over.

'Here, get your laughing gear around that,' he said, dropping bottles into their laps before crouching down and slipping a small purple pill into her hand.

Standing again, he blocked her from view while she put it on her tongue and swallowed.

'Well, come on, what are you waiting for?'

As she followed him back to the dance floor, she felt something drip onto her bare shoulder.

Roland leant forward to shout in her ear, 'That's sweat and steam,' while pointing up at the glistening ceiling.

She shuddered at the thought of someone else's sweat running down her back and couldn't help thinking that the club in Liverpool felt more... civilised. This seemed primal; people losing their minds to music in the subterranean basement of a manor house on the edge of the South Downs.

But then she began to feel herself loosen and move, to feel herself shift out of her body to make way for her alter ego, the one without inhibitions, the one who felt there was nothing to lose.

Within this sea of bodies, dancing to the pulsing beats, she felt a wave of intense euphoria swell through her. It seemed to surge in time with the music and she had the sense that if she focused too much on it, tried to hold it for a moment too long, it would float away. And she didn't want this sweet joy to leave her. Not ever. Because here, her inner and outer selves melted into one. Her inner voice was no longer at odds with the one she presented to the world. She could say what was in her heart with no fear of how it would be heard by others.

It was when they left the room to explore the upper floors of the house that she lost him.

Weaving through the mass of clubbers moving from one room to another, one moment he was in front of her, clasping her hand, and the next, someone crossed between them and his fingers dropped away. A group of lads surged against the crowd and she stood aside to let them past. And then she couldn't see him anywhere.

She kept expecting to find him. Surely he'll be waiting on the next landing, she told herself, searching the faces of those climbing the stairs. But no, there was nobody she recognised, just strangers in baggy t-shirts and jeans who, unlike herself, seemed to know where they were going and why.

Looking into a room, she was presented with a similar dark and confusing picture to the basement in that it was impossible to discern one person from another. The music was slightly less intense, different in a way she couldn't put her finger on. Was it jungle? Garage? She had no idea. Was this even the dancefloor he was looking for or had he gone up another flight of stairs to the top of the building?

With no idea of time – she could have been searching for minutes or an hour – she looked everywhere for him. There must have been hundreds of people, but she kept seeing the same faces, first on one floor, then on the next, then on the stairs, as if dimensions were layered on top of each other. Maybe he'd fallen away into another realm and the people she kept seeing were the ones, like herself, left behind. She knew she was being dramatic but with each passing minute, each futile search of a crowded room, she started to panic.

And then, with relief, she spotted Roland leaning against the wall. In this sea of strangers, he was at least a familiar, if not entirely pleasant discovery.

'Seen Nicki anywhere?' he asked, when she reached him.

'Not since we got here, ' she replied. 'And I can't find Ed. Is he with you?'

She thought she saw him grimace as he shook his head. He flung his cigarette onto the wooden floorboards and stepped on it.

He led the way and this time she kept up as they climbed up another flight of stairs to a dancefloor where the English Channel could be seen from the large sash windows. Retreating back down to the basement, they looked again, room to room, dancefloor to dancefloor.

It was Roland's idea to check the gardens.

Where the house was all noise and movement and life, the grounds were hushed and still. A group of figures sauntered across the lawn and disappeared into a straggly copse, the glowing ends of their cigarettes signalling the path they took. Against the balustrade at the edge of the lawn which bordered the car park, a girl cried while her friend sounded outraged on her behalf.

On closer inspection, the gardens were more populated than they seemed at first. Every now and then, a couple might emerge from the trees, clothes hurriedly straightened, or two lads might walk purposefully back towards the light, their deal done.

'Better have a look,' Roland said, walking away from her across the lawn.

As she followed him, they moved further and further away from the light thrown from the leaded windows so that by the time they entered the small wood, she couldn't see anything but the whiteness of his shirt.

Despite her desire to find Ed, she wasn't sure about this. Something felt wrong.

'We'd better go back,' she said, faltering.

'Thought you want to find him,' he said, continuing to walk.

'It's too dark to see anything,' she said.

'Yeah, well, maybe it's a good thing if they don't see us coming. You know, catch them red-handed.'

She stopped.

'What do you mean?' she asked.

He came close so that she could smell his aftershave.

'If you go down to the woods today, you're in for a big surprise,' he said, a sneer on his lips.

'He said you were all mates,' she protested.

He snorted.

'Do you mean they could be…?' she asked, hesitantly.

'Shagging? What do you think?' he said, stepping towards her.

His face was now so close that even in the dark she could see that something strange had happened to his eyes. His pupils had dilated so much that they looked pitch black. His eyes bored straight into her as he took another step towards her so that now, she could feel his breath on her face.

She stepped back until she felt the hard presence of a tree trunk against her back, and still he moved towards her, his jaw clenched so tightly she could hear his teeth grinding.

His eyes, so black and wide, stared at her so intensely now that her mind raced trying to think of what she should do next.

He leaned over her, his hand resting on the trunk above her head so that she caught her breath at the sour tang of his sweat.

'But two can play at that, ' he said, smirking.

She knew in a flash of clarity what he wanted from her. Act as if you don't know what he's suggesting, she told herself. Talk him out of what's in his mind.

'You know, I bet we've got it all wrong and they're in there somewhere. Trying to find us. In fact, they could be waiting at the car right now,' she persisted, willing herself to smile, to talk him down.

He narrowed his eyes in disbelief.

'Don't give me all that,' he sneered, tugging at the shoulder strap of her dress. 'You're not so innocent. Not dressed like that.'

She turned away, nausea rising and catching in her throat. Why hadn't she gone home with her friend, why had she followed him into these woods, why hadn't she run when she had the chance instead of standing foolishly, a rabbit mesmerised by a lamper's beam.

'I thought Nicki was your girlfriend,' she continued, trying to shift away from the fingers insinuating themselves under the fabric. 'The way she looked at you, I just assumed.' If she could just placate him, say the right thing to calm him down, change his mind.

'She's obsessed with him. Can't think of anyone else,' he hissed. His hand was now on the hem of her dress. She tried to remember what she had been taught in a self-defence class at school. Something about holding your door key between your fingers, how your elbow was the hardest part of your body, but none of it was of any use when she was pinned against a tree by a man twice her size.

Now the hand inserted under the fabric was pushing its way upwards. Kathryn felt the roughness of his palm on her thigh but was unable to scream for help, to do anything in fact but stay frozen to the spot, willing it to stop. Scream, she told herself, but she was terrified of what he'd do if she made a scene.

'No,' she said, wriggling away from him. 'I don't want to –'

He silenced her protests with the palm of his hand, flat across her mouth now as she struggled to breathe, panic coursing through her veins.

'Just shut up,' he hissed, turning his head to spit on the ground.

Kathryn saw a figure approaching against the glow of the house lights in the distance. They were clearly searching for someone.

Roland, sensing their presence, let go of her arm and whispered in her ear. 'Stay still. We're just having a bit of fun, aren't we? No need to make a fuss.'

His voice must have carried across the garden because the figure spun around and saw them.

'Hey!' It was Ed.

She knew what it must look like. A couple pressed against a tree, away from the path, determined not to be found. She hadn't made a sound. Why hadn't she screamed? Would Ed realise it was because she was terrified of further enraging Roland?

Roland recognised Ed's voice too. He cursed under his breath and stepped away from her.

'Mate,' he smirked. 'Where were you? We were looking for you.'

She still stood like she was pinned against the tree, strands of her hair loose where her hairgrips had been dislodged.

Ed swore and for a sickening moment Kathryn was terrified he might misread the scene and vanish into the night.

But after a split second of hesitation, he launched himself at Roland, grabbing his shirt and pulling him away from Kathryn. Caught off guard, Roland stumbled before a blow to the side of his head sent him reeling. He glowered and was about to say something when Ed lunged again. This time, Roland sidestepped him and ran.

It was only when he'd disappeared from sight that Kathryn realised the rattling sound she could hear was her teeth chattering uncontrollably. Tears of shame, fear and relief now ran down her cheeks.

'If you hadn't got here when you did,' she sobbed, yanking the hem of her dress back down.

'What did he do to you?' Ed asked, staring at the ground, unable to look her in the eye. 'Did he...?'

She shook her head, unpeeling her hair from where it had stuck to her tear-stained cheeks. 'I want to go home,' she said, shivering.

It was only when she felt his arms around her that she stopped shaking.

'The bastard. I'll kill him,' he whispered.

Chapter 9

Kathryn ran her hand over the rough stone of the bench where she sat waiting for Ed to come back. He'd found her coat in a pile on a sofa, wrapped it around her shoulders, and told her to stay there, that they'd go soon but first he had to find Roland.

She wished she could just leave; disappear into the night and let the darkness swallow her. She wanted to walk away from this portal; this frenzied world she didn't understand. She pulled her jacket tighter around her, feeling adrift and raw.

She wriggled one of her feet out of her sodden shoe to ease the stinging rub on her heel. She felt ridiculous, stupidly following Roland into the dark while Ed was with Nicki. She couldn't forget the look on Roland's face, jeering at her stupidity, her blind trust.

The stone felt cold against her legs. The bench had probably stood here for a century, maybe more, against the brick and flint front wall of the old house. A relic from the past, it had been here while the world changed – and kept changing. She closed her eyes and tried to tune out the relentless music pumping out through the doorway, wondering about the people who had sat here before.

She opened her eyes to see Ed in front of her, his eyes still flashing, his jaw clenched.

'I just want to go home,' she said for the second time that night.

'Let's go get a taxi,' he said.

She walked away quickly, unable to stomach staying a moment longer. Her shoes felt as if they had contracted even further and she hobbled along the tarmac, feeling like one of Cinderella's sisters trying to squeeze into the glass slipper to win the prince's hand. And, like the sisters, she too felt rejected.

Ed was soon alongside her but she couldn't look at him, keeping her eyes on their feet, watching how his trainers stepped in time with hers.

'Look, I'm sorry,' he said.

When she didn't reply, he fell silent.

The thin plastic soles of her shoes slapped on the road.

'I don't know how we got split up like that. One minute you were there and the next you were gone,' he said.

The silence stretched out again but she didn't care. She wished she hadn't waited for him, had left while he was trying to find his mates.

She remembered Elaine's words from earlier that night, 'you're throwing yourself away on him.' Nicki's face as she smirked, 'Not the knight in shining armour after all, is he?' They were both right. She'd been foolish to think she was anything to him except a vaguely interesting sideline until he found something better to do.

'You should have stayed in the house.'

She looked up and hissed, 'Oh, so it's my fault? You conveniently give me the slip and then blame me for what nearly happened back there? You think I'm something to pick up and put down when you feel like it?'

He stopped suddenly, grabbing her hand so she was forced to come to a halt too. She couldn't see his face in the dark but could hear his voice quaver.

'Kat, I know it's my fault. If I hadn't brought him down,

this would never have happened. I'm sorry.'

And now some small, hidden part of her wanted to be heard, to speak as it hadn't spoken before.

She shook her hand free from his.

'But you don't regret bringing her down, do you? Why would you when you were planning it all along.'

'What are you talking about?' His voice had hardened.

She remembered how Nicki had looked at him as she poured his drink earlier, that sly smirk as if there was a secret understanding between them.

Kathryn blinked back angry tears, knowing she had fooled herself into believing their relationship meant anything to him. At the same time, the thought of being without him made her feel sick, as if someone had come along and scooped out of her life the one person who meant anything to her. Nicki was everything she wasn't: artful, worldly, bewitching. How could she compete with that?

Wiping away the tears with the back of her hand, her words came out like a torrent.

'You can do what you want with whoever you want from now on because I've wasted enough of my time on you. Trailing up and down the country for what? To sit in your room and watch you smoke dope? You think that's what I want from life? To stick around with the likes of you? Elaine's right – I could do a lot better for myself.'

Even as she spat out the words with a vehemence she didn't know she was capable of, she knew she didn't mean a word of it. She wanted to punish him though for doing the thing she had dreaded most – choosing someone over her. There was nothing she could do but hit out and try to hurt him as she had been hurt.

Seeing the wounded look on his face, she immediately

regretted every word. And not only the words but the disdain in her voice too. Before she could try to pull the words back, to explain that she hadn't meant them but that, in this moment, she felt as if her life was being destroyed, they were lit up by the headlights of a car making its way down the drive behind them. Stepping out of its way, she decided she would apologise to Ed as soon as the car had passed. She would make it right between them, despite everything he had done.

But the car didn't pass them. Instead, it stopped and a voice called from the open window.

'Kathryn?'

Crouching down, she peered into the car.

'Mark?'

The last time she'd seen her sister's ex-boyfriend was last summer, shortly before Beth left for the States. He had been heartbroken and Kathryn had felt for him, even though she was secretly glad that he could move on and find someone who might appreciate him more than her sister ever had.

'I thought that was you. Need a lift home or are you parked further down?'

She was conscious of Ed standing a short distance away.

'A lift would be great if it's not too much bother.'

Mark leant across and opened the front door.

'You've a friend with you?' he asked, before calling out.

'Jump in, both of you.'

They clambered in and the car pulled away slowly down the hill.

'It's been a while, Kathryn. I heard you're away at university now?'

Kathryn nodded, unwilling to play catch-up when all she could think about was apologising to Ed. Mark could drop them at the seafront so she could make it up to him some-how. And anyway, maybe Roland had got it wrong. She only had his word for it that Ed was up to anything.

'I didn't have you down as a clubber,' she said to Mark with a forced brightness.

'You're right. But it's one of the lads at work's birthday and one thing led to another. I've left them to it. Couldn't stand another minute of it. What's it now? Fourish? I've only got three hours before I need to be up,' Mark said, groaning theatrically before glancing into the mirror.

'I'm Mark, by the way.'

'All right mate.' Ed's tone made it clear that he didn't want to have to conduct a conversation with a stranger at the moment.

'That accent's not from around here. You two studying together?'

Kathryn mumbled, 'Ed's from Liverpool.'

'A lot of good things have come out of Liverpool,' said Mark. 'The first overhead railway, Dinky Toys, the Beatles.'

'Trust you to know about the first overheard railway,' Kathryn said, softening it with a smile. He'd always been this way, easy company, interested in other people's lives. She had never been able to work out why her sister had found it so easy to leave him behind.

'Had a good night?'

They answered in unison.

'Yes,' she lied.

'No,' Ed mumbled from the back seat.

'Okay,' Mark said indulgently as if humouring two squabbling children.

As they neared the centre of town, he said, 'Where am I dropping you, Ed?'

She understood why he asked. In the three years he had gone out with Beth, he had never stayed the night. It would never have occurred to him. And, while it might have occurred to Ed, it was still not an option because her parents would have a fit and, more than that, because he'd just cheated on her.

'Okay if you drop me at the station?' Ed said.

She looked out of the window and blinked back tears. She could tell that Mark was glancing across at her inquisitively but she wouldn't let him see her crying.

'You sure? I'm guessing you need the train to Victoria?' Mark said.

When Ed didn't reply, he continued, 'As far as I can remember, the first train that will get you to Victoria is at half five. So you'll have a bit of a wait if I drop you off now.'

'I'll be okay.'

Mark pulled up outside the train station. Kathryn's car, her overnight bag still in the boot, was the only other car on the street. She'd have to get the bus in later after a few hours' sleep to collect it and by then, Ed would be long gone, maybe even back home in Liverpool. Or Epsom.

She wanted to say something as Ed opened the door. But Roland's brutal words were still ringing in her ears, 'Shagging – what do you think?'

'Thanks for the lift,' Ed said, climbing out.

'No trouble at all,' said Mark with a smile.

He's not even going to say anything to me, Kathryn thought, a lump catching in her throat. He's cheated on me on my birthday and he knows he's been caught out but he's just going to walk away.

The door clicked shut and he knocked on the window.

As she wound it down, he crouched alongside the car.

'I'm sorry, okay?'

She nodded but before she could reply, he stood up, tapped the roof of the car and walked away.

As they drove away, she saw him go into the deserted train station. Then she began to cry.

It was hard to imagine as she drove through the quiet streets with Mark that a few miles away, on a hill overlooking the town, the party continued. Her ears were still ringing from the loud music and her mouth felt dry. If Linda had been with them, she would have made sure she had enough water.

Linda's other words of advice came back to her as she stared out at the houses, in darkness except for the occasional porch light. Give him a nudge, she had suggested before adding, 'not that he usually needs that.' Had he slept with her too? It wouldn't surprise her. And to think she had believed she meant something to him when all along, she was just one of a number.

'Want to tell me what's up?'

Wiping the back of her hand across her eyes, she turned to look at Mark.

'I don't know what you mean.'

He stared ahead, drumming his fingers on the steering wheel. She had forgotten that habit of his.

'Kathryn, I've just picked you up looking, dare I say, bedraggled and emotional. Clearly something's happened to you. You listened to me before when I was in a bit of a state after Beth. How about I return the favour?'

Sniffing, she nodded and, a street away from her house, he pulled the car over and turned the engine off.

'But you've to get up in the morning,' she said. 'It's late already.'

'Or early, depending on which way you look at it,' he quipped, turning the key in the ignition so the digital display lit up. The clock showed it was now half past four. He shuddered in jest and turned the key so the car was once again in darkness. 'Don't worry about me. I might even throw a sickie. Now, spill the beans.'

He opened the glove compartment, producing a can of Pepsi which he handed to her.

'I expect you're parched.'

She nodded and tugged the ring pull. The brown liquid shot out of the can and fizzed all over the front of her dress.

As she wiped her dress with a duster Mark produced from the door pocket, she thought how typical it was that he had a proper cloth to wipe the windscreen instead of just using his hand. He was like her dad; tidy and exacting.

'It's my birthday and…'

'I know. Your birthday is exactly a month after mine. That's why I always remember. But I didn't want to say it in case your friend had forgotten.'

'Well, he might as well have done. I got some beautiful flowers but it turned out they weren't even from him. The whole thing's been such a disappointment.'

'If I'd known the disappointment it would cause, I would have thought twice.'

Kathryn narrowed her eyes, confused. 'Thought twice about what?'

With a rueful smile, Mark said, 'I'm afraid it was me. The flowers. Remember, I sent Beth a bouquet on her twentieth birthday and you said no one ever bought you flowers and…'

Of course. Why hadn't she remembered? 'And you said you'd make sure I had flowers delivered when I was twenty.

Thank you. They were really lovely.'

'It came to me the other day. I remembered it was your twentieth coming up and thought how tickled you'd be if I sent them. I had no way of knowing it would help to put the kibosh on your big night.' He took his glasses off and rubbed his eyes. 'How about we just forget the flowers and you start at the beginning.'

By the time Kathryn had finished telling Mark about her relationship with Ed from their first encounter up to the present moment, she wondered if he was either bored or asleep because he hadn't said anything for what must have been twenty minutes.

When he finally spoke it was to say, 'He's not sleeping with that girl, you know.'

She jumped. 'How could you know that?'

He shifted in his seat. ' For a start, he wouldn't have even got as far as Chapman's tonight. He'd have just stayed in Epsom with her. Why bother coming all this way? And, from what you've just told me, it sounds like you've helped him a lot, maybe even inspired him. He'll have you on some sort of pedestal.'

'Come off it, Mark, that's not the way it is at all. It's more that he's turned my life around.'

'In what way?'

'He sees me. Understands me. When I'm with him, he doesn't harp on about studying and grades and careers. He makes me feel like I'm good enough as I am. Like I already matter. You know, not playing second fiddle.'

She knew he'd know what she meant. He'd seen how Beth had stolen the show as they grew up.

'Then why would he try to wreck it? From where I was sitting, and take it from one who knows what it feels like, he looked pretty wretched when he got out of the car.'

'But all he cared about was sorting out Roland,' she said.

'And why wouldn't he? I bet he felt guilty about leaving you alone with that guy, who, by the way, I think you should report. You won't be the first he'll have cut up rough with. No, I bet Ed's feeling sick that he let you down like that.'

'He didn't let me down.'

'That's better,' Mark said with a smile.

'But he didn't make it better either.'

'He told you he was sorry and he knows he messed up. He can't tell you how he feels about you because, well, most of us can't. I tried with Beth when she was packing her bags and look how far that got me.'

Kathryn didn't know what to say. She remembered how Beth had rolled her eyes when she relayed, word for word, what Mark had said when he pleaded with her to stay.

The car suddenly felt very cold and Kathryn shivered.

'I've got a jumper in the back,' Mark said, leaning back between the seats.

He picked up a brown chenille pullover that had fallen into the footwell, revealing an envelope underneath.

'For you,' he said, after clicking on the interior light and scanning the name on the front. 'Ed must have dropped it.'

She smiled when she saw the birthday card with a race-horse on the front. As she opened it to read the message inside, something fell out.

It was a ticket for a flight from Liverpool to Dublin, leaving the following weekend. She frowned, feeling confused as she unfolded a letter that had been tucked in the card with the ticket.

Dear Kat,

Happy birthday! By the time you read this, you'll be twenty and we'll have had a mental night in that ghost town you call home. I know you're probably wondering why I've sent you a letter as well as a card, especially because you know I don't find writing letters as easy as you do (I'm running out of space for all yours!)

It's just that I've got stuff to say this time. So here goes. The last year has been the best. Because of you. You go out of your way for me when there must be loads of other things you could be doing. That means a lot to me.

I'm the luckiest bloke I know because you bother with me and I don't know what I did to deserve that. You're the best.

So now it's my turn to bother about you. I hope you're up for it because I've already booked everything for Dublin! Sorry it's not Paris or somewhere romantic. Thought it might be fun though.

We'll talk about it on Saturday.

I love you.
Ed x

By the time she finished reading, they were driving back into town.

She looked across at Mark inquisitively.

'I thought you were dropping me at home?'

'When you get a chance of happiness, you've got to take it.'

She gave silent thanks that after their lives had diverged with Beth's departure, their paths had crossed again this evening.

'You were right, you know,' she said, willing him to put his foot down and speed up.

'In what way?' he asked, braking as a milk float pulled out of a side street.

'I shouldn't have doubted him.'

He glanced across at her and smiled.

'But you're going to put that right now, aren't you?'

Leaving Mark in the car, she jumped out at the station and ran in. She ignored her sore feet and didn't care that she was wearing a jumper that almost reached her knees; she just needed to find Ed and tell him how sorry she was and how she would never doubt him again.

The shutter was pulled down on the ticket kiosk but the door was open onto the platform. A clock on the wall above the timetables showed it was now ten past five and she marvelled at her lack of tiredness after such a long night. Catching sight of her reflection in the metal shutter across the ticket kiosk, she grimaced at her dishevelled appearance but then grinned. What did it matter? He loved her. Despite everything.

The station looked different at this time of the morning. Lamps hanging from ornate ironwork shed light that gathered in bright pools, while further along, where the station wall gave way to a chain link fence, the platform was in gloom.

She couldn't see anybody. Across the tracks, the benches were empty. But there was a length of platform further along that was out of view. Maybe he was there, waiting for the minute hand to make its way round to half past five when he could jump on the first train home.

Kathryn bit her lip. He was going back to the chaos and hopelessness he so wanted to put behind him. And before he could tell her of his plans for his – for their – future, she had jumped to conclusions, showing him that, when it came down to it, she didn't trust him and thought he was as devious as his family.

She had to find him and tell him what a mistake she had made. Running up the steps, she clattered across the bridge that arched over the tracks. From that height, she could see Mark's car, its engine now switched off, and the sleeping streets. It felt like they were the only ones awake in the whole town.

Past the benches and glass-encased timetables at the far end of the other platform, she could see a row of wheelie bins and a porter's trolley leaning against the wall. And there she saw the outline of a person, their back against the wall with their head in their hands.

'Ed!' she cried, the knot in her stomach unravelling at the sight of him.

But then she saw a sleeping bag and a hump of bags at his feet and her heart sank.

'Sorry, I thought you were someone else,' she said as the figure began to shift.

She was turning back to the bridge when the man called.

'A young bloke? On his way to London?'

'Yes. You saw him?'

The man emerged from the shadows and despite her in-built wariness of being alone with a stranger on the deserted platform, her heart ached to see someone so down on their luck. He looked about her dad's age but unshaven and very thin, so it was hard to tell.

He thrust his hands into the pockets of his tracksuit bottoms.

'Seemed in a bit of a bad way, girl. Waited on that bench for half an hour or so and then left. Last I saw, he was crossing the bridge towards the street.'

'Did you speak to him?'

'A bit. I asked him for a light. He looked right upset so I asked if he was alright. He just said he'd screwed things up good and proper.'

'Did he say where he was going?'

'No. Sorry, love.'

Mark's face dropped when he saw Kathryn coming back through the archway alone.

'He's not here anymore. He waited for about half an hour and then left.'

Mark leant forward to start the car and then, thinking better of it, sank back into his seat.

'Best to wait for him to come back then. The train will be here in a quarter of an hour. He won't want to miss it.'

She had to admit he was right. Ed wouldn't want to miss the train and would surely come wandering back along the street any minute. He'd probably just gone for a walk to kill time. When he saw her he would understand immediately that she wanted to make amends for what had happened.

They waited in silence as a couple of cars swung in, let someone out and then drove away again. A bleary-eyed young couple, rucksacks on their backs, emerged from the hotel and made their way across the street and into the station. Mark switched the ignition on to check the clock.

'Five minutes to go. He's cutting it a bit fine.'

Kathryn got out of the car and walked to the corner. Nothing. And that's when she remembered the taxi rank.

She approached a black cab whose driver had pushed his chair back and was asleep. She rapped on the window, startling him back upright again.

'Where do you want to go?' he asked, rubbing his eyes.

'Nowhere. I just want to ask you –'

He shook his head in irritation and started to close his window.

She put out her hand to stop its ascent.

'Did you see someone come out of the station? About my age. In the last half hour.'

'Yeah, wanted to go to London but didn't have enough cash on him. Mick took him though. Typical Mick, he'll never make money cabbying at this rate but he's got sons of his own so he's a bit of a soft touch.'

With that, he wound the window up, leant back in his seat and closed his eyes.

'He's gone. In a taxi to London,' she told Mark as she opened the passenger door.

'We can't do any more now, Kathryn,' he said wearily. 'First things first, bed for you and then we'll have a think.'

How different the streets looked as they drove back to her house. Less than an hour earlier, all had been shrouded in darkness as she'd excitedly rehearsed in her head all the things she'd say when she found him waiting for his train. Now, the sun was coming up and the houses were emerging once again. Her mind, despite its nagging tiredness, was in turmoil.

Mark dropped her at the corner of her street.

'If your mum and dad think you're with Elaine, they'll have lots of questions if they hear a car dropping you off at this hour. Better to sneak in quietly.'

'You've been so kind. Thank you for the flowers. And for everything.'

He dismissed her words with a casual wave of the hand.
'Get some sleep and I'll call you later.'

Chapter 10

Her room, its curtains still open, was ablaze with warm sunshine when she finally woke. Closing her eyes again, she put her head under the covers. The heaviness she felt in her body, still cumbersome from sleep and weighed down deep inside by last night's misunderstanding, seemed at odds with the promise of the day. If she opened the window, she knew she would hear the sounds of life going on as usual but she wanted to keep the world at bay for a little longer.

But more sleep wouldn't come, so she finally clambered out of bed and filled her mug at the washbasin. She drank thirstily, catching her own eye in the mirror above the taps. She looked away again quickly but not before she took in the blotchy skin, its foundation long since washed away by the tears she had shed last night, and the dry lumps of mascara in the corners of her eyes. A stray hair grip still hung in there – she had no idea where the others had disappeared to – and with a pang, she remembered Elaine's careful ministrations.

The phone in the hall was now ringing.

She heard her mother's voice. 'Kathryn? No, she's at her friend's house.'

Opening the door slightly, she called, 'Mum, I'm here. Won't be a minute.'

In her hurry to grab her dressing gown from the hook on the back of the door, Kathryn stumbled over her discarded dress and shoes on the floor and cursed.

Valerie frowned as she handed her the phone, her hand

over the receiver.

'It's Mark. Beth's Mark. For you.'

She did at least disappear back into the kitchen although Kathryn guessed she was probably just behind the door, trying to hear what was being said.

'Hi Mark, how are you?'

'Not feeling as rough as you, if your voice is anything to go on,' he said, brightly.

'Are you just up?' she asked, impressed by his energy.

'An hour or so. Had a walk along the seafront to wake me up and now here I am, recharged and at your service.'

'What do you mean?' she said, wrapping the telephone cord around her fingers.

'I'm at a bit of a loose end this weekend if you want some company on the road?'

'On the road?'

'Well, I'm assuming you're heading off to track down Ed.'

She let the cool shower wash away the grubbiness of the night before and, by the time she was dressed, felt ready to meet the day head on. Sitting on the bed, trying to pull a sock over toes that hadn't been properly dried, she tried to imagine where Ed might be. Was he in the kitchen at home, looking out onto their drab bit of garden? Or in bed, playing music and smoking a joint? Or maybe he wasn't home at all. Maybe he had tried to find Roland.

No, the taxi driver had said London, not Epsom. But why get an expensive taxi instead of the train? He wouldn't have got home any earlier. She tried to push these pointless ifs and buts aside as she dragged a brush through her damp hair and pulled it into a ponytail.

The radio was on as usual when she went into the kitchen. She had never worked out why her parents couldn't cope with silence. Maybe it was because the constant background hum of middle of the road classics and dull phone-ins, broken up by half hourly news bulletins, meant that talk between them could be bypassed while listening to the conversations and opinions of strangers.

Her mother was ironing. The iron hissed as it glided back and forth over one of George's work shirts. Valerie stood it with a clatter on the metal edge of the ironing board before folding the shirt and placing it carefully in the basket on the kitchen table beside her.

She looked up and, with narrowed eyes, asked, 'How did you get home? I thought you were with Elaine? And why was Mark ringing?'

Before Kathryn could answer, the newsreader's voice caught her mother's attention.

'A man was assaulted in Brighton in the early hours of this morning. He is in a critical condition and his family have been informed. Police are making enquiries locally and are asking anyone who was in the region of Kings Road between five and seven am to come forward.'

The newsreader's tone suggested these things happened every day. As he moved on to the next item, so did Kathryn's mother.

'Life will never be the same for some poor family. Anyway, go on, what happened last night?'

Before Kathryn could answer, the doorbell rang, giving her a welcome reason to avoid her mother's questions and to momentarily forget the nervous twisting of her stomach at the thought of Ed in a hospital bed with his family around him.

It wasn't Mark, as she expected, but Elaine standing on the doorstep.

'You're in one piece then,' she said.

'Only just. Wait till I tell you everything.'

Elaine couldn't hide her look of disgust at the unmade bed and heap of clothing and shoes on Kathryn's bedroom floor.

She picked up the blue dress and laid it over the back of the chair by the desk.

'Sorry about that,' Kathryn mumbled, 'It was a lovely present.'

Elaine held up a hand. 'Never mind the dress. Tell me everything.'

Aware that Mark would be here at any moment and wanting to bring her friend up to speed as quickly as possible, Kathryn glossed over the incident with Roland. As she was about to move on to the misunderstanding with Ed, the door opened and Valerie came in with two cups of tea and the biscuit tin on a tray.

As she put them down on the desk, she shook her head.

'Look at this room.'

Elaine tried to steer her away from her usual barrage of criticism.

'We're just talking about last night, Valerie. We had such a lovely evening but my parents had friends staying over so Kathryn decided to come home instead of staying the night.'

'And how did you get home?' Valerie asked Kathryn.

'By taxi,' Elaine chimed in. 'It was late by then, wasn't it? Must have been what, one o'clock?'

'Well, at least you got home safe,' her mother shrugged. 'You know we worry about you being out late at night. We can't get a minute's sleep until you're home.'

The girls exchanged glances and, after Valerie had left the room with the empty tray, Kathryn shook her head in disbelief.

'I never know what to say to my parents but you have them eating out of your hand.'

Elaine shrugged before taking a gulp of tea, 'Well, someone has to convince them that you're behaving yourself and not running around the country after some fella. Now, tell me, what exactly happened when you went into the garden with that Roland bloke?'

'Nothing much. It's not important anyway because we had a fight.'

'You and Roland?'

'No, me and Ed. And then Mark turned up.'

'Mark who?'

'Mark Johnson.'

'Beth's Mark?'

'Yes, although I wish you'd all stop calling him that. As if he hasn't any identity beyond the fact that he used to go out with my sister.'

Elaine shrugged. 'Fair enough. But we're talking about the same Mark?'

Kathryn nodded.

'Poor Mark. He's had a tough few months, by all accounts,' Elaine said, straightening a pile of magazines on the desk.

'He didn't say anything last night,' Kathryn replied.

'His dad's very ill. Cancer again. My brother knows Mark from work; that's how I heard about it.'

They heard a car stop outside the house and, peering out the window, saw Mark get out and walk towards the house before going back to check he had locked the doors.

'What's he doing here?'

'He's coming with me to Liverpool,' Kathryn answered, seeing the look of surprise on her friend's face. 'What? He fancies a break.'

Valerie had let Mark in and they were standing in the hall making polite conversation when Kathryn and Elaine came down the stairs. Despite the heat, he was wearing a navy blouson jacket and dark trousers. Elaine and Kathryn had always joked that however hard he tried, he always dressed like someone twenty years older; like someone who always made the appropriate effort for the occasion.

Nobody had ever understood Mark and Beth as a couple. Beth was popular and the centre of attention while Mark stood in the wings, full of admiration for her. It was always going to burn out, especially when she got the offer of working abroad for a summer; an offer they all knew would extend into something permanent. Only Mark clung to the hope that she would return and pick up where they left off.

He eventually realised what everyone else had already known – that she would leave her life, and everyone in it, behind. Her parents, their loyalties firmly with their oldest daughter, had grown weary of his phone calls and visits, but Kathryn had taken his side, sorry that he had been cast aside as soon as a brighter future had beckoned for Beth. Even as a teenager, she had understood that people as kind as Mark were rare.

Mark turned and smiled broadly. The picture of health, without so much as a hint of tiredness.

After offering Mark the customary cup of tea, which he politely declined, Valerie returned to her ironing. Their relationship had not been the same since Beth left. Kathryn had even heard her mother tell her father that if Mark had been worth staying for, Beth might not have left in the first place. Of course, they all knew that was ridiculous, that these were the words of a mother who wanted to blame someone for her daughter flying the nest, likely never to return. And he had become something of a nuisance, ringing repeatedly to ask if they knew when Beth might be home again. They had been relieved when he finally got the message and drifted away to pick up his life again.

As the door closed behind Valerie, Mark's shoulders seemed to relax a little.

'I think your mum's a bit thrown by me just turning up,' he said in a low voice before turning to Elaine, 'Hey, I haven't seen you in such a long time. What are we going to do with our lovesick friend here?'

#

They decided to pick up Kathryn's car then drop Mark's car off at his house before heading north.

'Sorry to hear your dad's not well,' Kathryn said, feeling her own problems pale into insignificance next to what Mark and his family were facing.

He nodded and smiled weakly. 'Thanks. We're just putting one foot in front of the other. No point going into it, you know?'

Understanding that he'd rather not talk about it, Kathryn hesitated before saying, 'Only come along if you're sure you're happy to. I don't know what's waiting for us when we get there. I mean, I don't even know if he's gone home.'

'Could you ring his brother?' Elaine asked.

'No, their phone was cut off again last weekend. Ed's been ringing me from a phone box.'

'Neighbours, friends? It just seems like a long way to go if he's not even there.' Elaine seemed unsure about their potentially futile expedition. 'What if he stayed in Epsom with his friends? I mean, I wouldn't want to be anywhere near those two but they are his mates. And it doesn't sound as if there's anything in Liverpool for him, from what you say, anyway.'

Kathryn thought of the envelope, safely zipped in her bag.

'No, he's definitely going to be in Liverpool because we're… he's flying to Dublin next weekend,' she said.

It was four o'clock by the time they set off on the road out of town. Elaine had been aghast at the idea when Kathryn suggested it but had agreed to come along because it was her best friend's birthday weekend, she had never been north of Oxford and not a lot happened at college on a Monday.

'How long does it take to get there?' Elaine had asked as she bundled her holdall into the back seat.

'Only four and a half hours,' Kathryn said lightly. 'It'll pass quickly, you'll see.'

Chapter 11

It was as they made their way off the motorway, following the signs for Liverpool, that Kathryn's thoughts turned to what lay ahead. The three of them had chatted for hours about the past, both shared and personal, and the present, hardly noticing the passing miles until they were on the ring road into the city.

'I can't believe this old car of yours has made this journey so often,' Mark said, glancing across at the milometer.

'I know how to change a tyre and keep the car topped up with oil and water. Beyond that, I trust to luck.'

'You used to freak out about driving across town. Where did this new intrepid Kathryn come from?' Elaine said.

Mark studied the map while Kathryn checked her mirror and swung the car into the right hand lane, which was signposted city centre.

'Do you think your mum believed we were all going to Southampton?' asked Elaine. 'She looked a bit dubious.'

'Where else would she think I was taking you?' Kathryn said, winding down her window slightly. 'It is where I've been living for the past six months.'

'From what I can make out, you're hardly ever there,' Elaine said. 'I told you before, you'll regret it when you fail your exams. And your mum and dad will go spare.'

'Elaine's not keen on Ed,' Kathryn said, looking across at Mark.

'And what do you make of him, Mark?' Elaine asked, leaning between the seats to catch a glimpse of the stretch of river in front of them.

'We only exchanged a few words but he seemed nice enough. And pretty smitten with our Kathryn here,' Mark replied, winking at Kathryn.

Elaine snorted and sat back.

'Yes, well, he'll have to convince me of that.'

Despite her friends' protests, Kathryn decided the best plan was to drop Mark and Elaine at Pier Head and then try to find her way to the house. She didn't want to turn up on Ed's doorstep with her friends in tow. It would only complicate things. It was enough to know they were in the same city if she needed them. But for now, she wanted to be alone.

Whenever she had driven to Speke before, Ed had directed her. She hoped the route would be familiar enough for her to remember which exits to take at the roundabouts, and whether to turn left or right at the T junction on the edge of his estate.

Across the river, the sun was now slipping down towards the horizon and leaving in its wake a sky ablaze, as if a child had dipped their paintbrush in yellow, red and grey and swept it across the sky without thinking to wash the bristles in between. It looked like the factories and industrial plants of Birkenhead across the water were on fire, so intense were the colours. And against this lurid backdrop, King Edward VII sat on his horse atop a granite plinth, cast into silhouette.

Elaine looked up at the towering building next to where Kathryn had parked the car. Its grey stone walls seemed to go on forever, storey after storey topped by two clock towers that offered a comfortable perch for the city's famous birds, one looking towards the Mersey, the other facing the sprawl of the city.

'The Liver Birds,' Elaine said, staring upwards. 'Now I

know I'm in Liverpool.'

She looked beyond to where the white Cunard Building and the domes of the stately Port of Liverpool kept watch over the river. 'I thought it would be a bit rough up here but it looks like New York. But are you sure you'll be alright without us?'

Kathryn nodded and looked back at the map Mark had laid out on the bonnet.

'I'm a bit bothered about what you'll do if Ed's not back,' he said, marking the route to Ed's house with a biro. 'Where will you stay? If you can wait a few minutes, I'll pop over and book into one of the hotels. That way I can give you a phone number where you can reach us if you have any problems.'

But Kathryn wanted to be on her way and dismissed his concerns with a wave of her hand. 'I'll be fine. His brother won't just leave me on the doorstep. Now go, have a nice time and I'll see you tomorrow.'

'You're sure? Because we could get a taxi out there later, just to check that all's well. We wouldn't make a nuisance of ourselves or anything,' Mark said, answered only by a frown, 'Okay, but take care, alright?'

After arranging to meet at the same place the next day at noon, Kathryn hugged them both and watched as they made their way towards the city centre. Elaine hurried along with Mark, weighed down by both their bags, following in her wake.

#

As she turned the final corner towards Ed's house, Kathryn felt that it was somewhat miraculous that she was here after only one wrong turning. Now that she didn't need to concentrate on the road, her nerves were making their presence felt. She tried to convince herself that everything would be forgiven as soon as he saw her on his doorstep.

But as she pulled up at the house, her stomach lurched to see that it was in darkness. She couldn't understand it. The kitchen light was always on and its glow could be seen through the glass of the front door. But not tonight. Every other house on the street had the look of life about it except this one.

The gate stood propped open since it had fallen off one of its hinges and, even in the dusk, she could see that the weeds had expanded their patch since her last visit. They straggled across the short concrete path, where tufts of grass pushed up through the cracks. This small patch of neglected land's only purpose was to separate the house from the road.

She knocked hesitantly at the door and strained to hear any movement within. If Terry was away and Paul had decided on an early night – unlikely, she had to admit, but not impossible – it might take something more than a gentle tap to wake him. She knocked again, this time louder and for longer. Still nothing.

Unsure of what to do next, she waited before knocking again. And again.

After a couple more minutes, a woman popped her head over the fence that divided Ed's front garden from next door.

'Are you okay, love?' she asked, 'I saw you out of the window. You look a bit lost.'

Embarrassed to have been spotted, Kathryn smiled faintly.

'I'm fine, thanks, but there doesn't seem to be anyone in.'

The woman shook her head. 'There's nobody there, love. They all left this morning. It was early, about seven o'clock I think. I was just letting the cat out when I saw them.'

The idea of them leaving the house so early seemed odd. Kathryn couldn't imagine what would cause such a departure. It had to be bad news. Illness or an accident.

And then Kathryn's mind spun back to the news bulletin earlier that day. But that was in Brighton and he wouldn't have been anywhere near Brighton, not if the taxi had taken him to London.

But what if the taxi driver had thought better of taking Ed as far as Victoria and had dropped him off in Brighton instead? Maybe he'd already made plans to meet up with Nicki and Roland in Brighton and just hadn't told her. Maybe she had been chatting and joking with her friends all the way up here not knowing that Ed was hurt and needed her in Brighton.

She felt faint, as if the ground under her feet might give way at any moment.

'Are you all right?' the woman asked. 'You don't look too well.'

'I'm fine, honestly. But I think something awful might have happened,' she tailed off, unable to say anything more because she thought it would come out as sobs rather than words.

The woman persuaded Kathryn to come in for a cup of tea. Nothing, she said, was so awful that a cup of tea and something to eat couldn't help. So, feeling weak after not eating for hours, Kathryn agreed. She would finish her tea and then get back on the road to find Mark in one of the hotels. He'd know what to do next.

While her mind raced, Kathryn's eyes took in the details of the room. She guessed that these houses must all be laid out in the same way. Carbon copy buildings but the lives within couldn't be more different. As she waited, she watched the blue flame of the gas fire flickering behind its steel bars. There were no chimneys on these houses. Fireplaces would have been seen as out of date when they were built in the early sixties. Who wanted to sweep up coal dust like past generations when you could have heat and light at the turn of a dial?

The woman returned with two cups of tea and a cheese and tomato sandwich on a small plate.

It turned out that her name was Sue and she had lived next to Ed's family ever since she moved to the estate with her husband and baby in the early 1970s.

'I didn't realise they'd lived here that long,' Kathryn said, biting into the sandwich.

'Yes, our Denise is the same age as Paul. She's a baby of her own now, lives over Kirkby way. And she's got a lovely fella. Met him at school, she did. Anyway, don't mind me. I do go on.' She picked up the biscuit tin. 'And what about yourself? Like I said, I looked out of the window when I heard someone knocking next door and saw you looking right upset out there.'

Kathryn didn't know where to start. 'It's Ed. I think he's been badly injured in a fight.'

Sue held the biscuit tin in mid-air and looked at her, shocked.

'Why do you think that?'

'There was something on the news today about a man being hurt. They said the family had been informed and now they've all gone together somewhere so it has to be –'

Sue put her hand across her heart and smiled. 'No, love, they've gone to see his mother. She's been taken into hospital.'

'Whose mother? Ed's?'

Sue narrowed her eyes as if trying to work out how much Kathryn knew about the family, 'No, the old lady. Ed's nan. Someone called over first thing – turns out their phone's been disconnected again. I was getting the milk in when I overheard them. Seems she's had a stroke.'

Kathryn felt relief rush through her veins.

'I shouldn't say it, but I'm so glad to hear that. Did they all go?' she asked.

Sue settled back in the armchair beside the fire.

'Terry and Paul, and that girl that hangs around.'

'Ed wasn't with them?'

'No, love. I haven't seen Ed for a few days. Could be that he's been around and I haven't spotted him, but it's unlikely. I tend to see most of the neighbours' comings and goings.'

He hadn't come home. What if he had got into difficulty somewhere? Been mugged, had no money to get back. He'd have no way of calling anyone to help him.

Sue studied Kathryn's face and, shaking her head, smiled. 'You're sweet on him, aren't you?'

Kathryn could feel herself reddening.

Sue laughed, kindly. 'Don't mind me. I'm only teasing. He's the only one who's all right out of the lot of them. He's a good lad – he came over here after that bad storm a few years back, made sure I had enough of everything. He does that sort of thing. I've seen the two of you together and I'm right glad that he has a nice girl. Janet would be glad too.'

'Janet?'

'His mum.'

Kathryn's eyes widened. 'You knew Ed's mum?'

Kathryn felt impatient to know more. 'What was she like?'

'Well, she was… a lady, I suppose is how I'd describe her.

Had her ups and downs like all of us but didn't deserve the life she had with him.'

Kathryn wanted to hear more about this woman who nobody ever mentioned.

'And what sort of life was that?'

'Other women, drinking, gambling. And I always had a feeling he gave her a clout. She'd try and hide it but you can't hide some things, can you?'

Finally, someone who could colour in the outline of Ed's mother, someone who remembered the woman's trials, her struggles, someone who could put a name to the person who was elsewhere, dismissed because she had walked out on her children.

Kathryn wanted to know everything Sue could recall about Ed's mother. She might not have another opportunity to find out about his mother but shouldn't she be doing something to find Ed instead? Ringing someone? But who? The older woman, glad that her mine of information and observations of her neighbours were finally of interest to someone, had returned to the kitchen to put the kettle on again and, after a couple of minutes, was back with a fresh pot of tea.

'I'm worried about him, Sue. I think I should ring the hospital in Brighton, just in case.'

Sue put a hand on Kathryn's arm.

'Sorry, I shouldn't laugh but listen to yourself, girl. Why are you so sure he's come to harm? He's probably just knocking about with some mates. That's what young fellas do when they haven't a care in the world.'

Kathryn hoped she was right but Sue didn't know Ed. Not really. And she really didn't want to explain what had happened last night, how there was someone he wanted to find and punish, and also how she had spurned him. So, glancing at the carriage clock on the mantelpiece, she told herself she would make her way back into the city at half nine but, until then, she would drink her tea and hear about the woman whose disappearance had left a hole in her son's life so large that nobody could fill it.

The next time she checked the clock, it was nearly ten. She had been so engrossed in Sue's memories that she had lost track of time.

'I never did find out what happened to her. She'd come in with the baby every morning and we'd sit and have a cup of tea. Like you and me are doing now. Except we'd talk about things you talk about as young mums. I remember one day she was in an awful flap. Said that Eddie had fallen out of his high chair and hit his head on the side of the cupboard. Blood everywhere. She was that panicked. No wonder, the poor little mite needed stitches all across here.' She ran a finger across her temple.

Kathryn nodded. She had wondered about the faint scar but had assumed it was from his time in Feltham. She'd thought he must have been fighting, getting into bad company. When would she stop getting him so wrong?

'But then one morning she didn't come in. And then the next. And then next thing I knew, Terry's mother was taking the baby out in the pushchair. I didn't like to ask. I'd heard enough about Terry to steer clear. But a couple of the women down the street – they've all gone now, there's only us two families left. If you can call us families, that is...' she tailed off, as if another thought was now occupying her mind.

'The other women?'

'Oh yes, well I saw them down at the corner shop a week or so later and they'd heard that Janet just upped and went one night. Disappeared, never to be seen again. Not round here anyway.'

'You don't think anything, you know, sinister happened to her, do you? I mean, it happens to some women, doesn't it?' Kathryn asked.

'It did cross my mind, I won't lie. But she wrote to me. Just the once. Maybe a year or so later. Just a few lines. She'd met someone and was starting anew. Down in London, I think.'

Ed had already made it clear that, whether his mother was dead or alive, there was nothing to be gained from finding out. He'd lost her either way. But Kathryn's eyes widened as she considered the idea that Ed's mother was still alive, living the life she left her boys for.

'Do you still have the letter?' she asked, already guessing what the response would be.

'No, I've had that many clear-outs over the last, what would it be, seventeen years? There's no chance I've kept it. But I hope she's doing all right. She was different to most you find around here. Gentle, intelligent. Can't think how she ever got mixed up with the likes of him.' She jerked her head in the direction of the house next door. 'I never understood how she could leave the little ones though.'

Kathryn drank the last of her tea and stood up. 'I'd better go, Sue.'

Sue looked at the clock. 'Goodness, is that the time? I've been talking that long?'

It was only when Kathryn bent the truth a little and told her that she was meeting her friends in town, that Sue felt comfortable letting her go. She stopped in the hall and scribbled her phone number on a piece of paper from a pad next to the telephone.

'You're sure your friends are staying in town tonight? If

not, there's a bed here if you're stuck.'

Sue stayed in the open doorway, the bright light behind her, as Kathryn made her way down the garden path and it was only when she climbed into her car, that the older woman retreated with a wave and closed the door.

Kathryn looked at Ed's house, still in darkness. It looked vacant, as if waiting for council workers to make it tidy for its next tenants. She thought of Janet, walking down the path for the final time. Did she look back at the window of the bedroom where her children lay sleeping? Or did she ease the front door closed and slip away so quietly that nobody heard her as she hurried from one life to the next?

Who was she to judge this woman who probably had a child, maybe two, by the time she was twenty? What did she know of being saddled with responsibility and despair and what that could drive someone to? But she couldn't help wondering about the children left to cobble their lives together without the woman who should have loved them enough to worry and fuss over them. She wondered what Ed would have been like if she had stayed.

As she turned the key in the ignition, she felt so weary that she wondered how she would keep her eyes open on the way back into the city. The company of her friends and then Sue had kept the tiredness at bay, but now she just wanted to lay her head on the steering wheel and sleep.

What could she achieve tonight even if she found Mark and Elaine? She could hardly start travelling south at this late hour. And where would she even drive to? London, Brighton, Epsom? He could be anywhere.

Not wishing to alert Sue to the fact that she had not driven away, she parked the car around the corner. She'd sleep now and think again in the morning.

She knew she would find the house key somewhere. As she slid the chipped plant pot back into position, she shook her head in disbelief that someone as streetwise as Terry would hide it in such an obvious place. He probably knew that anyone who wanted to get access to his house wouldn't bother with a key when a brick through a window would do the trick.

It was a relief when the door opened and she slipped into the dark hall. She had never been here alone before and, for a moment, without the sound of the television or music blaring from Paul's stereo upstairs, it felt as if she was in the wrong house.

She switched on the lamp at the bottom of the stairs rather than the main light. If someone passed on the road outside, they might see the glow through the front door but Sue wouldn't see it from next door. The light, dim as it was, cast the house into familiarity again.

They had clearly left in a hurry. Taking a glass from the cupboard and washing it under the tap before filling it, she looked around. Bread had popped up in the toaster and had stayed there. Two cups of cold tea, the colour of rust, were on the draining board, an unopened carton of milk beside them, while on the table there was a half-eaten bowl of corn-flakes, soggy and deserted. She felt like Goldilocks stumbling into the three bears' cottage.

She switched the lamp off, plunging the debris back into darkness, and made her way upstairs. Her exhaustion swept away any doubt about letting herself into the house. She just wanted to climb into his bed and sleep.

She leant back against the door in Ed's room and closed her eyes. 'Please let him be safe,' she murmured to who or what she didn't know.

Chapter 12

In her dreams, she saw a coastline and a lighthouse at the tip of a jutting shard of land. She saw it from above as if she was a bird in flight and then she was in a room, not this one or the one at home or university but a room she didn't recognise. Without turning, she knew there was an expanse of glass behind her, stretching the width of the room, and that the flash which illuminated the white walls and the bleached floorboards wasn't lightning, it was too regular for that, but that it came from the lighthouse on the cliff.

The next flash came and didn't leave, the light remaining bright and warm. She heard birdsong high above her head, the swish of leaves, and now she was walking out onto a hillside where someone she knew lay in the grass in the distance.

And then she was being pulled away from him at lightning speed and was dropping down, as if a trapdoor had opened at her feet, and the wind was roaring in her ears until she hit the ground with a jolt that shot up through her legs and spine.

But when she opened her eyes, she wasn't crumpled on the ground but in bed. Ed's bed. She strained to recapture the dream, tried to identify the room with the glass, the lighthouse on the cliff, before they floated away out of reach.

A rattling sound. Like a drawer being pulled out downstairs. Then it stopped and a hissing took its place. Her body stiffened and her jumbled mind, now tugged into the present, remembered that she was alone in his house. In his bed.

She knew, of course, that she had to check where the noise was coming from. Her dream had evaporated and this sound was real. The room was still dark and she had no idea how long she had slept but guessed it hadn't been long. Inching out of bed, she crept across the room, eased the door open quietly and edged down the stairs slowly, one step at a time.

All was in darkness and, for a moment, Kathryn froze, unsure of what to do next. But she couldn't stand here forever, waiting for daylight. Maybe if she slipped out of the front door, she could get away but her car keys were on the kitchen table. Or she could go next door, wake Sue up. She said that she should let her know if she was in any difficulty after all.

A memory struck her, of her father under the sink at home looking for the stopcock as water hissed out of a burst pipe. Maybe that was it, a leak somewhere, and so nothing to panic about. But that didn't explain the earlier clatter. She continued to tiptoe through the hall, stepping around the trainers she remembered were strewn across the floor.

Hovering at the doorway of the kitchen, she realised that the noise had suddenly stopped and it was the cessation of the sound which made her stomach twist. A burst pipe wouldn't have stopped. Not in an empty kitchen.

She heard a click from behind the door, and then a footstep and she now knew what it felt like to be helpless and scared. More scared than she had been against the tree with Roland's hand across her mouth. There was someone there and they hadn't switched a light on because they didn't want to be seen.

She couldn't move, her legs feeling as if they could barely hold her up, let alone take another step. And then she saw a figure silhouetted against the window and the sky's faint yellow from the city lights.

'Who's there?'

He spoke first, in a voice as anxious as she had just felt. Her panic though had now disappeared, replaced by an intense wave of relief.

'Ed, it's me,' she said, not caring about anything other than the fact he was here and safe. She threw her arms around him but he tensed in her embrace.

'What are you doing here?' he said, stepping back.

'I was so scared that you were hurt. We went looking for you at the station but you'd gone and then I found out you'd gone to London in a taxi and someone was attacked in Brighton and I thought it was you so we came up straight away.'

'We?'

'Mark and Elaine came with me. They're staying in town. I needed to see if you were back and then you weren't here and I didn't know what to do when the place was empty. I didn't have a clue where to look next.' She knew her words were coming out in a torrent but she needed him to know how worried she'd been, how sorry she was.

'Yeah, well, I'm back,' he said, turning away.

He crouched by the sink, opening the cupboard doors to search for something underneath. She wondered why he didn't just turn the kitchen light on.

She heard the click of his lighter and then as he turned back to her, she saw the glow of a candle in his hand.

Even in this dim light, she could also see a black bruise surrounding his half closed eye and spreading down towards his cheekbone. His lower lip was cut, the blood around the wound black and congealed. And from the sharp intake of breath he'd given while straightening from the cupboard, she guessed his injuries extended beyond his face.

'Electric's been cut off again,' he muttered.

'But it was on earlier,' she said, staring at the damage to his face.

'Yeah, they usually turn it off after midnight.' He turned his head away and went to the table where he pushed the breakfast debris aside and put the candle down.

She watched him lift the pan of boiling water from the back ring of the cooker. Reaching up to the cupboard for cups, he winced, bending over with his hands on his hips to catch his breath.

'Come and sit down. I'll do that,' she said, wanting to take his hand to guide him to the chair but feeling unable to, as if an invisible barrier had appeared between them.

Tea made, she carried the cups over to where he sat, hunched over and flicking his lighter open and closed.

'Paul and your dad have gone up to Blackpool. Your nan's been taken ill.' She wondered why they were skirting around what had happened to him in the hours after he got into the taxi.

'Yeah, I know. I saw Linda's mum at the taxi rank. It's happened a few times before but she's usually okay once they get her medication right,' he said.

Kathryn took a mouthful of tea and winced at the sour taste. White flecks were floating on top of the liquid.

'Milk off again?' he murmured.

She stole a look at his face as he pushed his mug aside to join the deserted breakfast bowl.

'Who was it?' she asked.

'Have a guess.'

'And did you…?'

'Did I what? Give him a hiding? Yeah.'

'You stopped off in Epsom?'

He shrugged and went to the fridge to grab a can of lager. He held one out to her but she shook her head.

Peeling the ring pull back, he lifted the can to his mouth and drank thirstily.

She repeated her question.

'What does it matter? He's sorted, okay?'

'How is he in hospital though? What did you do to him?'

He looked up. 'Look, Nicki said they might go on to The Zap in Brighton.'

'The Zap?'

'It's a club we used to go to… anyway, I got dropped off there and went looking for them.'

'I was so scared that it was you in hospital.' She shook her head, at a loss to know whether she should feel relieved, shocked that he could attack someone so viciously or grateful that he had punished Roland for what he had done to her. 'Will he be all right?'

He shrugged.

'He's critical, the radio said.'

'Yeah well, he lost his balance. Hit his head on the kerb. It wasn't my fault. Not really.'

Kathryn wished he had stayed in the back of the cab all the way to Victoria Station and left Roland to his own devices. What good had his actions done? It was probably only a matter of time before the police came knocking at the door.

'Will you get into trouble?' She knew how she sounded; clueless and naïve without any idea of how the world worked. A world away from her disdain of the previous night. That's what had erupted from deep inside her – contempt. The likes of you, she'd said. She recoiled at the memory.

'No. She'll sort that out for me. It'll be his word against ours.'

She didn't need to ask who he was talking about. Nicki, always in the background, her eyes on the prize, biding her time. She hated the fact that it was thanks to her rival that Ed wasn't under arrest. And who was to say that she wouldn't change her mind in the future? What might Ed have to do to keep her sweet?

But all she said was, 'That's good of her.'

She picked up the candle and led the way upstairs, silently giving thanks when she heard his footsteps behind her.

She put the candle on the bedside table while he stood on the back of one trainer and dragged it off, then repeated it with the other. She sat on the edge of the bed, awkwardly, as he undressed. It was only when he struggled to unbutton his shirt, that she got up and helped him.

As she eased the shirt from his shoulder, he flinched and cursed quietly under his breath. She lifted the candle to his back where she saw a laceration zigzagging vividly across his skin.

'He had a go too,' was all he said as he went to the wardrobe and pulled out a t-shirt.

'With a knife?' she said, turning to lay the shirt on the bed.

Pulling on the t-shirt gingerly, he shrugged.

'Yeah, he'd be dirty that way.'

Ed brushed off her suggestion of going to hospital.

'It's just a scratch,' he said.

As well as his visible injuries, she could tell he was in pain when he moved. The way he wrapped his arms around his torso, it looked like a broken rib or, at the very least, internal bruising.

There was hardly standing space between the beds but

still the gap felt vast. As she lay staring at the ceiling in one bed, she listened to him shifting around in the other to get comfortable. She wondered if he would say anything more before sleep came and it was only when she was heavy-lidded and on the verge of slumber that she heard his voice in the darkness.

'You shouldn't have come.'

'What do you mean?'

'You've better things to be doing. You said so yourself.'

She didn't reply because he was right. She had said that.

'You've wasted enough time on me,' he continued.

'I know I said that but I didn't...'

'Come off it, Kat. You said it because you meant it. Because it's the truth.'

'I wanted to...'

'What?'

'I wanted to hurt you, Ed.'

The words hung in the gap between them. She heard him shuffle over towards the table. A click and then a spark before he took a drag on the cigarette.

'Look, I said I was sorry about leaving you on your own but it wasn't deliberate and I don't get why you blamed me after.'

'Isn't it obvious? Your mate wanted to get from me what...' she hesitated, 'what you were getting from her.'

'What are you on about?' he asked.

'He said, well, you know.'

'And you believed him? Just like that?'

She realised he still hadn't denied it.

'But did you?' she asked.

'What? Shag her? Course not.'

'But you were both gone for so long.'

'Yeah, well, while you were looking for me, I was looking for you but the place was that jammed, we must have kept missing each other. I only saw her five minutes before I found you. She said she'd seen you both go into the garden.'

'He trapped me, Ed. I couldn't move. If you hadn't got there when you did…'

'Yeah, I know and I'm sorry. I didn't know he was like that.'

She didn't reply, wondering if Nicki knew what Roland was capable of and had been happy to let it all play out anyway. Was she really that determined in her pursuit of Ed?

'But before, with her, in the past. Did anything happen?'

'What does it matter? Things are – I'm – different now.'

She bit her lip.

'When?' she asked.

'When what?'

'When did it happen with her?'

'What does it matter? I dunno, some night after racing last summer. It was nothing. Too much drink and she was having problems. Look, it was before we got together.'

She thought back to that day in Brighton when she had seen them on the racecourse, deep in conversation because – what had he said at the time – she was having difficulties with her landlord? Was it then? While she was at home reliving every moment of their conversation, had he fallen into bed with Nicki?

'It wasn't what I wanted. I could see that afterwards.'

'She doesn't seem to see it that way,' Kathryn said, shortly.

'Yeah well, that's not my problem.'

She felt sickeningly unmoored, like a boat, its ropes cut, drifting away from the shore. He had been with Nicki. And it hurt.

As he slept, she continued to scratch away at it in her mind as if she could dull the edges that pierced her inside. It shouldn't have been a surprise, she knew that. Hadn't she heard enough to know that he was like any normal lad of his age? But she hadn't see him that way. She'd wanted to believe he could turn away from temptation, see the likes of Nicki for what she was rather than be taken in by her sob story and her physical charms.

But then her inner voice chided her for her gullibility. Why wouldn't he want Nicki, bewitching as well as ready and willing? Or someone else in the future. Turning towards the wall and pulling the quilt up to her chin, she remembered lying here with him when he joked about forgetting him in years to come. She knew that if they parted, it would be because he was tired of her. This thought made her throat tighten. But then she reminded herself that tonight could have ended very differently. He was here and that was all that mattered.

Chapter 13

When Kathryn woke, the other bed was empty and, for a moment, she wondered if Ed had really come home last night or if she had dreamt it all. But as she got out of bed, she stepped on his suede jacket and their late night conversation came back into vivid focus.

The kitchen had been tidied, the cups and bowls washed and stacked on the draining board, and now the bright sunshine had quite transformed the room. She heard a key in the lock and the now familiar sound of the front door opening slightly before scraping over the patch where the lino had lifted.

'You're up then, sleeping beauty.'

His bruises were even worse in this light and, trying to smile, he winced and dabbed a finger at the cut on his lip which was bleeding again. He held up a carrier bag, a rueful look on his face.

'Breakfast?'

'Why not,' she said, filling the water pan for tea.

The day was so fine that they took their bacon sandwiches and tea outside.

'It's cracking the flags out here,' Ed said, groaning as he crouched down to put his plate and mug on the ground.

'Cracking what?'

'It's what we say up here when it's this hot.'

They sat side by side, their backs resting against the garden fence.

'About last night,' he began.

Kathryn shook her head, 'Look, you're back and that's all that matters. It's no wonder you were irritable – you can hardly move with the pain.'

'Yeah, but you'd driven all that way. Yet again. And after me letting you down so bad.'

'You didn't. And I didn't mean all those mean things I said.'

'You were only speaking the truth,' he bit into his sandwich and flinched as the tomato ketchup stung his lip. 'And I messed up big time. Again. Dragging you up there like that when you had other plans for us. I didn't know how to make it right again. All I could think of was finding him and sorting him out.'

'Do you know how Roland's doing?' She had to ask. What if he had died overnight? Would that mean Ed could be arrested on suspicion of manslaughter? Or worse?

'Nicki will ring if he gets any worse.'

Kathryn frowned. She didn't like the idea that Nicki had his number. For all she knew, she'd been here, maybe even during the weeks between her own visits. Would any of them have told her? Paul? Terry? They wouldn't have felt the need.

'I know what's going through your mind, babe. And you probably won't believe me because I've no way to prove it to you, but I've had nothing to do with her since we met.'

She knew he was looking at her but she looked away, tearing the crust off her sandwich and throwing it across the grass. A crow perched on the roof of a neighbouring shed hopped down, grabbed the bread and flew away.

'I've no way of proving this either,' Ed continued 'but I wrote you a letter. I must have dropped it somewhere. I know, it sounds like a likely story. But I said some stuff in it. Things I couldn't say to your face.'

'I know,' she looked at his bruised face. 'It was on the floor in Mark's car.'

'Right.'

'Did you mean what you said?'

'About?' he said, that familiar tease back in his voice.

'The bit where you said you needed to come clean and that...'

'Course I do.'

She grinned at him. 'And we're going to Dublin?'

'I don't tend to buy airline tickets for no reason,' he laughed.

#

The city centre took on a languid air on what was an unusually hot day for April. The sun blazed high in a pale blue sky, its heat seeming to pour through the streets, shimmering on the pavements and the buildings, so that pedestrians had to stop and rest awhile on benches and the cooling stone steps of monuments.

Kathryn was early so she sat on the grass in front of the grand buildings that made up the Three Graces to wait. The grass, scorched and spiky, prickled the sensitive skin at the back of her knees, bare from her last minute switch from jeans to the shorts she had had the foresight to stuff into her bag. It was too hot to care about covering her legs and as she leant back to stare at the skyline, she wished she'd remembered to bring her sunglasses too.

One Liver Bird, high up on the western side of the Royal Liver Building, continued to gaze out over the glittering waters of the Mersey to the chimneys and factories beyond. Constrained by thick metal cables that looked from this distance like puppeteer's strings, its wings were raised as if in readiness to rise into the sky in search of a cooling breeze.

But bound as it was, it remained eternally prepared for flight, its back towards its mate keeping a resolute watch over a city baking in the searing midday heat.

Bare-chested teenagers with t-shirts tied around their waists cycled back and forth on the pavement while the braver among them made their bikes rear like horses and showed off their wheelies to the admiration of the others and that of the three girls huddled on a nearby wall. Intent on hiding their interest in the boys' acrobatics, they licked ice cream cones and pretended to listen to each other.

The heat hung heavy all around her so Kathryn went over to the railings at the edge of the dock in search of cooler air. Less than half a mile away across the lapping waters of the Mersey, the factories and chimneys of the Wirral peninsula glinted and flickered in the brightness of the day. She picked out the dome of the town hall clock standing sentry over the town of Birkenhead and its water-front industry, and the dusky red silhouette of what looked like a place of worship but was, she had been told, the ventil-ation tower for the tunnel that ran underneath the river.

She noticed a flap of metal at her feet, rectangular and curved like the peeled back lid of a sardine tin. It glittered in the sun and then, picked up by the riverside breeze, it gambolled and fluttered into the distance, coming to rest briefly under the railings, its next stop the river's silver ripples below. Like a baby bird testing its wings, it seemed alive.

Here, along the river, there was a mysterious soundscape of booms, hums and, now and then, loud scraping noises echoing across the water. This was what she had imagined the North to be like, a place where things were still made and loaded onto waiting ships, where men toiled hard and emerged, weary and grime-coated, from the doors of high windowed factories before going home to their tea.

Kathryn was surprised out of her reverie by the sudden appearance of a melting ice cream cone.

'Here you go – you'd better eat it quick or it'll drip all over you,' Elaine said, biting the bottom of her own cone and sucking the ice cream through the hole.

'Hot enough for you?' Mark asked, taking his sunglasses off and putting them in the pocket of his shirt.

'It must be, because our Kathryn never shows her legs off,' Elaine laughed before looking around. 'So, where is he?'

Mark frowned. 'He did come home, didn't he?'

Kathryn was looking past them, so they both turned and saw Ed approaching.

'What on earth happened to him?' gasped Elaine.

Mark was already walking towards Ed, his hand out-stretched to take the carrier bag of fish and chips from him. While the two young men exchanged a few pleasantries, Kathryn took the opportunity to quickly grill Elaine.

'How did you get on last night? You found somewhere all right?'

Elaine nodded, and said in a hushed voice, 'You could say that. We only ended up in the Adelphi. Everywhere else was booked up. Mark paid for it.'

'I bet that cost him,' said Kathryn. 'I mean, two rooms must have really set him back.'

Elaine's raised eyebrows made Kathryn stop a moment and laugh.

'Elaine!'

'Well, we made the most of the hotel bar and one thing led to another. Please don't say anything. Mark wanted to keep it quiet... Hi Ed.'

Kathryn had got used to Ed's bruised face, but even she

had to admit that it looked worse in the bright sunshine. A woman pushing a pram along the riverside cobbles averted her eyes when she reached them, only glancing back over her shoulder when she was further along the walkway.

'You look different to the last time I saw you,' Elaine said, one eyebrow slightly raised.

Mark lifted the carrier bag. 'Who's for chips then?'

Ignoring him, Ed said, 'Had some trouble but it's all sorted now.'

Elaine shrugged. 'That's all right then. We don't want Kathryn getting caught up in any trouble, do we, Mark? I mean –'

Mark interrupted. 'We don't know anything about it, Elaine, so we should mind our own business. Come on, I'm hungry. Did you get enough for the four of us?'

Kathryn was grateful to him for steering the conversation onto steadier ground, 'Of course. Fish and chips, mushy peas and cans of Coke. Let's go and sit over by that wall where there's a bit more shade.'

Elaine softened as they ate, so that by the time the papers had been screwed up and put in the nearest bin, she was grilling Ed about all things Liverpool.

'So Ringo was a barman on the Mersey Ferry? What, like that one over there?' She pointed to the small nub-fronted blue and white ferry bobbing on the water at the end of the metal landing stage.

Mark, returning from throwing the rubbish away, sat next to Kathryn.

'Elaine's come round then,' he said, shielding his eyes from the sun with his hand.

Kathryn turned to him with a quizzical expression.

'She seems to have changed her mind about your Ed,' he said.

It made her glow to hear him described as hers. And yes, Elaine and Ed were certainly getting on better. Elaine, now listening attentively as Ed talked, squinted in that way she did when she was concentrating. Ed's hands moved as he spoke as if to demonstrate a point, and then he glanced Kathryn's way, as if aware that he was being watched. He smiled before turning his attention back to her friend.

'I'm glad it's all sorted out. I mean, he looks like he's gone a couple of rounds with Mike Tyson but at least he's safe and sound,' Mark said.

'For now, anyway. As long as Roland doesn't come looking for him. Or the police.' In a hushed voice, Kathryn told him what had happened in Brighton, describing how Ed had got the injuries that still seemed to be giving him some discomfort because, every now and then, he gave a slight grimace as he crouched on the grass beside Elaine.

'I imagine that he won't hear any more about it. I mean, it's not as if that Roland character is blameless.'

Kathryn wasn't so sure. 'I hope you're right. But Nicki's now got something over Ed and I expect it's a matter of time before she reappears. And by the way, you were wrong about one thing.'

Mark raised his eyebrows as he drank the last of his Coke.

'You said he wasn't sleeping with her. Well, he did. Last summer.'

'But he's not now. Come on, Kathryn, it's the present that matters most, surely? The past is done and dusted.'

The clock at the top of the Liver Building let out two resounding chimes. They would have to leave soon if they wanted to get home at a reasonable hour, but Kathryn wished she could freeze time. Life felt rather wonderful despite Ed's blackened eye and the tingling on her shoulders where the blazing sun had burnt the pale skin. On this glorious afternoon, her uncertainty dissolved and she remembered that he had said he loved her. Yes, life, right now, was more wonderful than she'd ever known.

It was perhaps not surprising then that she found herself easily persuaded to change her plans and, rather than drive south with her friends that afternoon, she waved them off on the four thirty train from Lime Street Station. Before Elaine could complain, Kathryn reminded her that it was just days before their trip to Dublin and so it made sense for her to stay in Liverpool.

As Mark removed their cases from the boot of Kathryn's car, he said quietly, 'Take care of yourself. I can see how much you're enjoying yourself and I know how life can be at home. You deserve to have some fun. But just be a bit careful.'

'Of course I will; I'm not stupid.' She hadn't meant her words to come out as sharply as they did. He was only looking out for her. But surely she was too old for a fatherly warning from someone just a couple years older than herself?

'It sounds as if you've been enjoying yourself too,' she added with a smirk, unable to resist.

Mark blushed before stammering, 'We were tired from the journey and the drink went to our heads. Elaine said we'd keep it between us.'

'Come on, Mark. At this rate, we'll miss the train,' Elaine called as she walked back from the ticket office.

As they watched Mark take Elaine's hand and help her onto the train, Ed nudged Kathryn.

'I could see those two getting together,' he said.

Kathryn grinned and Ed, catching her eye, snorted.

'What? Last night? You're having a laugh. They didn't waste much time, did they?'

'I wonder if anything will come of it?' Kathryn said as they got back into the car. 'I'm not sure they're all that suited.'

'Yeah, but forever's not for everyone, is it? Maybe it's just for a night, maybe a lifetime. Who knows?' he said, winding the window down.

When he saw her expression, he continued, 'I mean that for them. Not us. Saying that though, what would your old folks make of me? Some jobless Scouser living with his jail-bird father. Mark though; he'd do for them.'

Kathryn crunched the car into gear. 'Not really. They blamed him when Beth left. Said that if he had more about him, she might have stayed.'

'That's a bit unfair,' said Ed, flicking the ash from his cigarette through the open window. 'Mark's okay. He could do with losing the poncey gear because he looks a bit of a prat. I mean, what's with the floral shirt?' He sniggered before taking another drag on his cigarette. 'But apart from that, he's sound. What was he saying to you when you got their bags out?'

She rolled her eyes. 'He just told me to be careful. Typical Mark.'

'It's fair enough though. I mean, he knows what the score is with your old folks. And then he hears about the carry-on up here – me beating someone up, the old man just out of the nick. It's no wonder he thinks I could be a bad influence.'

She didn't want to talk about Mark and his concerns. She'd been happy to watch the train pull out of the station because it had felt spontaneous to change her plans, to decide against travelling back to university. And while she was feeling im-pulsive, she might as well continue in that vein.

'How about we do something different? You know, a change of scene before we go to Dublin? It's been a rough couple of days, maybe we could do with getting out of Liverpool.'

He had opened the glove compartment and was flicking through her tapes. Looking up distractedly, he said, 'Yeah, why not? You choose where. My giro's in so it's on me.'

'Okay but you've got to let me put something towards the plane tickets. I've got my student grant and you're not working at the moment,' she said. It had been on her mind since she had first found the card with the ticket inside.

'Oh yeah, like I'd let you pay for your own ticket. No way. And I'm going to treat you when we're away too. If you must know, I've got a bit of money in a Post Office account. My grandad left us both a bit when he died. Better to spend it on you than something stupid like drink or weed.'

'Well, if you're sure.'

'I am,' he said, sliding the stack of tapes back into the glove compartment before looking across at her and grinning. 'Now, what am I going to do with you, Kat? Your taste in music's about as lame as Mark's taste in clothes.'

As she drove, her mind was full of thoughts of where they should go. Pushing away concerns about her car struggling any further up the motorway, she thought about Manchester or one of the seaside towns on the Lancashire coast – Lytham St Annes maybe or Morecambe. She knew nothing of these places, just their names. Or how about the city of York or the Lake District? As they swung into the estate, it struck her that the problem with freedom was that it could be crippling. Too much choice and you may as well stick a pin in a map.

Or maybe it was pointless to waste such a glorious day in a sweltering car when they could just stay here. Basking in the late afternoon sun, Speke's harder edges softened so that the eye didn't settle on the casual neglect of its front gardens as it usually did, or the graffiti daubed across boarded up windows of the house across the street, but on the way the pale yellow light filtered through the leaves of the linden tree outside Ed's house.

At the end of the street, the verge widened enough for some boys to kick a ball between hastily-erected goalposts of discarded tracksuit tops. The ball, going wide, slapped against a car outside the last house in the street and a man, who had been carefully watering his hanging baskets, shouted at the gang.

Ed had already gone inside to throw some clothes in a bag and Kathryn was busy wondering if her thighs were tanning or if the skin below her shorts would end up peeling and sore when she heard the shouting. When she looked up, the man with the yellow watering can was staring at the kids, hands on hips and tightlipped, as they grudgingly scooped up their clothes, their game at an abrupt halt.

Now, his shouting was replaced by raised voices closer to home. She sat frozen, staring ahead as the boys shuffled along the street towards her nudging each other and pointing towards Ed's house. The door was suddenly flung open and Ed was pushed out by his father, who stood in the doorway raging and cursing.

The boys hurried past, stopping to gather and gawp further down the street, and Kathryn noticed the curtains move in Sue's sitting room window. She guessed she'd seen it all before. But Kathryn hadn't and she watched, unsure of what to do, as the shouting continued.

'You're out of this family, lad. You can piss off and never come back. You come in my house, not a care in the world and couldn't give a shit that yer nan's dying.'

'I didn't know she was that bad,' Ed yelled. 'She's been sick that many times. You said yourself that it was all her imagination.'

'Yeah well, she ain't making it up this time. They've given her a day or two. If she's lucky.'

'I'm sorry she's sick,' Ed said, quieter now. 'But I wasn't here, so how was I supposed to know? Look, I'll go see her now. We can change our plans.'

'We can change our plans,' Terry mimicked his son mockingly before spitting on the ground. 'Nah, fuck off. You're no good to anyone.'

'What do you want from me?' Ed asked, his voice cracking.

'From you?' Terry's eyes flashed. 'Nothing. Cos you're nothing to me.'

Ed flinched and took a step back.

Kathryn, her stomach wound in a tight knot, looked from father to son and back again, convinced they could hear her heart hammering in her chest.

Seeing the visible effect on his son, Terry warmed to his theme.

'The only thing you've ever been to me is a…' he hesitated, as if choosing his words carefully, 'a fucking disappointment.'

'Me a disappointment? Yeah, because Paul's done so well for himself,' Ed shook his head in disbelief. 'And what about you? Locked up for kicking a bloke senseless? You're fucking mental.'

'At least Paul's here with me and Linda at a time like this. Not like you, chasing some bird the length of the country to get yer leg over.'

Kathryn saw the expression on Ed's face and knew the cards he held. The revelation could bring his dad to his knees. But Ed just waited and said nothing, an odd smile on his lips.

'Wipe that look off yer face,' Terry spat. 'It's the truth.'

'You want to know the truth?' Ed said, a quiver in his voice.

'Go do one,' Terry waved his hand dismissively and turned to go back into the house. 'I've things to do. The taxi'll be here in a minute.'

'Paul and Linda. You know what they're probably doing right this minute?'

Terry stopped.

'What they've been doing every minute your back's been turned.'

Terry spun around.

'You're talking shit,' he said, his hands balling into fists.

'Yeah, right, if you say so,' Ed pushed past him into the house.

In seconds he was back, holdall in hand. His father was now blocking his exit.

'Get out of my way,' Ed said.

'You tell me what you mean. About yer brother and my... you tell me now.'

Ed turned and said wearily. 'What do you think?'

There was nothing more to say. As they drove away, their last sight of Terry was of him leaning against the door frame, his head in his hands.

Chapter 14

Neither of them said anything as she drove them out of the city. Kathryn stared ahead, her blood pounding in her ears, hardly noticing the road signs, feeling a slight breeze from the open passenger window, where Ed rested his elbow and stared out at the houses as they turned into edge of town retail parks and then an expanse of canary yellow corn fields. He switched on the radio, turning the dial until it settled on Radio 1.

She wondered if Ed regretted delivering the blow that Terry might never recover from. His favoured son and Linda. They had betrayed him in a way he could never have imagined. In his own eyes, he was still virile, feared, top of the pile while Paul was easy to like because he was no threat, hopeless, maybe even a bit of a joke. He could have coped if it had been Ed who had deceived him, but Paul? No, he wouldn't get over that.

They came to a halt at some traffic lights. As the car hummed, Kathryn glanced across at the car revving in the next lane. Its windows were wound down and pop music was booming out. The lights flicked to green and it roared away, giving her a good view of a lurid green sticker on its bumper and the words 'No Regrets'.

She smiled. No regrets. This had to happen, sooner or later.

When Ed finally spoke, it came as something of a shock because he didn't sound remorseful.

'So, that's that.'

She sensed that he was watching her.

'You think your dad will be all right?' Kathryn asked, keeping her eyes firmly on the road.

She saw him shrug out of the corner of her eye before looking back out of the window.

'Do you think he'll go mad at them?' she asked, braking slightly to allow a car to pull out of a slip road in front of her.

'Expect so.'

'Poor Paul. He won't be expecting that.'

'He had it coming. And anyway, the old man would have found out some time. At least he didn't walk in on them.'

She supposed there was at least that.

'I was half expecting him to take a swing at me though. Not just sag like that. I never thought I'd see the old man look like he'd given up on life,' Ed said, staring at his fingernails. 'I suppose he's not what he was.'

'You'll make it up with him. Just give it some time.' She wondered why she was talking like this, when she couldn't possibly know what the future might hold.

'Come on, Kat. You know that'll never happen. I'm done with them now. A new start. I've been on about it for long enough and now it's happening.'

She glanced at him, saw how his smile hadn't reached his eyes.

'Just you and me now, babe.'

#

She would look back on the days that followed as the happiest time of her life. Endless hours of sunshine and freedom, where, for the first time she didn't have to leave to return to Southampton or home to her parents. Just day after day of being together, going where they chose, when they wished. Free of the constraints and expectations of others. Maybe this was what adult life was like. Yet when she said this to Ed, he gave her a doubtful look.

'Don't think so, babe. Any adult I ever came across, spent their time either grafting, off their heads or drinking their days away.'

Kathryn stared up at the powder blue skies and disagreed. After all, her dad seemed content enough to do his forty hours a week in an office where he was well-liked. Her mum spent her days keeping house and didn't seem to feel in any way imprisoned. She pulled herself up from the springy bed of heather where they lay and looked down at him lying there, his eyes closed contentedly against the sun.

'I don't think that's everyone's reality, Ed.'

She watched his mouth move into a smile.

'Fair enough. But do people really look back and think they're exactly where they wanted to be when they were our age? Like they couldn't wait to get there? Or are most of them gutted with the way things have turned out?'

She had to admit he was right. Again.

'So how are you going to do things differently?' she asked, staring over the expanse of tufted moorland to where the land suddenly plunged into the depths of the dale and beyond to the rolling hills on the other side of the valley. She could see why Yorkshire was called 'God's Own Country'. In this high land, the heavens were at their fingertips.

'Who says it's a given that we'll even get there? There are plenty of kids who become teenagers and get no further. They never make it as far as jobs, mortgages; the whole boring grind of life.'

He must have seen Kathryn's expression because he grinned and continued. 'I'm not talking about you and me. All I'm saying is that nothing's certain. But okay, you asked me how will I do the whole grown-up thing?'

Kathryn nodded, a shadow having passed before it could land on her fully.

'The opposite of any adult I've ever known,' he laughed, pulling her back down onto the mattress of heather.

#

A few days earlier, they had come off the motorway at the signs for the Lake District but instead of travelling west, they had turned eastwards. It was new territory for them both, which was as good a reason as any to head in that direction. As the sun set behind them in a peach-tinted sky, they sped along narrow roads winding through the darkening hulks of the Pennines.

The road sometimes bent at a right angle across a river and then, a mile further on, twisted back over the same stretch of water before climbing into the hills so that Kathryn thought they would never reach civilisation. The lights of solitary farms glittered across the dark landscape and on they drove, hoping to reach somewhere resembling a village before they got completely lost or ran out of petrol.

They drove along the bottom of a valley for many miles, passing through the occasional huddle of houses, when the road suddenly rose and immediately dropped down to a sign announcing their arrival in a village called Reeth. Even in the darkness, they could see that at its centre was a wide village green, bordered on one side by a row of tall three storey buildings. Two were pubs, one offering rooms, which was a relief as Kathryn had feared they might struggle to find somewhere comfortable to sleep that night.

Breakfast was served between seven and nine but whether it had been the long drive up or the drinks they had brought up to the room, the light of mid-morning was spilling into the room by the time Kathryn woke.

Ed was at the window, opening the curtains. The slash across his back was fading but she could now see the shadow of bruising across his ribs. As if he could sense her eyes on him, he turned and she didn't know if it was his grin or the promise of the days ahead that made her heart skip. He flicked on the small kettle beside the bed and climbed back in beside her.

'There's so much space, babe,' he said, stretching his arms across the pink brocade bedspread of the double bed. 'Not that we need it.' He moved closer and Kathryn only half protested.

'We really should get up.'

But there were no demands on their time, no place to be but here under the covers and, by the time they had disentangled from each other, the kettle had long since boiled, its water now barely lukewarm.

#

And so each day passed. Time was of no consequence and their lives elsewhere were forgotten about. They walked miles across high moorland before dropping down into Wensleydale for a pint. Another day they drove so far east that they saw the sea at Scarborough. But by night, they returned to the village, hidden away in its steep sided valley, and sat out on the expanse of green, watching the sun set behind Calver Hill.

It was on the bench beside the grey stone war memorial

one evening that Ed said, 'You know what, Kat, let's come back here every year.'

'Yes, we should,' she said. 'Our special place.'

'Away from the madness,' he said, leaning down to retrieve his pint from the tray they had brought out from the bar. 'Imagine us sitting here in twenty years' time.'

He put the pint on the arm of the bench and pressed the buttons on his watch.

'Today's April 20th and in twenty years it'll be 2013.'

'We'll be forty then.'

'Bloody hell. I wonder what we'll be like then? Except old, that is!'

She didn't want to think about next week, never mind two decades into the future. If they could only stay here, living each day to the full, pulling every last joy out of each hour rather than returning to the flat greyness of daily life. Not for the first time, she wondered why magic had to be so fleeting, slipping between fingers so that all that was left was the ordinary. No. This was how life should feel. Jewel-like, with colours so rich as to make you catch your breath, the thrum of joy pulsing through the veins so that you wouldn't trade this moment for the world. Her sense of magic was now inexorably linked with Ed, and sometimes she wondered how she could ever make her way through the world without him.

Her life before him had been empty; a canvas remaining resolutely blank as the years passed. Now, her canvas was splashed and daubed with every colour imaginable. The brightest of hues against the darkest. But always colour. She knew, finally, what joy was. And above all, she had discovered that to have felt was to have lived. She couldn't face any other way.

'So, you up for it?'

Pulling herself back from her thoughts, she nodded.

'Never been more up for anything. But let's think about now, shall we? Like shall we get an early night or have another drink?'

#

Kathryn and Ed were determined to make every moment count on their last morning in the Dales. They even managed to be the first guests down for breakfast, which they devoured hungrily before dropping their key into reception and packing their bags in the car.

They headed for the high country, to a remote village called Keld at the upper end of the Dale, where they planned to walk part of the Pennine Way. The route would take them down to Kisdon Force and then up to the deserted ruins of Crackpot Hall. Apparently, the view from there wasn't to be missed.

There was a telephone box by the car park and, as Kathryn was locking the car, Ed glanced back towards it, asking, 'Got any change? I've had a nagging feeling since breakfast that I should ring home. Check up on nan and stuff, you know.'

'Won't it keep until later?' Kathryn asked, fishing a fifty pence piece out of her pocket.

He frowned. 'Something just feels a bit odd, you know? Look, it won't take two minutes.'

She sat on a wall by a square stone building that, according to a carved stone set high up on the wall, was the village's Literary Institute until 1912. She watched the sun shimmering in a cloudless sky at the other end of the dale and felt its warming rays on her cheeks. It was going to be another hot day and she was glad they had made an early start.

Glancing back towards the phone box, she saw Ed twisting the phone cord around his finger and pushing at the heavy glass door with his toe so that it opened now and then, his words becoming momentarily less muffled.

A middle-aged couple in the uniform of serious hikers nodded pleasantly before clumping off down the lane, their walking poles clicking as they went. It made her impatient, eager to get going, and she wondered how much longer Ed was going to be.

She was staring after the couple, who had now stopped and were consulting their plastic covered maps hanging on cords like swinging necklaces, when she heard the sound of the telephone box door being pushed open.

'Everything okay? Shall we… ' But she didn't finish her sentence because she had seen the expression on his face.

'We've got to get back. Right now,' he said, walking past her towards the car.

'Why? What's so important?'

He turned, rubbing his eyes with the palm of his hand, and said, 'It's the old man. He's done something stupid.'

As they navigated their way out of the hills, Kathryn felt that everything had shifted again. When they had arrived, all they had seen was darkness surrounding them, dotted here and there with the lights of far off farms. Now the landscape looked less mysterious, more commonplace. A school bus, dawdling along the narrow lanes, held them up for miles. Urged by Ed to overtake, Kathryn pulled out but a tractor and trailer heading towards them made her pull back in.

'Christ's sake, we'll never get there at this rate,' Ed said crossly, unpeeling the cellophane from another packet of cigarettes and letting it drop to the floor.

'We don't want to end up in hospital as well,' Kathryn replied, trying to sound reasonable while, inside, disappointment and resentment swirled around in equal measure.

Terry had taken the news of his son's betrayal particularly badly. He had returned to his mother's bedside just minutes before she passed away, and afterwards discovered Paul and Linda in a nearby cafe. White hot with fury and grief, he had returned to the bed and breakfast where they were all staying and had taken a bottle of sleeping tablets, which he had taken from his mother's bedside, washed down with whisky.

'He couldn't even do that right,' Ed said, with a hollow laugh.

It turned out that Terry had fallen against the tea tray next to the bed and the crash had attracted the attention of the landlady, who scuttled upstairs to see who was wreaking havoc with her best china. She'd called for an ambulance and Terry was soon sat up in a hospital bed, feeling grim but not in any real danger.

It was this that made Kathryn feel most bitter. His stomach had been pumped and he was undoubtedly feeling the worse for wear but it was clear that he was going to be all right. She hated that his cry for help had reeled his son in so swiftly, shattering their plans in an instant.

They hardly spoke as they made their way back down the motorway. Ed was staring out of the passenger window and Kathryn couldn't trust herself to speak without saying something she would regret later. She turned her attention to their flight the next morning. Their trip to Yorkshire might now be behind them but they could still look forward to Dublin.

As they reached the outskirts of Liverpool, trading one

reality for another, Kathryn said, 'What I can't work out is how you knew there was something wrong this morning.'

'Don't you ever just have a sense that something's a bit off? You know, you can't put your finger on it but you're unsettled.'

Kathryn shook her head. 'Maybe you're psychic.'

'Yeah, maybe.' His laugh sounded hollow.

A few minutes passed before he spoke again.

'He's done it again, hasn't he?'

'Done what?'

'Clicked his fingers and here I am running back.'

'Well, he is your dad and he needs you.'

'But we were having such a good time, and now it's all over because of my family.'

'It's not your fault though, is it? I mean, it's not your fault that your family's…'

'An embarrassment? A disgrace?'

'I was going to say chaotic.'

'Yeah, well I'm sorry you have to put up with it,' he said, earnestly. 'These last few days. I won't ever forget them, you know. Or the nights.'

She stared at the road, a blush spreading across her face as she felt his eyes on her. By day, they had explored the ravishing landscape, and by night, each other. In that small room, dimly lit by the street lamp outside the window, he had made love to her. Quietly. Gently. And gradually, her shyness had left her so that she could open her eyes and watch him watching her as he brought her to that place for which there were no words.

As they drew nearer to Speke, Kathryn wondered what would be waiting for them. Paul had told Ed on the phone that Terry was home after spending a night in Blackpool

Victoria Hospital. But they knew no more than that.

Kathryn was surprised to hear that Paul was at home and had not been thrown out of the house. Maybe Terry had decided that dealing with the matter of his son sleeping with his girlfriend would keep. There was a funeral to arrange and he needed his family to pull together.

When they pulled up outside the house, Terry and Paul were sitting on the front doorstep, smoking.

'He doesn't look too bad from here,' muttered Ed.

She could see Terry looking at them and, even from this distance, she noticed something altered in him. Despite the midday heat, his brown jacket was zipped up and he seemed to disappear within it as if he had shriveled in the few days since they last saw him. He flung his cigarette to the ground and struggled to his feet before going into the house. Paul, a smirk on his lips, followed him and closed the door.

Kathryn wished they could turn the car around and head straight back out of the estate. Instead, she followed Ed up the garden path and, noticing the glow from Terry's cigarette butt, put her foot on it and crushed it into the baked earth.

Ed took a deep breath before opening the door, which had, at least, been left unlocked.

Terry was in the sitting room, another cigarette lit. An old black and white film was flickering on the television but the sound had been turned down so it was impossible to hear what was being said. He stared blankly at the screen.

'Sorry about Nan. How are you doing?' Ed said from the doorway. Kathryn, standing behind him, watched how his nails dug into his palms.

'Been better,' was all his father said in reply, leaving Ed to shift from foot to foot before escaping to the kitchen.

Tipping a bag of sugar on one side, Paul was scraping a

teaspoon into its depths.

'Leccy's back on again,' he said, as if it was a normal day and his secret fling hadn't been discovered. His gaze flicked over Ed and Kathryn.

'Kettle's boiled if you want a brew?' he continued, giving up on his exploration of the sugar bag and tipping its meagre contents into the cup before carrying it to the sitting room.

Kathryn felt the quiet of the house, only broken by the soft hum of the film and the sound of Ed pouring water from the kettle into two mugs.

Ed looked up as Paul returned, closing the sitting room door behind him.

'What about the arrangements?'

'Monday afternoon,' Paul said, leaning against the worktop. 'The crematorium in Blackpool. Rita got it all sorted.'

Handing a mug to Kathryn, Ed explained. 'Rita's the old man's sister.'

Paul lowered his voice. 'What happened to you, anyway? Looks like you picked a fight with the wrong fella.'

Ed touched the yellowing bruise under his eye and shrugged. 'More to the point, how come you're still walking?'

'You've seen him,' Paul nodded towards the closed door and grinned. 'He can hardly stand, never mind give me a slap.'

Kathryn looked up from her tea. There was something like mockery in his voice. Or maybe it was just relief, she thought, giving him the benefit of the doubt.

'He's all right now though? After...' Kathryn asked.

'After he tried to top himself?' Paul replied, rolling his eyes. 'His belly's raw but apart from that, he'll do.'

'But he's just lost his mother,' she continued.

'Yeah, well,' Paul said, sliding a look at Ed, 'that's nothing new round here.'

Ed looked away.

'What I can't work out is how he found out about us,' Paul said. 'We were pretty careful and then suddenly all hell breaks loose.'

Kathryn began to flick through a yellowing *Sporting Life* on the table, without seeing anything on its pages. So Terry hadn't told Paul it was Ed who had planted the doubt in his mind. After what seemed like minutes, she heard Ed reply, 'Yeah, well maybe he finally put two and two together.'

'At least I managed to talk my way out of it. He's not mentioned it since so I reckon he thinks he was imagining things.'

'It's not like him though. It's like all the stuffing's been knocked out of him. Before he'd have had you bouncing off the walls,' Ed said as he tipped the dregs of his tea down the sink. 'Anyway, we only dropped by to see what was happening.'

He turned to Kathryn. 'Shall we head off?'

Paul frowned. 'Where do you think you're going? Someone needs to stay with him and I've done my bit. I was only waiting until you got here.'

'Where are you going?' Ed asked, confused.

That smirk again. 'Where do you think, soft lad?'

'Can't you leave it alone? How about a bit of respect for a change.'

But Paul was already poking around inside a drawer.

'I thought there was a few quid in here,' he said before looking up at Kathryn. 'I couldn't take a lend off you, could I? A fiver would tide me over.'

When he had gone, it felt as if a buffer between them and Terry had disappeared. Seeing him alone with his thoughts, contemplating the loss of his mother, Kathryn suddenly felt sorry for him.

'All right if I join you?' she asked tentatively.

He shrugged.

She took the armchair next to the fireplace. He cut a depleted figure across from her on the sofa, where once she had seen the entwined sleeping bodies of his girlfriend and son.

'I'm sorry about your mother,' she offered.

He nodded.

'How old was she?' she asked, unsure if her questions sounded polite or probing.

'Coming up seventy-five,' he replied. 'Would have been her birthday next month.'

A silence descended which Kathryn didn't know how to break. She sipped her tea and, because she didn't know where else to look, stared at the television where the film credits were now rolling.

'He was wrong,' Terry said suddenly.

'Sorry?'

'Boy wonder. He either got it all wrong or was causing trouble. Paul and Linda weren't up to anything, you know.'

He picked up the remote control and began flicking from one channel to the next before settling on an afternoon chat show.

'How do you know?'

'Paul's too thick to lie. When he told me there was nothing going on, I'd have known straight away if he'd been lying,' he said, still staring at the screen.

When she didn't reply, he continued, 'I'm gonna let the other lad off this time. For all I know, he just got it wrong. But if I catch him causing trouble between Linda and me again, he'll know about it.'

'Where's Linda now?' was all Kathryn could think of to say.

'Her mum's sick again. They need her there so she won't be round for a few days.'

Until now, Terry had been kept in check either by Linda's presence or by the promise of her arrival. Now, he just sat and drank and smoked. His mug of tea untouched, he was now making his way through a six pack of lager. He said no more and, because there was nothing else to say, Kathryn left him and went upstairs.

Ed was taking his clothes out of his holdall when she entered his room. She hoped this just meant he was making way for fresh ones for their Dublin trip.

'It's going to be a long night,' he said, the late afternoon sun now slanting across the wall behind him.

Seeing her puzzled expression, he continued, 'He'll keep drinking now till two, maybe three in the morning.'

'Yes, but we'll be making a move soon, won't we? I know we can't go straight away but…'

He tipped the rest of the clothes out his bag and kicked it under the bed.

'I can't leave him, can I? I mean, look at the state of him.'

Kathryn looked alarmed.

'But what about Paul? He'll be back soon and then we can…'

'Come on, Kat. You know as well as I do that's the last we'll see of Paul until Monday, and that's if he even turns up then.'

She bit her lip and sat down heavily on the bed.

'I'm sorry, babe. It's a mess.'

'But we're meant to be going tomorrow. The tickets are in my bag. Our flight's at half nine.'

'Yeah, but we can't go now, can we? We can't leave him to his own devices. He might try it again.'

She knew he was right. If she was honest with herself, she had known their trip was in jeopardy from the moment Ed walked out of the phone box into the sunshine that morning. But to hear it confirmed that there would be no strolling through the streets of Dublin, no nights in a smart hotel, made her life flatten out once more.

Anger lay heavy in the pit of her stomach. She thought Ed had turned towards a new future but all it had taken was one phone call and he was yanked back to this world, where his life – and hers – was on hold.

'It was my birthday present,' she said, knowing how sulky she sounded.

'I know. Don't you think I haven't already thought of that? I'll make it up to you.'

She understood the predicament he found himself in but in that moment couldn't see beyond her own disillusionment. She had played second fiddle to her sister and silently gone along with what was expected of her at home for so long that now she had tasted freedom, she was determined not to subordinate her own happiness to that of someone else, especially not Terry.

'Yes, well, you say that a lot, ' she said, shortly. 'But somehow it never happens.'

'I didn't ask for this to happen.'

Ed retrieved a joint from under an old magazine on the bedside table.

'And we have just had a brilliant few days away,' he said in a conciliatory voice.

'Yes, but that was my idea, to while away the days before we left. It wasn't *instead* of Dublin.'

Ed shook his head and sighed. 'We can go another time.'

He lit the joint and handed it to Kathryn.

'One you prepared earlier?' She heard how critical she sounded and shook her head. 'I've a long drive ahead of me.'

She knew with a twist of gratification that he hadn't expected this. But she wanted him to feel as let down as she did.

He narrowed his eyes, 'When did you decide that?'

She shrugged with what she hoped looked like indifference.

'If we're not going to Dublin, I might as well go back to Southampton tonight. I've got a lot of work to catch up on.' The words felt as if they would stick in her throat as she pictured herself studying in her room instead of on a plane with Ed by her side.

'But what about the funeral?' he asked.

'You don't need me there. It's a family occasion. Sorry, but I need to get back.' She could hardly believe the words as they formed. She hadn't actually planned on abandoning him before his grandmother's funeral, leaving him with only his father and brother for company, but cruelty snaked in her stomach. Let him miss you, it whispered.

He turned away from her.

'You better go then. You don't want to be driving in the dark.' He was so distant now that she could have been a stranger.

She wanted him to plead with her to stay, to tell her he needed her. Those words would be enough for her to put her frustration about Dublin aside. She was thrown by this coolness – this detachment – and didn't know what to do. She'd backed herself into a corner and felt annoyed that she hadn't been more mature about the change of plan. It wasn't his fault. She knew that. If her dad had attempted suicide, she wouldn't leave him either.

She quietly let herself out of the house and was almost at the car when she heard Sue's voice calling from her open door.

Kathryn, feeling in no mood to chat, sighed as she waited for her to make her way to her front gate.

'I'm glad I've caught you on your own, love,' Sue said, glancing towards the house next door. 'I heard that kerfuffle last week and wondered if you'd both be back.'

'It's been a bit chaotic, Sue. I'm afraid Terry's mum's died and he's taken it badly.'

'Sorry to hear that,' she said, her voice softening, 'I know it's probably not the right time, but I've got something to tell you and I just didn't feel right saying it in front of Ed.'

Despite herself, Kathryn's interest was piqued.

Again, Sue glanced at Ed's house before continuing in a low voice.

'I found the letter.'

'Oh yes?' Kathryn answered vaguely, her mind still on what had just taken place in Ed's bedroom.

'With an address.' Sue widened her eyes for extra effect.

Kathryn suddenly realised what Sue was alluding to.

'Not Janet's letter? You said you'd thrown it away.'

'It must have escaped the clear out. I found it tucked inside an old diary. It's from a few years back and there's a good chance she's moved on. But still, you never know.'

Letting herself back into the house, Kathryn went back upstairs.

Ed was sitting on the bed, his head in his hands. He looked up to see her standing in the doorway with her overnight bag.

'I thought you'd gone.'

She shook her head and, closing the door quietly behind her, came and sat beside him on the bed. The joint, unsmoked, had been stubbed out in the ashtray at his feet.

She would have to leave at some point but, for now, she'd

stay and do what had to be done. Because deep down she knew he needed her; needed someone to love him unconditionally. And wasn't that what she had always wanted? To be needed by him?

As she took his hand, she thought of what might lay ahead. Finding his mother might turn his life upside down – and not necessarily in a good way – but whatever he faced in the future, she was determined to face it with him.

'Better check the old man's still breathing,' Ed said finally.

She lifted her head from his shoulder and rubbed her eyes. The light was fading and, when she checked her watch, it was nearly seven o'clock.

Ed said quietly, 'This life, Kat. I can't leave it. Not yet.'

She nodded. 'I know. But we've all the time in the world.'

Chapter 15

Kathryn awoke at her mother's house the next morning and turned the night's dreams over in her mind. It had been confusing – scenes from long ago, forgotten for years, interspersed with glimpses of the Irish coastline. The flash from the lighthouse. She had a sense of ebbing details, pictures becoming fainter at the edges of her awareness until they dropped away into emptiness. Combing through what she could remember, she searched for traces of Ed but drew a blank.

She knew she would have to get through as best as she could. Day by day. It was the only way. It had been the way she had coped in the weeks and months after she lost him all those years ago.

Enough, she told herself. The past needs to stay there.

Her mother looked up from her bowl of cornflakes when Kathryn came in.

'You slept in.' Unsure of whether this was meant to be disapproving or a statement of fact, Kathryn said nothing. Opening the cupboard beside the sink, she was confronted by plates piled high. Why did her mother keep enough plates for a banquet when she lived alone.

'If you're looking for a cup, they're in the next cupboard.'

Kathryn peered into a cupboard jammed with mugs of every colour. The tall chipped Portmeirion mug, with a smaller one lodged inside to save room, had been her favourite as a child. She looked at them all, stacked tightly, and was transported back to a place she hadn't visited in a long time.

'I never did throw things out.' Her mother's voice interrupted her thoughts.

'Nice to see them all again though,' Kathryn said. 'Like old friends.'

'I always worried that if I parted with any of them I'd regret it. Now, I'm glad I didn't because all our things keep your dad a bit nearer.'

When George died ten years ago, everyone admired how well Valerie coped. She seemed philosophical in the face of such a loss, reminding anyone who enquired after her wellbeing that she had enjoyed forty years of marriage, that nothing good lasts forever and that it was a mercy that he dropped dead while mowing the lawn he loved so much. She seemed convinced that this would be seen as a blessing in the long-run. After all, he wouldn't succumb to dementia like his father.

Of course, she collapsed weeks later. A sudden panic attack in the frozen fish aisle at the local supermarket. She had dropped her basket and rushed home, where she stayed for the next six weeks. Her sister from Yeovil had moved in, her two daughters too busy with a child and job to be able to return. Valerie told them both she was fine and it suited them to believe her.

But she had steadily edged her way back to what could be seen from the outside as a normal life. She had accepted help from her neighbours, started going to the local church and, when the time was right, her sister Joyce eventually returned home to Yeovil.

She decided to downsize five years after George died and seemed to be coping well in her new neighbourhood. Her churchgoing had declined and old neighbours now only stayed in touch at Christmas but the television gave a reassuring shape to her day. She had been to Ireland just once – she was afraid of flying and complained that the ferry took too long. So she wrote and Kathryn wrote back with photos of Alice and their home.

It was agreed that Kathryn would drive her mother to the station so she could catch the lunchtime train to Yeovil. The plans had been made when she was still in Ireland and she hadn't given the matter another thought. Now though, her memories had bubbled up from that deep place where they had been shut away, the people and places of her past had suddenly become so fresh that it could have been yesterday. Which is why when she turned the corner and saw the red brick façade of Worthing station, she felt her throat tighten. There was a parking space near the archway, probably the spot where she had parked her car the night of her twentieth birthday, but she drove on, ignoring her mother's puzzled expression, and parked across the road, where the taxis still waited.

She pulled her mother's case from the boot and carried it across the road. Valerie was talking animatedly about the journey ahead but Kathryn hardly heard her. She was focusing on her breath, in and out, in and out, to keep her mind from tugging her back in time. This breathing technique had worked when she needed an MRI scan a few months ago and the confines of the tube had made her heart race. Directing her mind to the rise and fall of her chest had kept panic at bay. And now it was doing the same again. In. Out. Think of nothing but that.

When she was walking back through the archway after waving off her mother, she glanced to her left and saw the cream walls of the hotel at the corner of the street.

The windows were boarded up, a For Sale sign was strung across the ironwork and the heavy glass door through which she and Elaine had rushed that night, had been replaced with plywood. She wondered how long it had been closed and, her breath forgotten, she was back there, twenty years old, watching Elaine storm off across the road to the taxis, hearing Ed's voice behind her and then the roar of Roland's car speeding around the corner and mounting the pavement.

Blinking, she turned away and walked back to the car. Push it from your mind, she told herself. It was so long ago. Everything's changed. I've changed. He would have changed too if he had been... You can't go back there.

Her thoughts were interrupted by the toot of a car horn. She had walked in front of a smart silver BMW edging out of a parking space.

Embarrassed, she jumped back and mouthed 'sorry', waiting for the car to drive away. But, instead, the driver's door opened and a man climbed out.

'I thought it was you.'

The voice was familiar but his face less so and Kathryn found herself staring blankly at him. He was smartly dressed, as if on his way to work in a bank or the sort of office where men still wore a shirt and tie. His fair hair was cut tight to his head so his receding hairline was less obvious and he was beaming at her.

'Kathryn Johnson.' It was his smile that gave it away – the family resemblance was unmistakable.

'Dave – I'm so sorry I didn't recognise you at first,' she said, baffled because now it seemed so obvious. She might not have seen him in more than twenty years but she should have recognised Elaine's younger brother.

'Well, I've probably put on a bit of weight since I saw you last.'

Kathryn shook her head politely but was surprised to see that Elaine's skinny little brother had grown into this stout figure in front of her.

'How's Mark?' he asked. 'You two still in Ireland?'

They spent the next few minutes catching up on family news across the roof of his car. He was still with the Inland Revenue, having joined straight from school – just a couple of years after Mark – and now lived on a quiet estate near the seafront. Kathryn gave silent thanks that Mark had escaped the clutches of this institution that pulled school-leavers in with the offer of decent pay, not letting them go again until they were ready for retirement, their best years swallowed within its walls.

A quick check of his watch brought Dave's reminiscing to an end.

'I'd better go – I was meant to be back in the office half an hour ago. You got Elaine's number?'

When she shook her head, he frowned, clearly unaware that they hadn't spoken for a long time.

Watching as Kathryn saved Elaine's number on her phone, Dave said, 'Life's tough at home for her, Kathryn. I'm sure she'd appreciate a call.'

#

Later that day, Kathryn's phone rang. It was Alice and Kathryn found herself complaining that the next couple of weeks were going to drag interminably.

'But Mum, you couldn't wait to get away and have some time for yourself,' Alice said.

'Was it that obvious?'

'You don't have to spell these things out. Anyone could see you were happy to have a change of plan all of a sudden.'

'I never could pull the wool over your eyes, could I?'

'No, and you never will. But try and enjoy your time at Nan's. You'll be home soon enough.'

It was the sort of thing a parent would tell an unsure child. But her wise daughter had always led the way. An old soul, Mark called her, and Kathryn was inclined to agree. She was wise, kind, sparky and Kathryn missed her.

Wise, kind, sparky – words that she would have once used to describe her best friend. Elaine had been a lifeline that Kathryn had clung to since the first day of primary school. They had parted ways when they were eleven, when Kathryn following Beth to St Mary's, the private school for girls on the edge of town, and Elaine went to the local comprehensive, but their friendship had continued unaltered in the hours after school and at weekends.

When Kathryn had first moved to Ireland, they had written often. But then as the years passed, the letters were replaced by emails, then annual Christmas cards, which were at least still chock-full of news filling the facing side of the card and over onto the gloss of the back. Gradually, the lines of scribbled news shrank to a *Happy Christmas love Elaine and Rob* and then in the last two years, no card at all.

Elaine told Kathryn about Rob five years ago, while they were still in the period of feverishly scribbling news. An older man with grown-up children, it had been clear that he wanted no more additions to his family, which Kathryn assumed Elaine must have agreed to. And yet, Elaine had been the one to lie on Kathryn's bed as a teenager, discussing the merits and otherwise of the boys at school, talking of weddings and the family she might have one day. Kathryn had never thought that far ahead, had never even felt the slightest interest in any of the lads she met. Until Ed. And when Ed came along, Elaine had disapproved. She even said dramatically one day that she sensed danger in him.

Elaine, Ed, Mark. The sum total of Kathryn's connections beyond her family. One of them was dead, and one still worshipped the ground she walked on. And then there was Elaine. She decided to text her. If Elaine didn't reply, then she'd know their relationship was over. And if she did, then they could go from there. What was there to lose?

Chapter 16

It was strange how the essence of a person could persist after so many years. That same sense whether a teenager lying on a bed, gossiping about boys, or a woman in her mid-years poring over her phone. Still so intent, so curious.

Kathryn hovered a moment outside the café, enjoying the advantage of seeing without being seen, checking if Elaine came close to the image she had held in Kathryn's mind for so many years. How had she not seen her friend in so long? It was just a short flight between them but she might as well have lived on a far off continent. Yet Elaine had been content to let the contact drop too. Was that what life did, when it came to it? Forced a space between those who had once been close, inching it wider year on year?

Kathryn pulled the glass door open to allow a woman to manoeuvre a smart black buggy out. Elaine glanced up as the bell above the door tinkled and spotted Kathryn. She waved enthusiastically.

She was slimmer than Kathryn remembered, with a gloss that felt unfamiliar. The long blonde hair once pulled back into a long ponytail was now cropped short. An elfin cut, wasn't that what this sassy style was called? Favoured by women of a certain age looking for something modern and sharp while they could still get away with it. Chic cuts making a statement without the need for words.

What do you say to someone who knew everything about you for twenty years and then gradually disappeared from your life?

'You look great, Kathryn. How are you?'

She didn't feel great. She hadn't in years. She was wearing her usual uniform of polo neck jumper and jeans. No need for thought. Her hair, hastily washed just half an hour earlier, still damp at the ends.

'I'm okay. It's lovely to see you. You've changed a bit.'

'You mean the weight? I knuckled down to it about ten years ago. Shifted three stone. And it stayed off, luckily. I think Rob would have left me otherwise.'

'Course he wouldn't.'

'Probably not. But you know, when I slimmed down, I decided to tidy myself up as well. Make up for lost time.' She beckoned a waitress who was clearing a nearby table.

The young woman came over and handed them some menus. As Elaine took one, Kathryn noticed her manicured, light blue nails, hoping her own, bitten down nearly to the quick, wouldn't be seen.

'It's a bit early for lunch, isn't it?' Kathryn said, glancing down the menu. 'A cup of tea and a cake will do me.'

'I was thinking of a spot of brunch. How about a Bombay omelette?'

'What's in it? Except for eggs, that is.'

'Tomato, onion, coriander and some nice green chilli.'

'Okay.'

The waitress scribbled on her pad and retreated to the kitchen.

'It was such a coincidence that I bumped into your Dave,' Kathryn said.

Elaine nodded and poured a glass of water for each of them.

'He was on the phone to me as soon as he left you.'

Kathryn looked around at the exposed brickwork and

the polished wooden counter, on which strawberry gateaux and chocolate cakes were displayed on bone china cake stands.

'Changed a bit, hasn't it? I remember when this was a Wimpy.'

'How long ago was that?' Elaine said, in mock horror. 'Back in the eighties?'

It was hard to know how to steer the conversation onto what mattered. Years of change from girl to woman – Ireland, marriage, a daughter. Where do you start? And how do you get up to speed on two decades of someone else's life? Go year by year? Or drama by drama?

They both skirted around the question of how their friendship had drifted to a halt. Safer ground could be found by searching further back, reminiscences of school days, names from the past, and the obligatory checking in about parents and siblings.

'Something's wrong.' Elaine's bright blue eyes looked at her intently. 'You can't fool me, you know.'

And in a jumbled relief, out it all came. Her life which had left her feeling so empty in recent years. Her daughter who she fiercely adored but whose independence had made her feel redundant and washed up on the shore of what had once been a busy family life. Her husband who fiercely adored her and yet couldn't reach her.

There was a momentary pause when the omelettes arrived and then Kathryn continued, 'So many women would give anything to have what I have but I'm bored to death, Elaine.' Kathryn took a mouthful of the delicate golden concoction, her eyes widening as she bit into a chilli.

Elaine smiled, pouring a glass of water from the carafe and handing it to her.

'Goodness, can I swap places with you, Kathryn? You can cope with Rob and I'll be bored with Mark.'

Elaine's elegant fingers held a fork aloft as she studied her friend.

'You never got over him, did you?' she said.

Kathryn stopped chewing and shook her head.

'No, Elaine, I don't think I ever did.'

'But he was trouble, Kathryn. And you'd have ended up in trouble too.'

This was typical Elaine and no more than Kathryn expected.

'I think I saw him.'

Elaine's eyes widened, a forkful of omelette suspended in mid-air. 'Saw who?'

'Ed. Yes, I know it sounds mad.'

'Well, yes. You could say that.'

Kathryn didn't reply.

'So go on, tell me what you saw,' Elaine urged.

When Kathryn had finished telling her about seeing Ed walking along the road beneath Chanctonbury Hill, Elaine caught the eye of the waitress and said, 'Two Southern Comfort and lemonades please.'

'What?' she said, laughing at Kathryn's raised eyebrows. 'We might not have seen each other in forever but I can still remember what you like to drink.'

'I thought you would have forgotten. It was so long ago. I remember that summer so vividly, but I wasn't sure you would.'

'That summer? Or do you mean that whole year when I hardly saw you because you were always with him?'

'I don't think I was always with him.'

Elaine nodded, albeit with a smile. 'You, my girl, were a

lost cause. If you weren't with him, you might as well have been because all you talked about was Ed. And, sorry to say Kathryn, but I just couldn't see the appeal. Not really. I mean, he was good-looking, I have to admit that much. But not reliable.'

Kathryn gave a half smile. She had lived for twenty years with reliability and found it rather overrated.

'And then, afterwards, you were inconsolable.'

Kathryn nodded. 'It was half a lifetime ago but that ache, it's never gone away. I mean, who's to say that we wouldn't have made a go of it?'

'And that you'd now be settled somewhere with him? Enjoying your life together? Rather than just wallowing in the memory of him? Because that's what you've been attached to all these years, Kathryn. The memory of him.'

What was it with Elaine and the brutal truth, Kathryn thought. Never one to consider how her opinion would land, Elaine said it as she saw it. It had been one of the things that Kathryn had admired when they were young, but now her words wounded her.

Noting her friend's expression, Elaine continued, this time more softly. 'Look, don't mind me, Kathryn. It's not everyone who gets to feel the way you felt about Ed. It's a gift. Of sorts. Maybe I'm just envious.'

It didn't feel like a gift. More of an aching hole that had never been filled.

'I lost all of his letters years ago. I'd give anything to read them again. It would mean so much. But I have no idea what happened to them.'

The waitress returned with their drinks and Elaine waited until they were alone again before replying.

'The letters in the green box?'

Kathryn was surprised her friend remembered such a small detail. 'Yes, I had it in my university room and I thought I brought it back home but it went missing and I was never able to find it. You must have quite a memory if you can remember the colour of a box on my desk in 1993.'

Elaine bit her lip and winced. 'Please don't go mad. But I took it.'

'What?'

'I did it for your sake, Kathryn. We knew you wouldn't move on if you kept reading those letters over and over again. You were obsessed. Trying to read new meanings into every word he had ever written to you. We thought it was the best thing.'

'We?'

'Your dad suggested it. I'm sorry, but none of us knew what to do with you.'

How was it that so many years could pass and yet the same feelings of frustration and anger, long buried, could rise? And so quickly. It was as if her time with Ed had been reduced to an interlude. A pause between her teenage years, in which she felt smothered by her parents' expectations, and her years in Ireland where she fitted herself around Mark's life. With the exception of her time with Ed, she had always done what others thought was best.

'He had no right to take my things,' she said icily.

'Don't blame your dad. It was both of us.'

Kathryn didn't reply because words were pointless and she didn't want to fall out with her newly rediscovered friend.

'I can fetch them for you now,' Elaine said nervously. 'I've kept them safe. Maybe I knew you'd come looking for them one day.'

Kathryn gave a tight smile and nodded.

'I'll just pay the bill and then nip off for them.' Elaine said, digging in her bag for her purse.

'No, I'll get it,' said Kathryn. ' Is your place nearby? Shall I come with you?'

A look of uncertainty flickered in Elaine's eyes.

'No, you stay there. Rob's working from home today. I'd rather not disturb him if I can. It's only round the corner. I'll nip back and get them and I'll be back before you know it.'

Elaine's phone had buzzed a couple of times in the last half hour and Kathryn now wondered whether it was Rob. In all these years she hadn't considered the possibility that Elaine might be with someone who was possessive, who wanted her to break contact with people from her earlier life.

Kathryn paid the bill and had just sat back down to flick through the local newspaper when, true to her word, Elaine was back, holding a blue cloth bag. She handed it to Kathryn who, glancing inside, saw the pattern of the box. Her heart started to race.

Kathryn felt sure that if she started reading the letters, she would be floored by the feelings that would flood through her.

'Look, I think it's best if you go read them when you're alone, without me breathing down your neck.'

Kathryn nodded. 'Elaine, I'm sorry. I shouldn't have been off with you like that. It's just that people have always thought they've known what's best for me. It was the story of my life… still is, to some degree.'

Elaine put a hand on her friend's arm. 'Don't apologise to me of all people. I remember how it was back then and I also know what it's like to feel like you're locked down by life. In a kind of prison.'

'A gilded cage.'

Elaine smiled faintly. 'Got it in one. But you know what Kathryn, sometimes you just have to forge ahead with what's right for you. You know, take no notice of everyone around you, however well-meaning they might be.'

Out on the street, Kathryn hugged her friend and agreed that they'd meet again, and next time for longer. As she watched Elaine cross the road and walk away, she wondered about the life her friend had created for herself, and the discontent she'd alluded to. Would she be able to take her own advice and put her own needs first?

They would talk more before she returned home, but for now, with the letters safely in her bag, Kathryn knew where she needed to go.

Chapter 17

The car park at the bottom of Chanctonbury Hill was larger than she remembered, its spaces marked by freshly painted white lines. A pay and display machine now stood on a raised island in the centre beside a sign bearing a list of instructions: keep your dog on a lead, put litter in bins, beware of nesting birds. As Kathryn pressed the key fob to lock the car, she wondered where she might find instructions for opening doors into the past. How could she do that correctly?

The chalk showed through where centuries of people had trod the turf. The white trail wound its way up the grassy slope, beckoning Kathryn onwards. She had transferred Ed's letters into her coat pocket and slipped her hand around them, touching the paper he had once touched.

As she walked on, she noticed a couple coming towards her, their golden spaniel darting across the grass, probably on the scent of rabbits. They passed her without pausing their conversation as they walked on downhill.

She was glad to be alone on the hillside, to be able to turn off the path to where she knew the dewpond lay waiting. The turf, more springy and alive than the clay farmland around her home in Ireland, rose gently before the land tipped down into a hollow in which a clear pool of water lay. A hawthorn hedge sheltered two sides of the pond and there was room to pick a spot and sit down, sheltered by the sloping ground and the straggling hedge.

Kathryn felt the grass under the palms of her outstretched hands. She looked up at the bright blue sky and felt at home in the quiet. She unlaced her boots and peeled off her socks. She felt the grass tickle her feet as she pressed them into the turf. Closing her eyes, she lay back and wondered what she should feel.

'Where are you Ed?' The words formed in her mind and she felt a flush of embarrassment. Surely it was daft to be this preoccupied with the memory of him? What could it possibly achieve?

She put the letters on the grass beside her. After a deep breath, she unfolded the first one and began to read.

Dear Kathryn,

See, I said I'd write to you! This is the first letter I've written to anyone. Ever! The others are down the pub and I told them I'll be down later on. Couldn't tell them I was writing a letter to a girl, I'd never live it down. Hope university is ok. Bet it's a different scene to racing.

It was so pukka to see you at Brighton last week.
Thanks for the card. I've got it up on my shelf.
Love Ed

She smiled at her younger self for clearly filing the letters in date order. She remembered how she had felt when this first letter had arrived, holding it with a sense of disbelief. He might have promised to write to her that evening at Brighton Racecourse, but she hadn't really expected to hear from him again. Reading it repeatedly as she walked to lectures in that second week of term, she felt as if her heart might burst.

Folding it carefully and putting it to one side, she picked

up the next one, then the next, smiling in places, wiping away a stray tear elsewhere. The letters felt like a record of long ago events, of how their relationship had deepened as the months passed. In the early letters, he spoke of stable yard news and life in Epsom, but gradually they shifted in tone, page after page about how he felt about being back in Liverpool living with his brother, and then his father. The writing became less neat, less self-conscious. She tried to imagine where he had written them. Was he crouched at the small table in his room? Or in the kitchen, a hand shielding the contents from Paul's prying eyes?

Unable to resist, she picked up the envelope at the bottom of the pile, with its peeling stamp and faded Liverpool postmark. The letter inside was short, on lined paper, and the ink had faded so that the words were almost ghostly. It was the last letter she had ever received from him. How she wished he had had time to write more. That she could have carried his words with her as she moved through the years.

Hi Kat,

A quick note because I want to catch the post. I can't talk properly when I ring you with the old man in such a state. He's always in the background and I don't want him hearing our conversations.

Seeing you is the one thing I have to look forward to. I was thinking of coming down at the weekend. What do you think? Might get the coach down to uni to see you.

Anyway, bye for now.
Love Ed x

She felt she was back there, in her room in halls, reading these words for the first time and knowing that she couldn't keep what she had discovered from him any longer. Who she had discovered.

Kathryn couldn't bring herself to read any of the other letters. If only she hadn't told him. He wouldn't have left when he did and what they had together wouldn't have been severed so that she was left with nothing but a grief, its edges so sharp and jagged that she could hardly move without it tearing her apart.

She decided she had spent long enough on the hillside and would head back to her mother's bungalow. Maybe find a fish and chip shop in the nearest town to save cooking, ring Alice and have an early night. There was no point sitting here reading old letters. It wouldn't change anything.

When she returned to the car, she carefully put the envelopes back in the small box. Although perhaps not carefully enough as the corner of one snagged on the soft fabric lining, pulling it away from the wood. As she pressed her fingers on the material to smooth it flat again, she felt a slight thickness. Gently lifting the fabric a little further from the wood, she found another envelope – small and square, like the tiny Christmas cards schoolchildren send each other.

Carefully taking it out, she noticed that this envelope didn't have an address and a stamp on it like the others. It simply said *Kat* in his handwriting. She had never seen it before.

The envelope flap was tucked in rather than stuck down and she was glad not to have to tear it. On the card inside was a cute teddy bear cuddling a heart under the words Thank You. Kathryn guessed it must have been bought in a hurry because cute teddies weren't Ed's style. She opened it and read.

Kat,

*I thought I'd leave this in your room for you to find –
maybe tomorrow, maybe next week, maybe years from
now if I hide it well enough! I expect you're reading this
now thinking what is he on about. But whenever you
read this, I know I'll be thinking about you. And I'll be
remembering what we've done together and what you've
done for me. It's nearly a year since we met and I'm
already planning what to do for our anniversary.
This time I won't mess up, I promise.*

*What you don't realise is that you know me like nobody
else does. I see who you really are too. That inner fire.
Don't ever change.*

*All my love,
Ed x*

Her eyes filled with tears and the words started to swim.
It was too much to take in. She let herself cry. The box had
sat on her bedside cabinet in her room in halls, his letters and
other keepsakes inside. He must have slipped the card into
the box the morning he left. Hours before he died.

She needed to walk. To cast off this feeling of being buried
in the past, in something she couldn't change, no matter how
much she wanted to. She would climb the hill and sit for a
moment. The view had always been worth the effort and
would help to settle her mind.

She had been here once with Ed. They had climbed the
hill from the northern side. As she walked, her mind cast
back into her memories of that day. What if she could have

done something back then to alter what came next? Made different choices. Made him stay.

She thought again about the figure she had seen walking along the road. She had been convinced it was Ed, but time had rubbed away at that certainty and she now told herself that it couldn't possibly have been him.

Even though something similar had happened before. Once, she thought she had spotted Alice across the street, only to discover when she got nearer that it was another young woman animatedly talking into her phone. The puffer jacket was the same shade of plum as her daughter's, the girl's hair plaited in a similar way, but it wasn't Alice.

She wondered what Ed would have thought of her now, whether he would have seen the change in her. Would he even recognise her if he passed her here today? Twenty years can make an ocean of difference between what you were and what you became. The woman who had seen her life for what it was and was now looking back at the girl she had been.

She reflected on how much of middle age involved covering up. Not only the signs of age, but its frustrations too. How silent she had stayed as she felt her life peter out into the flatness of routine. She had raged inwardly but her fury had stayed muted. Would her future be any different?

The Ed she had frozen in her mind was on the edge between a teenager and a man. His teenage years were coming to an end but she would never know the man he might become. Their time together had been such a brief snapshot but had remained fast within her as she moved on through the years.

Not for the first time, she played out various scenarios in her mind of how Ed might have aged. Would he have had a family? Would he have settled down and found himself a regular job? Would the light in his eyes have dimmed as he weathered more of what life had in store, as her own light had dimmed?

She was now at the edge of the Ring. Once a ditch protecting the fort, it was now a low, wide indent that rose up gradually to meet a low rampart following the curve of the fort before levelling off into a wooded area.

It seemed a pity to have climbed this far and not to explore the trees. She had plenty of time. Nobody was demanding her return or wondering where she might be.

The late afternoon light, watery and grey, sifted through the branches so that she had to pick her way carefully along the dim pathway. The gnarled and twisting roots of the trees threaded through the earth like tentacles, a web of probing and searching claws that, here and there, emerged through the soft soil, ready to trip anyone who didn't have their wits about them. The trees towered at either side of her, their branches crisscrossing above to create a ceiling under which there was silence.

As she walked further along the path she realised the silence had been replaced by a low hum, soft at first but gradually becoming louder. She quickly dismissed it as the wind whistling through the trees, but as the sound intensified, it became shriller. She stopped, closed her eyes and discovered that the sound, now high-pitched and piercing, felt as if it was coming from within her.

When she opened her eyes, the trees around her were swaying even though she felt no breeze. The sky, glimpsed through the branches, was no longer a soft grey but seemed to shimmer and sparkle. And, all the while, her head was throbbing with this insufferable noise.

And then it stopped.

The track was now bathed in bright light where it re-emerged on the hillside. As she walked on, the light became more intense. The sun's rays threaded their way through the branches, dappling the path with light and warming her face. Looking up, she noticed the green canopy of leaves rustling in a gentle breeze.

And then, finally reaching the rampart at the northern edge, she stopped and gazed at the panorama before her.

Chapter 18

Beyond the earth bank, the hillside was bathed in blazing sunshine. Under a cloudless and brilliant blue sky, the downland was a lush green speckled with buttercups and dandelions. Cow parsley swayed in the soft, warm breeze and a bee busied itself in the delicate honeysuckle clinging to the sign pointing along the South Downs Way.

I could see a family further down the hill. A woman was packing plates into a basket while a man threw a ball with two small children. Their laughter was faint.

And then I heard a voice.

'There you are! Where've you been? I thought you'd deserted me.'

Looking around, I saw a young man lying on the grass in the distance. He was propping himself up on one elbow and looking towards the trees a little further along from where I stood.

And then I saw a young woman wandering over to where he lay and dropping to the grass beside him. She looked so familiar, so much like myself. She was...

My heart began to pound harder and harder and my knees felt as if they might give way so that I too might drop to the sun-baked ground. There, in front of me, was my younger self. Her hair, wavy from her first and only perm, was pulled back into a brown butterfly clip from Woolworths and Beth's black sunglasses – borrowed and never given back – were pushed up on her head. And there he was, bare-chested in the heat of the afternoon, his silver chain glinting in the sunshine.

What was this? I couldn't make any sense of what was in front of me; who was in front of me. I wanted to turn and run away, back to a place where life made some sort of sense, but I was rooted to the spot, unable to take my eyes off them.

His back was tanned and strong, his small red devil tattoo visible even at this distance. As I watched, he reached across to press play on a CD player propped against his companion's bag.

This had to be a dream. Yes, that's what it was; I was dreaming in bed back at my mum's house and this was nothing more than a movie playing out in my mind.

The loud, tinny beat of one of his dance tracks came pulsing from the small machine.

He rolled over, murmuring, 'Banging tune.'

Kathryn rolled her eyes.

He grinned, his eyes closed against the sun. 'You'll get a taste for good music one day. And hopefully a better stereo.'

He folded his arms under his head, nodding to the throbbing bass.

I waited a short distance away and watched them – us – together. His head was thrown back in the full glare of the sun, a slick of sweat glistening on his brow before trickling lazily into his closely-cropped hair. Kathryn sat beside him, picking the petals from a daisy she had just plucked.

I watched him with a lump in my throat. Those hazel eyes that danced and gleamed in a way that could spark an intense ripple of excitement and delight within me. The way he held his head slightly to one side, as if deeply interested in what I was saying. How he would bite his lower lip and narrow his eyes to roll a spliff, his fingers dexterous and assured. How it had made me feel when I made him laugh.

I remembered how Elaine had wasted no time in spelling

out the dangers of someone like him.

'You mark my words, Kathryn, he's only after one thing. When you come back pregnant with your future in tatters, don't say I didn't warn you.'

As he sat up blinking in the harsh light, for a startling moment I thought he was addressing me. 'So shall we make a move or what?'

She hesitated before saying, 'Okay then. It's an hour's drive so I suppose we'd better get going.' It was clear she wanted to stay longer, to hold on to this perfect moment and keep real life at bay.

I watched her with the experience of an older sister, recognising her need to impress him, to fall in with all of his suggestions. I remembered how that was.

As they carried their bags back down the hill to the car park, I followed at a distance. I watched her walking beside him, noticed the tan of her shoulders in her black and white checked sleeveless shirt, and the way she tugged it down self-consciously over her jeans to cover what she imagined was plumpness but which I now knew was just the softness of youth.

I couldn't ever remembering watching myself in a dream before but maybe this was something else, something more lucid. Perhaps that meant I could alter the day; rewrite it to get the ending I wanted. In the morning, the past would still be as it was, set in stone. But maybe, just for now, I could dream a new ending.

#

The motorway had always been busy on a Sunday evening. Cars clogged each lane as people returned home from visiting family, out of town shopping trips, days out in the countryside; heading back to get ready for work as the weekend freedom drew to a close.

They – we – stopped at a petrol station near Portsmouth. He had run out of cigarettes. I smiled as she hastily brushed her hair, watching him intently in the rear view mirror as he crossed the forecourt, pulling the cellophane from the gold box.

How was it possible that this could feel so strange and yet so familiar? The car, so old-fashioned at first with its corded turquoise upholstery, red plastic box of tapes between the front seats, and air freshener swinging from the mirror, soon felt as familiar to me as when I first climbed into this small red Metro.

Ed clicked open the box of tapes and started rifling through them.

'Nice one,' he said, sliding one into the cassette player on the dashboard.

'So the Lighting Seeds meet with your approval then,' she said, smiling across at him.

'Yeah well, at least they're from Liverpool,' he said, turning the volume up.

My dream time didn't seem to run as usual but jumped, like a video on fast forward. We were now pulling into the car park at my old halls of residence; a journey of an hour reduced to mere moments. I spotted Mary whose room had been down the corridor from mine. She was getting into her dark green Mini with bright yellow sunflowers painted on the doors. I hadn't thought of Mary and her Mini in a long time.

As they crunched across the gravel of the car park to the path that turned and twisted under a wooden trellis of young wisteria, I recognised it all. Looking up at the first floor, I could see my own window, where a lava lamp sat, a Christmas present from Elaine. The details of a half-forgotten earlier life.

I knew then that they wouldn't go directly to the room. They would head for the student bar instead. I also knew that after two pints, I would hear him say that he didn't expect to live much longer.

They sat at a table by the window overlooking the road that ran through the campus. It was busy for a Sunday night. Across the bar, a group of students were huddled, chatting. I remembered their faces but had never known their names. Like many third years, they had returned to halls for their final year. It was supposed to be more conducive to studying. Or so the prospectus said. Halls kept the rookies safe from harm while they figured out how to be adults, while those on the cusp of the real world were kept safe from the more enjoyable distractions of life.

The ash on his cigarette was growing. A split second before it crumbled onto the table, he flicked it towards the ashtray between them and the grey powder dropped onto the glass. I had always marvelled at his judgment and how he never seemed to miss. He put the cigarette back to his lips and, after a moment, exhaled a thin line of smoke that curled artfully to the ceiling.

I watched him lean towards Kathryn, his elbows on the table.

'Can I tell you something weird? I mean, really weird. Deep down, I've always had this feeling that I'll die long before my time.'

His words hit me in the chest. And I watched as confusion clouded Kathryn's face.

'It's okay though,' he continued. 'I mean, we all have to go some time.'

'But you're only twenty.'

'Kat, I just know it.'

I studied his expression, that unflinching gaze of his, and I saw that he knew.

When Kathryn went to the bar to fill their glasses, I watched him more intently. There was no need for the snatched glances of my youth, stolen when I thought he wasn't looking.

He stood out from the other young men in the bar. There was a universal ease about them, as if they were teetering on the brink of adulthood but still cosseted by institutional life. Ed, on the other hand, might have been the same age but he had the careworn look of someone who had seen what adult life had to offer and was already disappointed.

His attention was fixed on the television high up on the wall, where a football match was underway. I wondered what he was thinking in that moment as he picked at his fingers, his eyes following the ball on the screen. He fished in his pocket for his lighter, turning it over in his hand to read the engraving and gently rubbing his finger across the words.

Noticing Kathryn returning with their drinks, he quickly put it back in his pocket. But I had seen it and my heart had twisted. The lighter I had given him as a Christmas present had meant more to him than I realised. Could it be that I too meant more to him than I ever understood? I would have gone to the ends of the earth for him, but I could never really understand what he saw in me. Maybe I'd got it all wrong.

'No crisps or anything? Are you trying to starve me?' His smile didn't quite reach his eyes.

Kathryn was clearly not ready to change the topic of conversation just yet. 'What you said a minute ago. You can't just drop a bombshell like that and expect us to carry on like nothing's happened.'

'There's no point in talking about it.' He lifted the glass to his lips and drank thirstily.

'But you said you knew that you were going to…' She let the sentence trail off.

'Die? Well, you know what they say…' he hesitated, teasing. 'What?'

'Live fast, die young.'

'Is that what you mean then?' she said, her shoulders relaxing a little, 'That you just don't want to get old? I get that. We all think like that sometimes.'

He didn't reply at first, but glanced up at the TV again.

'I mean, it's not like you've had a premonition or anything,' Kathryn said, studying her fingers before looking at him again.

When he still didn't reply, she said, 'You haven't, have you?'

'What?' he turned his attention back to her as if he had been distracted rather than deliberately avoiding looking at her.

'A premonition. It's nothing like that?'

'No, Kat. Nothing like that,' he said.

She missed it, but I caught the shadow that passed across his face as he turned away towards the screen. As he turned back to her, he made a deliberate effort to brighten his face, to give his voice a lighter tone. 'So, what do you fancy doing now? It's still early.'

Chapter 19

As they left the bar, I looked at Kathryn and knew that her mind was now racing. Tonight had to be the night she told him about his mother. She had kept the information to herself for long enough, waiting for the right moment, and had decided it was best to tell him on neutral ground away from his father and Paul.

'How about the cinema? We haven't seen Jurassic Park yet.' Ed suggested.

I knew how close she was to putting it off, letting the days move on until another suitable time arose when she might be able to tell him but when might that be? And surely it was right that he should know and as soon as possible.

'No?' he said. 'We could go to one of the clubs in town?'

He must have wondered at her lack of enthusiasm as usually she relished the chance to go somewhere with him.

'How about we just go back to halls?' She said it so quietly that I barely heard her.

'What, already?'

'Well, if you don't want to, that's fine.' I could hear how defensive she sounded.

Was it the tone of her voice or the blush that spread upwards from her neck that he noticed? A look of confusion passed over his face and he said quickly, 'No, no, course I do.'

They walked back to the halls in silence.

She fumbled with the key in the lock of the main door before Ed stepped forward, 'Here, I'll do it.'

Loud music was coming from Stephanie's room along the

corridor. A chair had been dragged out to wedge the door open and, next door, Joanna had done the same. They did that sometimes when they were getting ready to go out. I remembered being envious of how at home they felt, treating halls like a shared flat, but it was their final year and they had obviously shrugged off the uncertainties I had felt as a first year.

Joanna came out of her room in a dark red dressing gown, a towel wrapped around her black curls, her eyes peering out of the ghostly mask of a face pack. She was clutching a bottle of wine as she turned into Stephanie's room.

'Not smuggling men into halls again are you, Kathryn?' she called along the corridor.

'Of course not. We just came back to get something,' Kathryn replied hurriedly.

'A likely story. Don't take everything so serious, Kathy. You're allowed to have fun you know.' With that she sashayed into her friend's room and nudged the chair aside to let the door clunk shut behind her.

Kathryn glowered while she waited for Ed to unlock her door. She could hear laughter from Stephanie's room and she scowled at the floor.

'The cheek of her,' she said crossly as Ed pushed the heavy door open and switched on the light.

'Well, this beats my room,' he said, looking at the shelves where she – I – had spent ages positioning photos, books and ornaments just so. I remember feeling a need to make an impression, to give a sense of confidence and taste, and to be careful not to appear too studious, too pretentious. Some books were hidden under the bed, others artfully displayed. A strip of photos taken in a booth in Albert Dock was propped up in a prime spot on the bedside table.

He crossed the room to the turquoise fractal poster she had bought in the Student Union market that week.

'This is wicked,' he said. 'It's so comfortable in here. How can you leave it and come up to mine? Talk about slumming it.'

She shrugged. 'Yes, well, you're there, aren't you?'

He looked surprised, as if he couldn't quite believe that he was enough of a reason, which made my heart ache for him. But now I could see that Kathryn had made a decision and was reaching in her bedside drawer for an envelope.

'I've something for you.'

Holding it out to him, she said, 'But I have to tell you what it is before you open it.'

'Well, I know it's not my birthday, so what's with the mystery? Have I won the pools?'

I knew how Kathryn was feeling. The gnaw of anxiety in her gut as she prepared to turn Ed's world upside down.

'It's from your mum, Ed.'

'What?'

'Your mum,' she repeated.

'It can't be. You know I haven't heard from her in twenty years.'

'We traced her.'

'We?'

'Sue next door came across an old letter with an address and then she…'

'If this is some sort of joke, Kat, it's not funny. And it's really not like you to mess with me like that.'

'I wouldn't joke about something like this.'

'But why would she contact Sue and not bother keeping in touch with her own kids?' He was now shaking his head. 'No, there's been a mistake. She's gone. Out of our lives.

Disappeared into thin air.'

'But she didn't,' Kathryn murmured. 'We followed up on the old address and it turned out she hadn't lived there for fifteen years so we thought we were at a dead end. But Sue's son-in-law was in London for work and she got him to go along, knock on a few doors and…'

He threw the envelope onto the bed. 'No, this isn't happening. Sue's wrong. Neither of you had any right to go meddling.'

'Ed. We found her.'

He was still shaking his head, refusing to believe what he was hearing.

'Who said it was okay to go digging in our lives like that? Why didn't you tell me? Not a word and then you just throw it at me like this.'

I could feel his anger. It was aimed at her, but it resonated across time, across the dream-like world that held us all captive.

'I didn't want to get your hopes up. Somehow, I thought it might be what you wanted,' Kathryn said quietly, tears pricking her eyes. 'But we can throw the letter away, pretend it never existed.'

He paced up and down the room, his fists clenched, before stopping suddenly and sitting down beside her.

'I'm sorry, okay? Don't cry. It's just it's a big deal, you know?'

She wiped her eyes with her sleeve and nodded. 'Of course it is.'

The letter lay unopened on the bed. How I wished I could snatch it away; hide it again so they could move on with their lives and avoid what I knew was coming.

He sat for some minutes, his head in his hands, before

reaching for the envelope. He opened it carefully, in the same way he had opened the card at Brighton Races.

And for a moment, I vividly remembered how I had wished we had never found her. If his mother didn't want to know him, if her life was now too complicated to risk being turned upside down by the appearance of a son – two sons – twenty years of coping would be shattered and he would never recover.

His lips moved slightly as he shaped the words his mother had written. He turned the page and continued reading while Kathryn sat and waited for a reaction.

But he simply folded the pages and slipped them back into the envelope, leaving it on the bed. He stood up and pulled his cigarettes from his jeans pocket.

'Can I smoke in here?' he asked distractedly.

'If you open the window and sit on the sill, the smoke alarm won't go off,' she said.

Perched on the ledge next to her desk, he lit a cigarette. He stared out onto the quadrangle and inhaled sharply, letting the smoke wind out into the night air.

Kathryn shifted on the bed, drawing my attention away from Ed and his attention back to her.

'So, she's alive then,' he said, stubbing out what remained of his cigarette on the outside ledge and flinging it out onto the gravel below.

Kathryn nodded.

'And living in Balham.' He shook his head as if this fact baffled him more than anything else. 'That's less than half an hour from where I was living down south. I mean, I even went clubbing in Balham. I might have passed her on the street and not even known it was her.'

'I guess so.'

'She's got a kid. A daughter.' His voice wavered and he turned away again to gaze out over the quadrant and the students drinking and chatting in a huddle below.

'Oh? How old?'

'Fifteen,' he said. 'Didn't waste much time in replacing us, did she?'

I saw Kathryn flinch, wondering why his mother hadn't saved that information until she met him. If she wanted to meet him at all.

'Did she say much else?'

'Only that she is on her own again. Her and the kid. And other stuff.'

'And did she explain why she did what she did?'

'No. But she said she wants to meet up.'

She smiled, relieved. 'That's good, isn't it?'

'I dunno, is it?' He turned away again. I watched the rise and fall of his breath, trying to guess what could be running through his mind and feeling a knot twist in my stomach at the thought of what lay ahead.

'Was I wrong to try and find her?' Kathryn said. I knew she wanted him to put her mind at rest, to tell her she had done him a huge favour in tracking down his mother so they could make up for all the lost years.

But he said nothing. As I knew he would.

After some minutes, he slid down from the window sill.

'Maybe we should just get some sleep,' he said, avoiding her eyes. 'Got the keys? My stuff's in the car.'

When he had left the room, I watched as she quickly snatched the letter from the envelope. The writing was girlish, the letters plump and round.

Dear Eddie,

I've thought of you so often and have always hoped you were getting on well in life. As the years passed, it was harder to get in touch. You have a sister now. Kerry's fifteen. I hope you get to meet each other.

I hope this isn't a shock and that you don't hate me. It has been such a long time. You probably thought you would never hear from me.

I'm so sorry if I'm not making sense – I just don't know what to say in a letter to my little boy.

We both heard the door open downstairs and Kathryn hurriedly slid the letter back into its envelope, carefully positioning it where he'd left it. She went to the window, putting distance between herself and the confidence she'd just broken.

Ed came in with his red bag, which he took into the bathroom. The latch clicked.

As a mother myself now, my heart ached for the small child – Eddie – whose mother had walked out one day and never returned. And also for the woman who surely had to be running from something terrible – someone terrible – otherwise how could she have left?

When Ed came out of the bathroom, he sat on the side of the bed and rifled through his bag. Kathryn went and brushed her teeth and, when she came out, he was in bed, his back turned to her. She pulled the curtains and clicked off the light before sliding into the narrow space beside him.

How I remembered that decisive turn of his back, the tug

of the duvet over his shoulder, how it had left me in no doubt that he didn't want to discuss this evening's revelation any further. I had wondered if he was asleep because his breath was so even but then he would clear his throat or rub his face and I knew that he was awake, thinking.

Yet I was still surprised when Ed sat up in bed. I watched him press the buttons on his watch so that a faint glow illuminated his face. He edged out from under the quilt, clearly to avoid waking the sleeping girl beside him. As I watched them, sadness flooded through me. The last words I had heard him say were about getting his bag from my car. The last word I had said to him as he lay beside me – sorry – hadn't been answered, leaving me sorry for evermore.

Why hadn't he told me he was going? I would have gone anywhere with him, surely he knew that? Whatever he had to face, I would have been by his side.

He quietly pulled on his jeans and t-shirt. And my heart swelled to see him put his fingers to his lips and then touch them lightly to her forehead.

Kathryn shifted in bed, turning her face into the pillow he had just been lying on. I kept that pillow for months afterwards, holding it close, until the scent of his aftershave was gone.

After a moment's hesitation, Ed retrieved a small white envelope from the side pocket of his holdall. Opening the lid of the green keepsake box on the desk, he pushed it inside. He then eased a page out of one of Kathryn's notebooks and began to write.

'What are you doing?' she asked, drowsily.

I didn't remember waking up. I was sure I hadn't woken up. His back stiffened but he didn't turn.

'I've gotta go, Kat.'

'Go where?'

'I need to catch the train. The earliest one. I didn't want to wake you.'

He held the piece of paper aloft as if to prove that he had planned to tell her rather than just walk out with no explanation.

'No, wait,' she dragged herself out of bed and, grabbing her clothes from the chair where they were draped, she disappeared into the bathroom.

'Promise me you'll wait?' She said, keeping the door wedged open with a towel while she washed her face.

He was sitting on the bed when she came out. He smiled weakly.

She picked up her keys. 'So where to?'

Chapter 20

As the door closed behind them, I found myself staring at the ivy-patterned duvet he had been sitting on moments earlier. My mind was racing. I had no memory of waking and leaving with Ed that morning. None of it made any sense.

All I remembered was finding the note the next morning and knowing he had gone. For him to leave without warning like that, I knew he thought what I'd done was unforgivable. He wouldn't thank me for chasing after him, however much I wanted to. So I gave him some space to let the dust settle. When I eventually plucked up the courage to ring him, Paul told me the news that turned my world upside down.

But now my dream was telling me a different story, showing me a different way. Was there a version in which he survived? And could that version somehow become a reality?

I knew that some people believed that for every left turn we make, another version of ourselves turns right. The same with any decision we make so that, in theory, there could be an infinite number of versions of ourselves living parallel, equally real lives. But that was ridiculous, surely?

The alarm clock on Kathryn's desk said 5.30am, but what time was it in the real world? Would I be waking up soon … in twenty years' time? My head felt too fuzzy to think straight.

And in that moment, the light began to shimmer and flicker, the walls, desk, and ceiling seemed to quiver in front of me and the room folded in on itself and everything went dark.

I expected to see the familiar striped wallpaper of my mother's spare bedroom when I opened my eyes. But I wasn't in bed, I was sitting on a park bench. As if propelled by an invisible force, I got up and started to walk along a path that weaved through a wide expanse of grass, too cultivated to be farmland but wilder than a lawn. Through the beech trees on either side of the track, I looked out across the landscape, shrouded by early morning mist. It felt deserted, like I was alone in a silvery world between night and day.

But as I walked on, car headlights began to momentarily pierce the gloom ahead, disappearing almost as soon as they appeared, so I knew the path was leading to a main road.

There was another noise now, a *whoosh* of movement, and it was only at the last moment that I jumped onto the grass as a cyclist sped past. Head low, pedals spinning, he was now streaking away as quickly as he had appeared.

Moments later, there was a screech of tyres on the road ahead, a cacophonous bang, and then silence.

But then the silence was broken and a voice emerged in the distance, shouting, panic-stricken. They kept yelling and, with my head spinning in confusion, I closed my eyes.

When I opened them, I had a bird's eye view of the scene below. The bicycle that had passed me only a minute earlier was now strewn across the road, one wheel buckled and the other torn from the metalwork and spinning in the road. The cyclist, previously so intent on speed, was now hobbling towards an oncoming car, waving his hands wildly.

And then I saw my car. It had crumpled, concertina-like, as it had slammed into a lamppost. The red bonnet had folded upwards and steam hissed from the engine. I strained to hear any sound, however muffled, from within the car, but all I heard was the cyclist frantically yelling for help to a young man climbing out of a black Toyota Supra.

The driver picked his way over shattered glass to reach the passenger door of my car. He hesitated and then opened it, immediately taking a step back. Even from a distance, I saw how his face had blanched. I wanted to scream, to help, to do something, but, with the rapidity of a camera shutter blinking open and closed, I was once again sitting on the bench looking out over the common.

The scenes were flicking one into the next, speeding then slowing, as if someone was directing my dream like a movie. I had the strangest sense that I was both the observer and the observed. But as to who was observing me, I had no idea.

I looked back towards the main road, expecting to see blue flashing lights, to hear the wail of sirens, more voices, more panic. But there was nothing, just silence.

And then I saw a bicycle speeding towards me once again. As if there was a finger pressing the rewind button and then releasing it to play the scene over again.

The strange thing about making your way through a dream is that you don't have a chance to question what's possible or even what's explainable. All I knew was that I couldn't let this scene play out the same way again. Except that everything was happening so quickly that before the thought could even make itself known, I found myself propelled into another scenario. I grabbed a fallen branch and flung it across the path. The cyclist braked so severely that the bike skidded and he tumbled to the ground. Swearing, he pulled his bike upright and checked the tyres and the chain before climbing on and proceeding at a less ambitious pace.

My thoughts were tangled in knots and I was unable to grasp what had just happened. I stared towards the main road, waiting for the sound of a car slamming into the metal lamppost.

In this version of reality I was in the car with Ed. But did I die with him or not? Even as soon as the question began to form in my mind, the path beneath my feet slid away so that I found myself dropping as if through a trap door into a blank, empty space. Screwing my eyes shut, like I used to do as a child on the highest, scariest rides at the funfair, my head started to pound and I wondered if this was what death felt like, being yanked out of the present into a void through which you then plummeted into the unknown.

Tentatively opening my eyes, I discovered I was now in the back seat of my car – the car I had just seen caved in and hissing against a lamppost – but which was now making its way steadily along the road at the edge of Southampton Common. In the front seats were Ed and Kathryn.

'Maybe you should put your foot down a bit?' he said.

She checked her watch before shaking her head.

'You know Ed, if you'd snuck off as planned, you'd be getting there later than you will now. Hitching a lift or walking would have taken way more time than me driving you.'

'Fair enough,' he said.

What was this? Why was I locked in a loop, experiencing constant reruns of this early morning car journey from every angle? Was I now going to experience what it was like to be in a car crash? Would I feel the force as we slammed into the lamppost? Would I have to watch the man I loved die?

And yet there was no fear. Was I dead already? Was this what happened? Do we just keep reliving the moment of death, like some sort of repetitive purgatory?

'How are you feeling now?' Kathryn asked.

Ed shrugged. 'I'm scared to say it, you know, tempting fate and all that, but it kind of feels like the end of something and the start of something new.'

Was this the last exchange they had before impact? Was this why she – I – didn't see the bike as it shot out from the common? Because her eyes were on him instead of the road?

And then as the car passed an avenue of trees, I spotted someone on a bicycle, slowing to a standstill and waiting for us to pass.

Ed glanced over to where the cyclist waited.

'Mental, out on a bike this time of the morning.'

Kathryn shrugged. 'Maybe it's safer when there's less traffic.'

A sleek black sports car swept past in the opposite direction at that moment and I turned to see its brake lights as it slowed to let the cyclist cross the road.

'Nice motor,' Ed said, admiringly.

My mind began to spin as I realised that yet another version was now playing out. One in which no one had died on that misty morning. There was nothing for it but to stop trying to make sense of it all. What I needed to do right now was surrender to it because, on some level, I knew there was no other way.

Would I shortly wake with a jolt, twenty years in the future, and for a split second think that the past had been rewritten, before slowly and painfully realising that it was all a wild, if cruel, dream. Or having been transported from scene to scene so seamlessly that it felt I was following a narrative arc, could it be something else?

And then darkness fell.

Chapter 21

2013

It felt like forever since she had laid on the grass and watched the clouds drift. Wasn't that for children and young couples in love?

They were down by the lighthouse where the land suddenly ended, giving way to the Atlantic waters far below. At night, the lighthouse beam lit up the landscape for miles around, but today, in the warm April sunshine, the shaft of light was invisible.

'I hope you realise how lucky you are to live somewhere like this,' Elaine said. 'I mean, it's a bit of heaven, isn't it?'

'You could say that,' Kathryn replied. 'But it took me a long time to appreciate it.'

Elaine sat up, wrapped her arms around her knees and looked down at Kathryn.

'We tell ourselves stories about the way things are, or at least how we imagine them to be. And you know what? That's usually exactly what they are. Just stories.'

Kathryn, seeing her reflection in Elaine's sunglasses, looked away, out across the sparkling blue waters. She waited for her friend to elaborate.

'Like all those years we were apart,' Elaine continued. 'I thought you were too busy having a whale of a time in your own little paradise over here in the middle of nowhere. I thought you'd left me behind.'

Kathryn pulled herself up.

'And I thought you were wrapped up in Rob and that I was just someone from your past. That your life had moved on.'

She looked back towards the house where Rob was sitting, wrapped up in a duffle coat despite the balmy temperatures. His wheelchair had been pushed to the edge of the paving, and he now lifted his arms to allow Mark to tuck a green tartan blanket over him.

'I was wrapped up in him but maybe not quite as you imagined,' Elaine said, lifting her sunglasses, her eyes following Kathryn's.

'You should have told me. I could have come over; given you a break.'

Elaine smiled. 'Yes, well, I probably wouldn't have let you. He needs me but I need him too. I wouldn't have had it any other way.'

'And to think that I actually thought he was abusive to you, when we met. I feel awful about that now.'

'When he was texting me, you mean? He'd fallen. That happened a lot back then, which is why I couldn't leave him for long.' She pulled her sunglasses down and her voice quivered. 'But hey, we've gone beyond that now.'

Kathryn lay her hand on her friend's arm.

'You know we're always here. Or I can come over to you. But when the time comes, you won't be on your own.'

Elaine nodded. 'I know.'

#

It was later that evening, when the sun had set and the house was quiet, that they finally spoke about it. Mark was out walking the dog and Elaine had settled Rob in the downstairs bedroom, leaving the door ajar so she could hear him if he needed her.

'When did you go all posh with a teapot?' Elaine asked with a wry grin, watching Kathryn pour tea into two cups. 'Teabags were good enough in our day.'

'It's an Irish thing,' Kathryn explained, pushing a cup over to her friend.

Elaine took a chocolate biscuit from the tin.

'You always did have nice biscuits,' she said, taking a bite. 'I never got out of the habit of buying plain ones, like my mum.'

'Habits,' Kathryn said, 'Who says we need to shake them off?'

The lengthening shadows of evening made the room seem less muddled than it looked in daylight. Since taking on staff and, more recently, a partner in his accountancy firm, Mark had been able to take more of a back seat at work. It didn't stop him littering most of the surfaces in the kitchen and sitting room with files and papers though. Although Kathryn had suggested it, Mark had not been able to bring himself to convert Alice's bedroom into a home office, despite the fact she hadn't lived there since leaving for college three years ago.

'Mark was telling Rob earlier that Alice is enjoying her new job,' Elaine said, shifting in the armchair to tuck a leg underneath her.

Kathryn smiled, as much at the sight of Elaine sitting in the same way she had as a teenager as the news of her daughter's latest adventure.

'And how's she getting on with her aunt?' Elaine asked, one eyebrow raised.

'If I told you they got on like a house on fire, would you believe me?' Kathryn replied, rifling in the biscuit tin.

'Knowing them both, it doesn't surprise me one bit.'

It had surprised Kathryn when her daughter had sent a flurry of texts enthusing about her aunt, who had graciously offered to put her up until she found her feet in Boston. Aunt and niece had not met before and the young woman Beth met off the Shannon flight at Logan Airport was a virtual stranger but, still, an instant rapport had been established.

'Funny that she never came home. And all those years we thought she was living the high life. I suppose it's easy enough to keep up the pretence through letters and photos. I mean, to think that her life was nothing like we guessed,' Elaine said.

They had all been surprised to discover that Beth's fortunes had taken something of a turn for the worst in recent years. Relationships had come and gone, lasting a couple of years, until finally she was alone. Her career had dwindled as her place as the young star of the office was snatched by a succession of ambitious, media-savvy twenty-somethings. And yet it had never been an option to come home. Not that she regarded England as her home anymore; she had left it so long ago.

'Beth's been pretty good,' Kathryn conceded. 'She's really taken Alice under her wing. Actually, Mark was saying the other day that Beth is probably getting as much out of it as Alice.'

'Well, at least you'll know that Alice is well-chaperoned. I bet Beth won't give her a minute's peace,' Elaine noticed Kathryn's expression, 'What?'

Kathryn shook her head, pushing the biscuit tin across to her friend.

'Nothing,' she said affectionately. 'Please don't ever change.'

Elaine looked around the room appreciatively and gestured towards the black stove in the corner, laid with paper and sticks for the next cold day.

'I always fancied a stove but there isn't room in our flat. As it is, it's like a hothouse. You know what it's like in modern buildings.'

'I can light it if you'd like? It's getting a bit chilly and it really cheers up the room.'

Kathryn took a box of matches from the shelf above the stove. Shaking it, she realised it was empty. So she fished in her pocket and pulled out the square, silver lighter. It sat in her pocket always, so she could feel the pressure of it against her skin. A talisman of sorts.

Pushing the lid open with her thumb, she struck down on the small metal wheel and a flame flickered. She opened the door of the stove and held the flame to the paper until it caught light with a satisfying *whoosh*.

'What's that you've got there?' Elaine asked, inquisitively. 'A Zippo?'

Kathryn felt the familiar weight of it, smooth in the palm of her hand.

'Let's have a look. I haven't seen one of them in years.'

Hesitantly, Kathryn handed it over. Elaine frowned as she held it up to the light.

She read the engraved words and then looked back at Kathryn, puzzled.

'This is Ed's lighter?'

Kathryn had turned back to the stove, closing the door gently with a click.

'So if you gave it to him – what? – twenty-odd years ago. How on earth do you still have it?'

Watching the flames licking and darting around a glowing

log, Kathryn caught Elaine's reflection in the glass of the stove. If she turned to face her, she'd have no choice but to tell the truth. But maybe if she stayed like this, absorbed by the fiery display, Elaine might lose interest in a lighter from long ago, and a name from the past. They hadn't spoken about Ed at all. There was no reason why they should. In Elaine's eyes, he was simply a sad remnant of their youth.

But no, Kathryn wouldn't allow him to be left there. In the past.

Feeling the heat on her cheeks, she turned to her friend.

'I've wanted to tell you so often, but it never felt right. I suppose now's as good a time as any. I'm warning you though, you might not believe me.'

Chapter 22

She had felt rather as she imagined someone who had spent years in a coma might feel when they finally came back into the world.

Unsure of what was real and what was imagined, having to believe what you were told rather than what you remembered. Not for the first time, her world felt upended and as if everything that had once made sense had been scooped out, so that all that was left was an outline of what her life had been. Vagueness was now her safest bet. That way, she didn't say something that led to that look, now familiar, of concern in the other person's eyes. It was barely perceptible but she knew it was there. She knew what they were thinking. That she had gone mad.

Looking back, she wondered if she had suffered something like a nervous breakdown. Could you have something like a nervous breakdown or was it a case that you had one or you didn't? Again, she didn't know. That was a common theme in the weeks and months that followed – how much she realised she didn't know. And so she withdrew into herself, stayed on safe subjects. Like what happened yesterday, the weather, her shopping list.

What she did know was that on a late afternoon in November she had walked into the trees at the top of Chanctonbury Hill and, the next moment, she was sitting in her car at the bottom of the slope with no memory of how she got there. On the horizon, a pink layer of sky encroached on the darkness above, hinting at the light to come. Shivering in the damp chill of the car, she turned the key in the ignition to light the dashboard and saw that it was seven o'clock in the morning.

And just like that, fifteen hours of her life had evaporated and her mind felt wiped of thought.

'Pull yourself together,' she muttered, picking up her phone from the passenger seat.

There were three missed calls and two text messages. Gripped by an unfathomable guilt, as if she had been caught getting up to something, she opened the first text, sent at nine o'clock last night. It was Elaine.

I've tried ringing but no joy. You OK?

She had texted again two hours later.

I'll try you in the morning. I'm dying to know if you've read all the letters yet.

The box of letters. There it was, on the passenger seat.

Had it really all been a dream then? Had she had found her way back to the car after her walk, fallen asleep and dreamt of him again? But the ringing of her phone would have woken her, wouldn't it?

She decided to drive back to her mum's, grab a couple of hours sleep and then text Elaine. It would put her mind at rest and that would be that.

Except that wasn't that.

When she fell back into the single bed in her mum's spare room, she slept so deeply that when she finally woke, it was dark again and she only had the energy to have a quick shower and feed the cat before climbing back under the quilt. She felt jet-lagged, aware that she should get up but craving sleep and, above all, just wanting to be left alone to piece together the fragments of scenes that flashed across her mind without her bidding – a bicycle speeding along on a misty morning, steam rising from the twisted wreckage of a car, the patterned cover on her bed in university.

When she thought of him, she began to cry. She remembered the funeral. How worn and hollowed-out his father had looked, clutching Linda's arm. Ed's mother hadn't been notified – Terry wouldn't hear of it and Kathryn hadn't had it in her to push the point. Paul had sat next to her in the front pew, staring blankly as the priest summarised the life of someone none of them really knew. She had felt a hot, burning rage inside at that point and had to sit outside and feel the breeze on her face to calm down before retaking her seat. They hadn't ever had a clue about who he really was. None of them had.

His funeral now felt like a scene from a movie that had ended up on the cutting room floor, discarded as superfluous to the storyline. And there were others too. Like sitting in the kitchen days after Ed's death, trying to read a book and ignore the gabble of the television her parents were watching when the doorbell rang. It was Mark. He had followed her to her room, produced a box of tissues and a bottle of wine and sat with her as she sobbed until her eyes stung. But now, when she tried to focus on it, the scene faded so that she couldn't even be sure if it had happened.

She hardly knew what was real anymore.

And then something happened that swept all doubt away.

Unable to face talking to anyone yet after her dream-like lost hours, Kathryn had managed to keep Mark and Elaine at bay with text messages. She told them she had eaten something that didn't agree with her, probably some chicken her mum had left in the fridge, and was staying in bed until she felt brighter. She crawled from her bed to the sitting room, where she watched television behind closed curtains and wondered how she could ever step into her old self again and show her face to the world outside the front door.

It was on the third day that daytime television lost its appeal to such a degree that she couldn't bring herself to switch it on. Kathryn looked around her and wondered what she could do to kill time. With few options to choose from, she decided to put a wash on.

She picked up her jeans and navy cardigan from the dressing table stool at the bottom of her bed. The knitwear was new so she wasn't sure if she should risk putting it on a normal cycle, and was just checking the label when she heard something drop with a thud onto the carpet.

Clearly the room had either escaped the gradual redecoration of the bungalow or was on the end of a long list because the geometric pattern of the carpet wasn't her mother's taste. What had fallen from the cardigan pocket lay almost camouflaged among the grey and white oblongs and stripes.

If she hadn't heard it fall, she probably wouldn't have seen it there next to the leg of the bed and it could have lain undiscovered for years. The thought sent a shiver through her. Because then she wouldn't have ever known. Not for sure.

She felt the cool smoothness of the lighter as she turned it over to reveal the words she knew were engraved across it.

\#

It was reassuringly easy to fool her mother when she arrived home from Yeovil a few days later. With the high spirits of someone who had enjoyed a change of scene and company after so many years of solitude, Valerie filled her daughter in on every last detail of her time away. Kathryn was relieved to hear her mother's enthusiastic chatter because, if nothing else, it kept the attention off her and how she had spent her time. When the question finally came, as she knew it would, she had at least had enough time to come up with something that would allow the conversation to slide onwards again.

'And you weren't bored? Not even a little?' her mother persisted.

'Bored?' Kathryn had replied, feigning surprise. 'The time just flew. I met Elaine a few times, her brother as well. I got a few books out of the library, went walking each day. I can't believe the fortnight's over.'

She didn't meet up with Elaine again before she left. Knowing that she would have to come clean, that her friend would immediately spot that something was amiss, Kathryn avoided her calls until, after a week, they stopped. Knowing that Elaine would feel hurt, even shunned, weighed heavy on Kathryn but she couldn't speak to her. Not at the moment. Because she knew that Elaine wouldn't believe her and she couldn't face the doubt on her friend's face. She wouldn't have believed it either, if she didn't have his lighter in the breast pocket of her shirt.

She was sitting in the airport lounge waiting for the departure gate to be announced when she felt her phone vibrate in her pocket. She jumped, jolting her cup so her tea spilt onto the silver-topped table in front of her and dripped onto her jeans. She had been debating whether to get a fresh pot, even though this was the third one she had ordered since she'd arrived. She had been far too early. Even her mother had suggested that she shouldn't drop the hire car back at the airport so early because the problem with arriving early at an airport was that you ended up spending money you didn't have on perfume and whisky you didn't need.

Checking the phone, Kathryn frowned at the strange number. But a thought, buried deep, and one she hardly dared to bring into the light, struck her. She should answer it, just in case.

'Hello?'

'I thought you might pick up if I used a different phone.'

Elaine sounded put out and Kathryn didn't know how to respond. She watched the dark patch of tea spread across her thigh, irritated with herself for daring to hope that it could be – who? Someone who died long ago but who she happened to dream about lately?

'Kathryn? Hello? Are you there?' Elaine's voice, the hurt dropped, was now concerned.

'Yeah, sorry. I've just thrown tea all over myself.' It was all she could think of to say.

Elaine laughed. 'You're at the airport in plenty of time then. I called your mum and she said I'd probably catch you.'

After another minute of small talk about Valerie's trip, there was silence.

'What did I do, Kathryn?' Elaine eventually said, quietly. 'Was it because I didn't let you come back with me to the flat?'

'What? No, of course not.'

'Because it's not what you think. I mean, I've a lot to tell you but now's not the right time. It's one of the reasons I wanted to meet up again. To explain.'

But there was no time for explanations. The departures board was now flashing 'gate number in 2 minutes' next to Cork.

'Look, I'm sorry Elaine, but they're about to announce my gate number.'

'Okay, I'll let you go. But we'll speak soon? Promise? There's a lot we've to catch up on.'

'Of course. And Elaine?'

'Yes?'

'I'm really glad we've found each other again.'

'Me too. My mum used to say that as we get older, we should keep around us, those who knew us when we were young.'

Kathryn was now gripping the phone between her shoulder and chin while she reached for her small case under the table. 'We're still quite young, Elaine.'

'Yes, I know, but we couldn't even imagine being this age when we were kids, could we?'

'I don't know. Probably not,' Kathryn answered distractedly, checking her bag for her boarding pass. Why, when she'd been sitting in the airport for so long, had she not found it before? It could only be in her bag. Although, wait a minute, she remembered folding it. She checked her jean pockets. Still nothing.

Kathryn tried to think when she had last seen the boarding pass and if it could have been mixed up with the rubbish she'd emptied from her bag into a bin outside the terminal. She swallowed hard and saw Gate 14 flick up on the departures board. Maybe if she hurried, she could return to the desk, but that would mean going back through security and she was pretty sure that once through, there was no going back.

And now Elaine was talking again, like someone who didn't have to be anywhere soon, who had an empty afternoon to fill, who hadn't noticed that the person on the other end of the phone was in a hurry.

'We wouldn't have had a clue what being forty was like. Except old, that is.'

Kathryn froze.

Those words came tumbling down through the years. A different voice in a different place. And in that moment, her search for the boarding pass faded into insignificance. Elaine's inane chatter had just dredged a brief exchange from the far reaches of Kathryn's memory. Back then, it had been forgotten in an instant. The conversation had moved on swiftly but it was as if those words had drifted onwards across the years, into a new century, to be repeated by Elaine.

Kathryn spotted the boarding card poking out of her book and smiled. She'd get on the plane, return home, catch up with Elaine properly on the phone in the next few days and, most importantly of all, allow this glimmer of hope she was feeling to flicker into life.

Chapter 23

Nineteen weeks. That's all she had to wait, Sometimes she counted the days. One hundred and thirty eight to be precise, from the moment she had understood that there was a chance, a slim chance admittedly, but the one lifeline that remained.

Sometimes she deliberately held off checking her diary. If she denied herself the daily ritual of crossing off another day, she felt the deep stir in her stomach that came when she realised she was closer to the date that she thought.

She occasionally allowed herself to skim through social media but always came up blank. It turned out that there was a surprising number of people in the world with his name, most of whom had next to no information on their social media pages. The others' photos showed they were either much younger, much older or just not him. She typed his name into a search engine sometimes but found nothing.

Christmas came and went, providing something of a distraction if only because it was Alice's first time home after leaving for college in September. She came back as she had left, with a flourish, her energy rebounding off the walls of the house that had been so quiet without her. Not that Kathryn minded the silence. In fact, she had started actively seeking it out. If Mark was in the house, she would take Charlie for a walk along the path that traced the peninsula. It took a little under two hours and, in that time, with no traffic and few walkers, she could indulge herself with thoughts of a certain place and a certain time.

If she hadn't had the date fixed in her mind, a far off light she was making her way steadily towards, she would have felt bereft. The date, the lighter and the box of letters were all that was keeping her going.

She hadn't dreamt of him in months, not since that night in her mother's bungalow, before events took a turn, pulling her into their shared past. But what of the present? The future?

At times, she doubted if any of it was real. He had died on August 18th 1993. Everyone knew that. She was the only one spinning out a fantasy that he was still out there somewhere. A fantasy based on glimpses, dream-like, from an in-between world where she had visited their younger selves. And like dreams, the more she tried to remember details, the more the memories slipped away, into a misty landscape where nothing was clear.

But all the while, she kept the lighter close to her skin. Solid and real, it was her one indication – her one piece of evidence – that something had happened that evening that she couldn't make sense of but which she chose to believe.

Kathryn's spirits finally lifted one morning in late March when, unusual for this southernmost tip of Ireland, frost still coated the ground, icing over puddles and freezing the cobwebs on the icy bars of the galvanised gate leading down to the lighthouse. Watching her breath captured on the chilly air, she smiled as Charlie scooted through the crackling grass.

She sighed when she turned into the driveway and saw Mark's car was still there. He had said he had an early meeting this morning and she was looking forward to having the house to herself, at least for an hour or two, and so it was with a frown that she pulled her wellingtons off in the porch and pushed the door open.

She could hear Mark's voice from the kitchen and guessed he must have decided against driving into town because the roads might be icy. Typical Mark. Cautious to the point of neurotic. No doubt he would complain, as usual, that the gritter lorries would have been out before dawn back in Britain to make the roads safe. And once again, she would reply that a light scattering of frost was hardly worth gritting.

She shrugged off her coat and hung it on the hook behind the door. She noticed that Mark's voice stopped suddenly when Charlie pushed his way into the kitchen. And by the time she got to the kitchen, Mark was perched in the chair by the stove with a newspaper open on his lap. If he had been holding the newspaper upside down, he couldn't have looked more like someone who had just narrowly avoided being caught red-handed.

Kathryn put the kettle on.

'Who was that?' She asked, knowing that she had walked in on something he would rather she knew nothing about.

He looked up from his newspaper, affecting surprise.

'Oh, nobody in particular. Much of a frost out there?'

'Not really.'

'Martin said he'd be delayed so we moved the meeting to ten,' he said. 'Don't worry, I'll soon be out from under your feet.'

'You're not under my feet, Mark.'

He picked up his phone from the table and slid it into the pocket of his trousers. Charlie waddled over and stared up at him with that adoring look that only Labradors can give and Mark bent down and scratched his chocolate brown head.

'Was that Martin on the phone?' She knew she was probing but he was acting so suspiciously that she couldn't resist. Usually an open book, he couldn't keep a secret if his life depended on it.

'No, it was Elaine.'

He picked up a mug from the table and carried it over to the dishwasher.

'Is everything okay?'

Rearranging things in the dishwasher in an obvious attempt not to make eye contact, he said, 'Yes, they're fine.'

'So why did she ring? We only spoke last night.'

He hesitated for a moment, before straightening and turning to look at her.

'I rang her, Kathryn.'

Kathryn frowned, confused. As far as she could remember, Mark had never rung her friend before.

'What for? I mean, you could have spoken to her last night.'

He turned and slammed the dishwasher door shut, his reaction catching her off guard.

'She was the only person I could ask,' he said, running his hand through his hair.

'Ask about what?'

Mark now took a deep breath and closed his eyes.

'About the flight and hotel you've booked a few days after your birthday.' He opened his eyes and looked at her directly. 'About why you're keeping things secret.'

Kathryn's heart hammered in her chest. Of course, she was going to tell Mark at some point. Wasn't she? It was her past that she was trying to work out, not an affair she was hiding from him.

'It's not a big deal,' she said. 'Really it isn't.' Even as she spoke the words, she knew it sounded as if she was lying. Because she was. This was more than a big deal. It had consumed her ever since she returned from England.

Mark pulled out a chair and sat at the table. 'I wasn't

prying. I had to go on your laptop to find the plumber's email, you know, to ask him to come out about the tap in the bathroom, and a new message flashed up. It was a flight reminder for a few days after your birthday, which seemed strange so I had a look.'

They had always been truthful with each other in their marriage. She had never lied about who she had met, where she had been, what she had spent. There had never been any need. She had never needed to keep anything from him, except perhaps her thoughts, her regrets. But her visit to England had changed all that. She hadn't told him about her experience on Chanctonbury Hill, the peculiar discovery of the lighter, the fact that Ed's letters were now buried underneath a pile of jumpers at the bottom of her wardrobe.

Her mind trawled through people she could pretend to be visiting but the problem with someone knowing your life as thoroughly as Mark knew hers, was that he knew everyone she knew, both now and in her past. She toyed with the idea of telling him she was paying her mother a surprise visit, but knew he had seen that she was flying to Liverpool Airport, five hours north of her mother's home.

'I rang Elaine because I thought that maybe you had planned something together,' he said. 'But she knew nothing about it.'

The kettle was now hissing and Kathryn watched the water bubbling behind the glass as it reached boiling point.

'You couldn't have just asked me?' Kathryn could hear how cold her voice sounded.

'Maybe I didn't trust you to tell the truth.'

'When have I not told you the truth?' she asked, playing for time while her mind raced.

'Well, that's just it, isn't it? How would I know?'

Kathryn's face flushed with annoyance, but the sight of Mark with his head in his hands, looking so defeated, made her feel guilty.

'Kathryn, are you having an affair?' he said.

'Of course not,' she replied, wearily.

He rubbed his eyes and she could see tears glistening on his cheeks.

'We've ticked along for years but I know these things happen. People get in a rut. Bored. What I'm trying to say is, well, I've sometimes wondered if we're becoming that couple. You know, looking elsewhere for something new.'

How could she tell him that she wasn't looking for something new but wanted to find what she had lost so long ago. How she had no idea if she was deluded or whether there was really someone out there who only existed because she travelled back twenty years to change the past.

'If you must know, I just wanted to get away for a day or two, a birthday present to myself.'

'It's just when I saw Liverpool, I thought that...'

She cut in, the story taking shape. 'I wanted to go to Manchester, go along to the museums, do a bit of shopping, and it was easier to catch an early flight to Liverpool and get the coach than wait for a later flight to Manchester.'

His face brightened and she could tell he had chosen to believe her.

'I didn't think you'd mind.'

Mark nodded, 'Why didn't you just tell me though?'

Kathryn, feeling guilty that it had been so easy to fool him, turned back to the kettle unable to answer.

'I know you must have thought about him over the years.'

'Who?' Kathryn asked.

'Ed.'

His name made her start. 'Well, yes, of course I've thought about him.'

And then he spoke the words that confirmed that something had altered, something she would never be able to fathom.

'I suppose I just always thought there'd come a point when you'd try to find him. To reconnect. It's something I've always dreaded. I'm just surprised that you never tried to find him. You know, what with it being so easy these days with social media.'

Mark was worried about her reconnecting with a person who was alive, making his own way somewhere out there in the world. As she stood staring at Mark, it felt as if the world was tilting and that nothing was as it seemed. Ed wasn't dead.

Chapter 24

So how do you mark the day you meet again after twenty years apart? Divided not by death but by a moment, not yet remembered, when one of you decided to leave, to unravel two paths so that they diverged and stretched away into the future, into opposite directions.

Or the day when you have to face your own delusion?

Kathryn's thoughts had darted between the two realities for weeks and now that she was here, just hours from her answer, she told herself to settle down. After all, if she was deluded, nobody in the world except Elaine would ever know and she could fall back on her mythical trip to Manchester, as she fell back into the knowledge that her life with Mark was all there was and that she would just have to make the best of it.

She tried to distract herself with the display rack of postcards in the corner of the village post office. Glossy photos of purple moorland, wildflower meadows, stone walls crisscrossing steep grassy hillsides. She picked a selection, then glanced at her watch. Was he making his way here? Her heart skipped and she told herself again not to tempt fate. The chance of him being here today was slim. She knew that.

Did the evidence really add up to Ed being alive? It was all so unbelievable, so far from what most people called normal life, that her sensible side often stepped in and tried to convince her that Ed was dead and nothing had changed.

And even if the past had been rewritten and he was still alive, he could have forgotten all about their plan to come back here on this date. After all, if Elaine hadn't said something, by complete chance, to jog her memory, wouldn't Kathryn have forgotten it too?

She flicked through the books in the shop and considered for a moment whether to pick one for Alice before reminding herself that this was a break from her real life and for the next two days she was not Kathryn Johnson, mother and wife, she was just Kat. She could be responsible for the remaining three hundred and sixty three days of the year. For now, she was giving herself permission to forget her life and focus on what lay ahead.

The shop was a small treasure trove, so different to how she remembered it all those years ago. Then there had been a pile of newspapers and probably the same display rack, but with less glossy postcards and a few dusty birthday cards. Now, as she was poking through a pile of woollen hats, she caught sight of herself in a mirror on the wall in front of her. She looked tired. But no wonder, as she had left home so early. It hadn't felt real, none of it, until she found herself in the hire car making her way out of the airport. Liverpool Airport, of all places. She hadn't booked her flight out of sentimentality – it was simply the nearest – and hadn't given much thought to how she would feel when she found herself half a mile from Ed's old home. But as she drove out past the housing estates of Speke, along the same roads she had driven in her old car with Ed by her side, she was gripped by a fierce sense of nostalgia.

There was the pedestrian crossing they had crossed to catch the bus into the city; the lane that led through the industrial estate to the wood where he had told her about his mother; the convenience store – now a mobile phone shop – where Paul had been caught shoplifting. Just a year.

That's all it had been. But those days were preserved in aspic in her mind while the years that had passed since now felt blurry and indistinct.

After checking that there was nobody else in the post office, except for the elderly postmaster busy stamping parcels, she looked more closely at herself in the mirror, running her fingers through her hair and noticing its subtle golden highlights picked out by the sun shining through the open doorway. Her stylist had been right about the layers and fringe, they did make her feel like a new woman. Or partially right, because as well as the new look, it had been the promise of the day ahead, which was proving to be so revitalising, her North Star.

It was a Saturday and the parking spaces on the edge of the green were gradually filling. Two cyclists were pulling their mountain bikes from the rack on the back of their car, while outside the newsagents, an older couple were fussing with bowls of water for their two cocker spaniels, which yapped and spun, eager to get out onto the footpaths into the wild country beyond. A colony of hikers marched in formation up the road, their sticks clicking on the tarmac as they spoke to each other in low voices, conserving their energy for what lay ahead.

There was a sense of sanctuary here. It was a place where people gathered before exploring the surrounding remoteness, only to return for refreshments before taking the road back home to their lives. As Kathryn watched life playing out on the grass in front of her, she knew she too would be returning to her life tomorrow night but, in the meantime, the magic of this place could do its work. If it came to nothing and she was here alone, then she would just have to make the best of it.

After checking in at the old inn, she stood for a moment to look at her watch. Why did she keep checking the time? He had suggested they meet on April 20th; he hadn't got as far as suggesting a time. She couldn't sit on the bench all afternoon, waiting. She had to trust that if he was coming, he would find her. And if he didn't appear at all, then she would fly home tomorrow night and do her best to put this all behind her. There didn't seem to be another choice.

She decided to walk down to the swing bridge that straddled the fast-flowing expanse of the River Swale and then take the track through the fields to the ancient church of St Andrew's. It was along this path that the dead had been carried during the years of the plague and for centuries it had been known as the Corpse Way.

But it was hard to imagine such darkness as Kathryn unclipped the gate on top of the bridge and wandered across the wooden slats, watching the water glint below. In her mind's eye, she saw flashes of Ed rolling his jeans to his knees before crossing the river as a dare while she laughed on the bank, demure and covered up, despite his teasing.

She now squinted against the sun at the high moorland above and remembered how he had pulled off his t-shirt to bask in the heat on one particularly sweltering afternoon before pulling her to him. They had stayed there for hours until hunger made them dress and become respectable again. Deeply buried memories now surfaced, feeling just a fingertip away.

She wandered inside the church and because there was no reason not to, she squeezed into the back pew and sat down. Looking around with the self-consciousness of someone who rarely went to church, she was relieved to see she was alone. She closed her eyes.

'Dear God.' She cringed at the childish-sounding words, but continued. 'Please let him remember and please let him be here today. I don't know how I'll cope if he isn't. Amen.'

She dipped into her pocket for a pound coin. On the rare occasions she had been inside a church, she always seemed to be asking for something and as she pushed the coin into the slot of the collection tin and heard it hit the bottom with a metallic clang, she felt a little easier.

Opposite the church was a pub with a sign welcoming dogs and dirty boots but, although she was hungry, she walked on. The village was only a mile away and, glancing at her watch, she worked out that she would be back at the green by five. Cars passed steadily and serious-looking cyclists pedalled by.

Her phone beeped in her pocket. Mark always told her not to keep her phone there. Something about electromagnetic radiation.

All ok?

She texted as she walked.

Yes, checked in and just setting off now.

His answer came back quickly.

Have fun. There's an exhibition on Ancient Greece in the museum near Manchester University. Might be worth a visit.

At the bottom of the hill, she was faced with a fork in the road. From her earlier explorations, she knew that if she swung up to the right, she could take a cobbled shortcut that came out near the post office. It was shorter but steeper and, at the top, she stopped to catch her breath. From this vantage point, she could see that there were more cars in the village now and her heart raced at the thought that one of them might be his.

Calm down, she told herself. Remember how unlikely it is that he's here.

When she reached the green, she could see that the bench by the war memorial was empty. She wandered over to it and sat down. She watched an elderly lady emerge from the congregational chapel across the grass, a broom in her hand. Further up the green, three teenage boys cycled around the bandstand, their voices carrying on the breeze to where she sat. A young waitress came out of one of the pubs and gathered plates from the picnic tables, shouting something across to the boys with the familiarity of youngsters who had known each other all of their lives.

Checking her watch again – ten past five – she told herself there was still time. No need to give up hope yet. She would go back to the inn, tidy herself up, maybe get something to eat and then come back out with a book. Anything rather than sit and wait and wonder if she had got it all wrong.

After a little deliberation, and because it was still warm, she picked the bright red sleeveless shirt from her case and changed into the Levi's she had bought in a vintage shop in Cork city a few weeks earlier. As she stood in front of the bathroom mirror, pulling the mascara wand through her lashes, she felt excitement swirling in her stomach. Maybe, just maybe. And if so, she wanted to look her best for him.

She hadn't worn perfume in years but had recently bought a bottle of Calvin Klein Eternity, which she had worn when she was young. Now, as she sprayed it at her throat, the scent pulled her back to that year with him. Their relationship had been so intense, but what if he turned up and wasn't the Ed in her memory? What if they had nothing to say to each other, searching for golden memories which, pulled into the present, faded and disintegrated in front of them?

Her excitement receded and she wondered again if she was making a mistake. She felt the day's earlier promise slip away and reminded herself that, whatever happened, at least she'd tried. She had honoured her part of their youthful agreement and could return home to come to terms with the fact that it was over and he was gone from her life forever.

She had opened the window earlier to let the sun into the room and now, as she reached up to slide the sash down, she glanced across the green. There were the usual dog walkers, a young couple dismantling a buggy, the boys on their bikes still egging each other on and, on the bench by the war memorial, someone sitting alone.

She knew instantly that it was him.

They had changed the past and he hadn't forgotten.

As she hurried down the stairs, through the empty bar and out into the sunlight, she felt that oddest sense of being out of her body, just as she had that first day she saw him at the racecourse. With the rhythmic drum of blood pounding in her ears, and a delicious squirm of excitement in the pit of her stomach, she crossed the grass.

She would have known him anywhere. Sitting as he used to, leaning forward, his elbows on his knees, he was looking into the distance in a way that reminded her of the first time she had driven to Liverpool to meet him. He had waited for her then as he was waiting for her now.

'You probably thought I'd never get here,' she said. It felt like a script from long ago, from a grey winter afternoon beneath the statue of Queen Victoria, the past overlaying the present.

He looked round quickly, jolted from his thoughts. He had hardly changed; maybe a little fuller in the face, a little broader in the shoulders. His hair, still cut short, was flecked here and there with grey but, searching his eyes, she saw the lad she had known and loved.

'You're here,' he said, jumping up.

Emotions surged through her that went far beyond happiness or excitement. He was here and she was home. After half a lifetime – and for the first time in what felt like forever – she remembered what it was to feel pure, unchecked joy.

She was her nineteen year old self again catching his eye over the racecourse railings, feeling that same delicious thrill as she stared at him, the world seeming to judder to a halt. All that existed in that moment was the two of them.

'Yes, I'm here,' she said, laughing.

Before she could say another word, he pulled her into a tight hug. His neck was warm against her cheek and she could smell his aftershave, more expensive than the Lynx he had used years ago. Standing back, holding her at arm's length, his eyes took her in.

'You're just the same,' he smiled, shaking his head as if he couldn't believe that she was standing here in front of him.

It was flattery but she grinned anyway.

It was then that she spotted the ring on his fourth finger.

So he was married. She hadn't been expecting that. Maybe his wife was with him, watching her husband meet an ex-girlfriend from long ago, giving them time to say hello before coming over to join them.

She glanced over her shoulder.

'Looking for someone?' he asked.

'Are you on your own?' she asked.

'Course. Why wouldn't I be?' he said, and then his eyes followed hers to the golden band glinting in the sunshine.

'Long story. I've got so much to tell you, Kat.'

Her heart skipped to hear him say her name – the name he had given her – once more.

Chapter 25

They were staying in the same inn and when Kathryn came down from her room before dinner, she could see he had beaten her to it and was sitting at the table by the fireplace looking at a menu. She hesitated a moment, taking in the way he chewed at a fingernail, the way his shoulders hunched. Habits that remained.

She had thought about changing yet again but couldn't decide what to wear. The discarded tops and skirts lay in a heap on the floor of her room and she was still in the same jeans and red shirt. Shaking her hair loose, she had combed some mousse through it to give it a wilder, more carefree look, and added a daring slick of red lipstick.

As she reached the table, he glanced up and she thought with a dart of pleasure that she saw his eyes widen a little.

'Cider?' he said and, when she nodded, he smiled and went to the bar.

She looked around, trying to appear detached, casual, before letting her gaze fall on him as he stood with his back turned waiting to order. He had changed into a green flannel shirt and different jeans. He'd made an effort, she noticed with a thrill.

He came back with two pints of cider. She hadn't drunk a pint in years.

'So,' he said, putting the glass down in front of her. 'We're here. How did that happen?'

He looked at her with a faint smile that she tried to read and failed. She needed him to take the lead, to give her a sense of what had led them here because she was completely clueless.

Finding him had obliterated all of her ideas about how the world worked.

'Okay,' he said, straightening the fork beside his placemat. He hesitated and looked up at her again. 'I don't know what to say. How much you know? How much do I know, come to think of it.'

They were interrupted by the waitress arriving to take their order. When she had gone, Kathryn decided to ask Ed the question that had been on her mind since she saw the ring on his finger. There was so much to talk about but she needed to get this question out of the way.

'Who's the lucky lady?'

He began to fidget with the fork again.

'Not so lucky,' he said quietly.

'Come on, Ed. She's the luckiest woman I know if she's married to you.' The cider was obviously starting to have an effect. She wanted him to know what he meant to her – then and now.

'Was the luckiest woman.'

Kathryn frowned, confused. If he was divorced or separated, why was he still wearing his wedding ring? 'She died.' His voice was now barely audible.

As Ed told her the harrowing details of how he had lost his wife, Kathryn listened intently, her heart breaking for him. He had only known Louise for a year before they got married quickly, and they were only a couple of years into their new life together when she was diagnosed with an aggressive form of cancer.

'She didn't have a chance,' Ed said, looking away. 'It was too late to operate and we lost her three months later. She was only twenty-seven.'

'Oh God, Ed,' Kathryn began, but he held up a hand to stop the flow of sympathy before it began.

'It was a long time ago and I'm managing okay. Really. And at least Simon was young, so most of it went over his head.'

'Simon?'

'Our boy. He was only a toddler.'

Kathryn was thankful that Ed had someone, a boy who needed him.

'Who's looking after Simon now?'

'He's with my mum. Only too glad to get rid of his old man and be spoilt by his nan.'

'It's worked out then. You and your mum. What about Paul? Linda? Your dad?'

The conversation flowed as he explained how Terry was much the same, still drinking like a fish, still trying it on with women young enough to be his daughter. 'He hit rock bottom when Linda found a fella from Cheadle and moved away. Paul too. They're as bad as each other but I suppose they've propped each other up over the years. Still living in the same house. Still driving the neighbours mad.'

Kathryn laughed. 'I liked Linda. And Paul. Despite everything.'

In the glow of the fire – and of the cider she was now finishing – she wanted to tell him how happy she was that he was here, that against all the odds they'd found each other again, but was stopped in her tracks by the arrival of the waitress with their plates.

'Can I tell you something daft?' he said, looking down at his plate as he cut his fish, 'You might think I've lost the plot though.'

'You can tell me anything,' she replied, glad that he felt

able to open up to her.

'It's going to sound crazy. I'm going to sound crazy. But I've had all these dreams over the years. And they were so real they really messed with my head.'

She stopped chewing. 'Go on.'

'It was really odd. And always the same. Remember that night you gave me the letter from my mum? You were well annoyed that I went to London to meet her without you. Remember?'

How could she tell him that she remembered something very different? That he had died when the taxi he was travelling in collided head-on with a lorry on its way from Balham station to his mother's house.

He didn't seem to notice that she hadn't agreed, and continued. 'In my dream, which I've had over and over again for years, I never got to my mum's. I was just snuffed out somehow – in a car crash I think; something violent – and for the rest of the dream I'd be on the outside looking in. Watching life go on for everyone but me. It was well weird. I even saw a funeral – my funeral I think – and my mum hitting rock bottom. To be honest with you, I was always glad to wake up,' he continued, a degree of uncertainty entering his voice. 'It was all just too real.'

Kathryn was stunned.

A silence stretched between them. She stared down at her food, knowing he was looking at her but afraid to catch his eye.

'So, what do you think that's all about, Kat? Just my mind playing tricks? Because the thing is, it doesn't feel like a dream when I'm in it.'

She looked up and, unable to hide the truth, took a deep breath. Maybe he would understand.

'What you experience in your dream, Ed, is what I remember happening in real life.'

They held each other's gaze for a moment and it was Ed who spoke first.

'A crash? Me ending up...?'

'Except you didn't.'

He shook his head, flabbergasted.

'It's mental, isn't it?'

'Yes,' she replied, because nothing they could say could ever explain the peculiar experience they had shared.

Kathryn's phone vibrated in her bag.

Without looking up from his food, Ed murmured, 'So where does Mark think you are?'

'How do you know about Mark?'

'Maybe I'm psychic,' he said, laughing flatly.

She left the phone where it was.

'You saw me, Mark, Ireland, all of that in your dream?' she asked, shocked. When he nodded, she continued with a guilty smile, 'If you must know, he thinks I'm in Manchester. I could hardly tell him what I was doing, could I?'

He caught her gaze and held it. 'Because he'd think you were mad? Or because he might not trust us together?'

She felt herself colouring and glanced away.

'You're blushing,' he said, with that familiar tease in his voice.

After they finished their meal, Ed suggested they sit at the bar for another drink. Sitting next to him, she remembered how it had felt to be with him when they were young. Like a moth to a flame was how Elaine had put it. Kathryn felt the warmth of that flame again now. As he waited for the barman to finish pulling their pints, Ed tapped a bar mat on the counter just as he had in the past.

'What?' he said, when he saw her smiling.

'Where have the years gone?' she laughed.

As he turned on the bar stool towards her, his knee nudged against hers and she let it stay there, enjoying the sensation.

'So, are you going to tell me how you've filled all those years?' he said, looking at her intensely.

She didn't want to talk about Mark, about her life in Ireland, all the in-between years. She'd rather hear his version of their lives.

'Seems like you've seen most of what I've been up to already,' she replied lightly. 'I'm more interested in what happened back then. Between us. If you didn't die, why on earth did we split up?'

'You'd had enough of me. End of,' he said.

She couldn't imagine how that could have been the case.

'After I met my mum, I spent all my time down in London with her. It was like a new start. And although I was nearer to you, we just didn't get to see each other as much.'

She remembered how she had dreaded him moving away from Liverpool and what it would mean for them.

'And then you began to knuckle down at uni and that took up a lot of your time. And… and is all this really news to you?'

She nodded.

'Your folks were made up.'

It felt like she was hearing a story about someone she didn't know, parents she didn't recognise.

'And then you got a chance to study in Birmingham.'

'A Masters?'

He shrugged. 'Yeah, something like that. We managed okay because it was only a year but then you got this hot shot job up in Edinburgh. And that was that. You couldn't turn it down.'

What hot shot job? The highest rung of the career ladder she had ever reached was in a bookshop in the quiet little town near her home in Ireland. It had been interesting enough and had paid a few bills but she hadn't scaled any heights.

'So who called it off?' It felt as if she was asking about two strangers.

'How weird is this, that you have no idea? Anyway...' He held his hands up in mock surrender. 'I drove you away. I can see that now although I didn't at the time. I was scared to be with you now that you were mixing with a different sort. You know, they had a few quid, were going places. And I got jealous, rang a few times when you were out and accused you of cheating on me. It got messy and I started drinking again. It just turned sour. I wasn't surprised you never got in touch or anything because, to tell you the truth, I was well out of order. I just added you to the list of people who had walked away from me.'

She shook her head, as if she could dislodge whatever was blocking her memory.

'I'd never have done that,' she said. 'And I'd have come looking for you but I thought you were gone. Forever.'

'Yeah, well, I'm glad you've given me a second chance.'

She didn't react to his words but she felt a charge rush through her veins. A second chance. For what?

'It sounds so trivial. You know, what made us break up. I always thought you'd leave me for someone else. Especially as there was always someone waiting in the wings.'

He looked at her, confused.

'Nicki,' she said, the name still bitter on her lips. 'Whatever became of her?'

'God knows. I lost touch with her years ago. She tried to persuade me to pick up with her again, and when I didn't play ball it got a bit nasty, saying she knew things that could make life hard for me.' He rolled his eyes. 'Last I heard, she was in Milton Keynes with some fella. Poor bloke.'

'She was mad about you, Ed. It was obvious. But blackmail isn't really the way to go. And what about Roland?'

Ed picked up his drink and took a gulp.

'Not my finest moment.'

'Beating him up?'

'And leaving you on your own with him. Turns out he recovered though. I think he got a job in Australia after. On one of the racetracks out there.'

He scraped his bar stool back.

'I need a smoke. You okay if we take these outside?'

As she followed him out into the darkness, she smiled. Typical Ed. Still smoking long after it became a social taboo.

He fished in his pocket for his cigarettes and then turned to her with a grin. 'I seem to have lost my lighter. Can I borrow yours?'

The lighter was in her shirt pocket, as it always was. She fished it out and handed it to him.

He rubbed his finger across the engraving and held the lighter against his cheek.

'Feels warm,' he said, turning to her with the trace of a smile.

'How did you know I had it?'

He flicked the lighter and held the flame to the end of his cigarette. Inhaling deeply and letting a thin trail of smoke curl into the night sky, he looked thoughtful as he took the cigarette from his mouth.

'I wasn't sure. But I'm starting to piece things together,'

he said, staring at the engraving before looking up at her. 'You came back for me.'

She frowned. How could he know – and how could she ever fully explain – what had happened on the last night of his life? She wasn't even sure what had happened herself.

'My lighter went missing,' Ed continued. 'I was gutted because… well, you know why.'

She glowed inside.

'It happened just after I'd had a really vivid dream. One where we were young again and I was watching us both. But you were there too. I mean, you as you are now. It was mad.'

He held her gaze steadily.

'I didn't realise at the time that it was all connected – the dream, losing this,' he nodded to the lighter glinting in his palm.

'I remember feeling that I was being watched but couldn't make any sense of it. Of any of it,' Kathryn said quietly. 'The only think that made sense was finding the lighter – your lighter.'

'It's so weird how it disappeared from my flat in Hackney and turned up in your pocket like that.'

'It's all weird,' she said. 'Everything. It's like someone else has been pushing the chess pieces around the board. Even down to the moment I saw you on the side of the road. Do you remember that too? Were you there?'

He nodded. 'I think I was, yes. If it's the same night I'm thinking of, I'd been feeling rough and went to bed early. I couldn't sleep because every time I closed my eyes, I had this picture in my head of you driving. It was raining and getting dark. You were looking for me, shouting my name. And then it all disappeared. I didn't know whether I'd been awake or dreaming. But it felt so real.'

'I told myself I'd imagined it, but you're right. It felt real. Like our connection was so strong that we could still be together even though we were miles – lifetimes – apart.'

He shrugged. 'We probably won't ever find out what really happened.'

Kathryn continued, 'I mean, one minute I'm sure I know what happened and then I'd think, how could I have walked into the past like that? That doesn't happen in real life.'

He smiled and shook his head.

'I don't think reality's what we thought it was. Thank God.'

'If I try and think about it all, my mind gets…'

'Tangled up?' he asked, smiling. 'Yeah, none of it makes sense, does it?'

'So, what's next?' she asked.

'Next?'

'Another drink?'

'Yeah, why not,' he laughed, stubbing out his cigarette and following her back into the bar.

#

Kathryn hadn't asked for the same room they had shared years ago but had recognised it from its view across the village green. The wallpaper had been updated, and the bedding was no longer floral but now fresh cream cotton. But there were still cracked tiles in the bathroom and the same burgundy carpet beneath her feet as she crossed the room.

She sat at the dressing table, brushing her hair back into a ponytail.

'Grow up, Kathryn,' she chastised herself. 'You're forty, not a teenager.'

But the words didn't stick because tonight she felt like a

teenager. Aware that Ed was waiting for her downstairs and not knowing what lay in store, excitement pulsed through her.

She hastily texted Mark.

Manchester's great. Having fun. Speak to you tomorrow.

And it struck her that it was exactly the type of message Alice sent them – brief, skating over the details, checking in because it was expected of her.

It had been Ed's idea to continue their night after the bar closed and Kathryn had silently given thanks because it had felt as if time was running out for them. Whenever she checked the clock behind the bar, they were nearer the unbearable moment they would have to say goodbye again.

He was holding a bottle of wine and two glasses. He jerked his head towards the heavy oak door, which she opened quietly as if they were errant teenagers trying not to wake parents.

They stepped out into the quiet of the village green. They were alone and it struck her, as it had twenty years ago, that while the village was alive with activity all day, sleep came early here and she was glad.

They walked through the village, past the shop at the bottom of the hill and the houses all in darkness to the sandstone bridge she had crossed earlier that evening. At the other side, they squeezed through a narrow stile and she followed him along the riverbank, thankful for the moon, almost full in an ink-black sky.

The only sound was the rush of the water tumbling over rocks glistening in the pale light and forging its way onwards between banks where beech trees stood, their roots exposed, tentacle-like in places.

It was dry so they sat on the ground which sloped down to the water. Ed began to uncork the bottle.

'Remind me to put this back on the bar when we go in,' he said, giving the corkscrew one last twist. 'Here, you hold the glasses and I'll pour.'

Holding them by their delicate stems, she remembered the warm Liebfraumilch they had drunk in his room years ago and smiled.

'So, you're a proper wine drinker these days,' she said.

'Nah, but we could hardly raise a toast with a pint, now could we?' he said and she saw that grin that used to make everything feel right with the world.

Watching the red wine slosh into each glass, she asked, 'A toast? To what exactly?'

Wedging the bottle in the roots of the tree under which they sat, he said, 'I don't know. That we made it this far? What do you think?'

She took a sip, held the wine in her mouth a moment before swallowing, feeling it slide down her throat.

'I suppose we could say… to friendship?' she said, feeling the wine began to warm her.

He was looking ahead into the water beyond them.

'Okay then,' he said, lifting his glass to his lips and drinking. 'To friendship.'

A companionable silence descended and Kathryn closed her eyes, telling herself to savour this moment because being here, hidden, with him would be a memory she would hold close forever. Having him so near made her feel like she had looped back to her younger life, but without the anxiety she had so often felt during their year together. With the future unwritten, she used to dread their time together coming to an end. Now, knowing how the future had unrolled, how it had brought them to this moment, she could relax and, yes, celebrate.

And yet, this time tomorrow she would be in another country, he would be back with his son and the life he had created for himself. And this patch of riverbank would be empty, with only the discarded cork to show they had ever been there. Bittersweet, she thought and opened her eyes to find him watching her.

'So, tell me about your life,' he said quietly. 'I mean, really.'

His directness surprised her and she was unsure how to respond.

'I'm lucky, I suppose. I live in a beautiful place, have a nice home, my daughter's doing well at university, Mark's business is successful,' she hesitated, knowing how flat this all sounded, how lacking in life. Had her ambition at twenty years old been to get to middle age and be well provided for? She didn't remember having any ambition or thought for the future. Maybe that was the problem, maybe that's why she had fallen into what had become a gilded cage.

Ed moved closer, as if sensing the unhappiness behind her words. Feeling his arm around her shoulders, she felt a lump form in her throat and knew she was going to cry.

'Ignore me,' she said, blinking her tears away. 'Really. It must be the wine because I am lucky, you know? I mean my life's good. And Mark is a really good man who –'

'You don't love.' His voice was kind and she knew he wasn't trying to score points.

'He's too good for me, really he is. All he wants is for me to be happy,' she said, rubbing her eyes with the sleeve of her jumper. 'I mean, you remember what he was like, don't you?'

She felt his hand stroke her shoulder.

'Yeah, course I do. He was dead sound.'

Picking up her glass again, she drank in the hope that the alcohol would numb the place from where the tears had sprung. When he changed the subject and began to talk about his son and his life in London, she was grateful for the opportunity to gather herself again.

When she told him how pleased she was that he had finally found happiness, Ed withdrew his arm.

'I wouldn't say that, Kat,' he said, emptying the remainder of the wine into their glasses. 'I mean, they say time heals, but it doesn't, not really. We live alongside the grief but we never quite get rid of it.'

'Louise?'

'Yes, but not just her.'

'Your mum.'

He nodded.

'We get on. Kind of. But only because I know the state of play. Like, there's this barrier I know I'll never get over. Not if I want to keep the status quo, you know?'

'Has she ever told you why she left? I mean, the full story,' Kathryn asked, surprised as she had assumed that twenty years was time enough to talk things through.

He shrugged. 'Yeah, bits. About the old man and the drinking and the women. That was way back when I first found her. But I've never been able to get her to tell me more than that. And if I ask her why she didn't take us with her, never came back for us, she gets emotional, says she can't cope with talking about it. She makes out I'm blaming her. So I've learnt not to bring it up. And besides, her health's not great these days. It's best to leave it, you know?'

'The hurt's still there though,' Kathryn said, feeling his pain all over again.

'Hurt, anger; it never really goes away. Not completely.'

'Are you glad you found your mum? I mean, do you wish we hadn't rewritten the past so you could be with her?' It sounded ridiculous to her ears, like something from a film. But it also felt like the truth. His past had been rewritten and, even if everyone else found it impossible to believe, it would connect them forever.

Gulping down the remnants of the wine, Ed turned to her and, even in the dark, she could see how his eyes flashed.

'Never, Kat,' he said with passion. 'I've you to thank every day of my life. We've all got to take the rough with the smooth. I wouldn't have it any other way. I know mum has her reasons for keeping me in the dark. Who knows what she's protecting me from? I mean, something must have happened to her to end up with the old man. I might not understand her but I don't blame her.'

They were quiet for a few minutes and Kathryn thought back to those long ago evenings in his room when he had played music and they had talked. She treasured those moments. They had shared their innermost thoughts as only the young can – serious and earnest, not yet knowing that life is rarely cut and dried.

'Sorry,' he said, after a while, 'this doesn't feel like much of a celebration, does it? You'd have been better off going straight to bed.'

'I wouldn't have missed being here with you for the world,' she replied, wanting to be near him again, to take his hand, but her youthful shyness had returned and she held back.

'Yeah?' he asked, as if he didn't quite believe her. 'And why's that?'

'Because I've missed you so much. This, tonight, is what we had when we weren't much more than kids. In all the years since, I've never found it again. Life has ticked along with the odd high point. Like my lovely Alice. But I never experienced that intensity we felt. So, I'd tell myself that those sort of feelings are just for the young, that when you get older and life settles down, it's not realistic to expect more.'

'And now?'

'I've missed feeling alive all these years.' Her stomach fluttered in that way it always had when she thought of the words sitting on her tongue. 'You always made me feel alive.'

He didn't reply but she felt his hand close around hers. He brushed away her tears, which had threatened for a while and were now rolling down her cheeks.

'We were good together, weren't we?' he said.

Kathryn nodded. It had been such a short span of her life – just a year – but it had been so good. Nothing and nobody had ever come close.

'But we were never quite able to say it, were we?'

'That's why I had to write stuff down. I'd have felt a div saying it to your face.'

'The bit about my inner fire?'

He frowned, confused.

'The card you hid in my box of letters.'

He laughed, tapped his temple. 'Yeah, I mean, hiding a card. What was I thinking?'

She wanted to circle back to what he'd written in the card, discovered after so many years. Wanted him to tell her if that's what he still saw in her.

'I think whatever fire you were talking about was quenched years ago.'

'No, because you're here, aren't you? It would have been so much easier to push everything away; to make out it was just your imagination. But you didn't. You chose to believe. I remember how you'd get in your car and drive all those hours to Liverpool just to be with me. Like now, getting on a plane on the off-chance that I might be here. I've always loved that about you. Underneath it all, you're kind of fearless.'

Fearless? If only he knew. She was afraid right now. Afraid that when they parted tomorrow, that would be that. That tonight was just a walk down memory lane, reminiscing about the past, swapping notes on the strange experience they'd shared. And that they would return to their lives as if nothing had changed.

But she was determined that, whatever happened, fear would not stop her from saying what she had to say. It was now or never.

'I'm in love with you,' she said and, suddenly embarrassed by her words, added with a laugh, 'There I've said it.'

As the words hung in the air between them, a car swept over the bridge, its lights shining on the water. Kathryn only saw Ed's face clearly for a moment before it was again cast into shadow again, but it had been time enough to spot the frown across his brow. She had said too much. Why had she blurted her feelings out to him like that? She was a married woman with a teenage daughter. He had always held her in such high regard, and now? He probably thought she was looking for an affair, trying to assuage a looming midlife crisis.

And still he didn't reply.

'Look, forget I said that. It's the wine, the fresh air. I hardly know what I'm saying.' It was all she could do. Salvage some sort of self-respect by blaming the alcohol and never mentioning it again.

He picked up a stick and started to dig it into the soil at his feet.

'I didn't come here expecting this,' he said, casting the stick aside. 'To be honest, I don't know what I expected. But when I saw you again it all came back, you know, those feelings. And then we fell back so easily into how we'd always been, and I remembered that, when I'm with you, I become somebody else. Somebody better.'

He turned to her. 'What I'm trying to say is… ditto.'

Seeing the confusion on her face, he said, 'Remember in *Ghost* when Patrick Swayze can't tell his girlfriend he loves her. Whenever she says it, he just says ditto. So, you know, that's what I'm trying to say. Ditto.'

Kathryn felt her heart race in a way it hadn't in forever. She was her twenty year old self again, with excitement coursing through her veins, blindsided by something beyond her understanding.

'What are we going to do, Kat?' he asked in a tone that suggested he wasn't expecting an answer.

Unpeeling his arm from her shoulders, he pulled his phone from his back pocket. The screen lit up his face.

'It's pretty late. Shall we make a move?'

They walked back to the village saying little. Kathryn felt that words might unbalance this delicate moment of expectation; this paradox of euphoria and nagging uncertainty about what lay ahead. But then again, hadn't it always been this way with them?

Ed put the corkscrew, bottle and glasses on the bar, which was now in darkness except for the flickering light of the smoke alarm, and they carefully made their way around the tables and chairs to the staircase where the light had been left on.

She followed him upstairs, an echo of that earlier time, her first time, but while dance music had blared then, now the pub was silent. Twenty years ago, she had felt she had something to prove, but now things were different. She knew she was standing on the edge of crossing to where everything changed. If it hadn't already. If she hadn't known it from the moment they met that afternoon.

He stopped at the top of the stairs and turned to her. His room was down the corridor to the right. Hers was to the left. He waited, his face giving nothing away.

'So,' she said, unable to resist a nod to the past. 'What happens now?'

'Obviously I want to kiss you goodnight,' he said.

She giggled at his politeness, which was so unlike him yet, in some ways, was reminiscent of the early days of their relationship.

'Obviously?' she said, enjoying how flirtatious she sounded.

He moved closer, his lips brushing against hers.

But then he hesitated. Was it because she was married, because he didn't want to overstep the mark? But Kathryn didn't want him to pull away. Maybe he read that in her eyes because he began to kiss her again so slowly and tenderly that time collapsed, the years between their first kiss and now dissolving in the feel of his lips on hers.

Finally, she pulled away, her mind spinning, and inclined her head meaningfully in the direction of her room.

'You're sure?' he murmured. But she began kissing him again so that he said no more.

Chapter 26

It was only when she finished relaying her story that Kathryn noticed the fire had gone out. Just the dying embers remained.

Elaine lifted her glass and drank the remnants of her wine. She shook her head when Kathryn pointed to the bottle on the table between them.

'If Rob needs me in the night, I need my wits about me,' she said. 'I'll just check on him. Put the kettle on though. I can't go to bed yet. My mind's...'

'Blown?' Kathryn said, crossing to the kettle.

'You could say that,' Elaine said, disappearing into the bedroom.

As Kathryn waited for the kettle to boil, she lifted the blinds at the window, so the room was lit up by the flash from the lighthouse. Regular as clockwork, she could set her watch by it. It was so reliable. And then she smiled.

'What are you thinking of to make you smile like that?' Elaine said, closing the bedroom door softly behind her.

'Oh, nothing much. Just something you once said.'

'What time is it anyway?'

Kathryn glanced at the clock. 'Very late. Or very early. Depending on which way you look at it.'

Elaine groaned. 'And we've got an early start too. Why couldn't you have hit me with the big revelation a few nights ago? I would have had plenty of time to grill you properly.'

'Exactly. I probably wouldn't have told you at all if you hadn't spotted the lighter,' Kathryn said, smiling.

The night was relatively warm and the wind had dropped so they took their tea out to the patio and sat facing the sea. The beam of the lighthouse swept inland, lighting up the house briefly before arching on out to sea once more and plunging them back into darkness.

Elaine turned to Kathryn, expectantly. 'So?'

'So what?'

'So what happened then? I mean, have you heard from him since? Or did he leave you heartbroken all over again?'

Kathryn shook her head. 'Not heartbroken.'

Even in the dark, Kathryn knew that Elaine was rolling her eyes.

'You might not agree with what I've done, but it's partly thanks to you. Everything changed after I met you in that café in town. Since then, I started to feel a glow in my life.'

Elaine squeezed her friend's hand.

'I get it – I do – but you need to get him out of your system. Obviously, Mark doesn't know so there's no harm done yet. Look, first love is fine and everything but it's not the same as making a life together. Don't swap something solid for excitement. You know it'll end in tears.'

As the lighthouse beam lit them both up, Kathryn considered how their lives had changed since she and Ed had found each other again. They had not made any promises but they both knew this wasn't the end of their story. On a trip to Dublin, she had sent Ed a postcard of the Ha'penny Bridge, a reminder of the birthday trip that Terry's drama had put paid to all those years ago. A postcard of the Queen Victoria statue in Liverpool had arrived a week later. And just like that, the threads of their lives began to weave together once more.

Chapter 27

It was late July and the hilltops had been scorched brown by the exceptionally dry summer weather. Rain was a distant memory and sun-baked days that seemed to stretch out forever had become the norm. Cloudless skies of shimmering blue arched over the parched earth and there was already talk of water shortages. In centuries past, shots might have been fired at passing clouds, but now it was more a case of checking long-range weather forecasts and knowing that this couldn't go on forever.

Kathryn and Ed walked passed the wall where she had waited for him to finish his phone call on their first visit. The telephone box was still on the triangle of grass but had long since been disconnected. Both mornings shared the promise of warmth. But on this particular morning, they could be pretty sure the temperature would keep rising to an almost unbearably hot zenith by early afternoon.

He unlatched the gate at the bridge and they clattered over the wooden slats above the waters of the Swale. The banks, hard and cracked, were bare in patches. Where the water levels had dropped, the dark river bed gave the water the appearance of liquid chocolate, but Kathryn knew she only had to cup it in her hand to find it as pure and clear as ever.

It was too hot for jeans so she wore a pair of shorts. Ed had clearly had the same idea that morning because he was wearing khaki hiking shorts and a white t-shirt, extra bright against the deep tan of his neck and arms.

The waterfall was spectacular, but they continued on,

clambering the stepped pathway alongside it. The sound of the cascading water dropping to the rocks below was loud enough to make conversation pointless but, at the top, they reached the Pennine Way and turned eastwards into the silence of the hills.

Sunlight bounced off an old tractor abandoned next to the track and, as they turned sharply to the right, they saw the ruins of a stone farmhouse looking out over the most breathtaking view of Swaledale. Far below, the river was like a silver snake winding its way along the valley floor between the sheer, stone wall-laced slopes of the fells. High up in this remote place, it felt as if they were on top of the world.

Ed gave a low whistle before shrugging off his rucksack.

They sat on the springy turf in front of the crumbling walls of the house and stared at the landscape in front of them.

'So,' Ed said.

'So?'

'We made it then.'

'The climb?' Kathryn replied, knowing that was not what he meant.

'Yeah, that too.' He smiled and reached into the rucksack.

She turned and, catching his eye, smiled back at him.

'It was worth the wait,' she said.

'Twenty-one years,' he said, handing her a bottle of water. 'We took our time.'

Time taken, rewritten. But here they were, looking out across these isolated hills, and forward to the rest of their lives. As she lay back on the soft turf and closed her eyes, Kathryn thought back to when she first met him, to when she lost him and then, decades later, to when she found him again. And in between, a marriage, a daughter and a life elsewhere.

That life had unravelled quickly. Just a week after returning home from Ireland, Elaine rang with the news that Rob had died in his sleep. The day had come sooner than expected and the news had shocked them all. In the months that followed, either Kathryn or Mark had flown back to stay with her at the weekends until, gradually, it was just Mark who made the journey.

The routine of their marriage had been shaken up by his frequent absences, giving Kathryn time to think and to consider her future. When she put the phone down after another long call to Ed, many of which lasted until the early hours, she repeatedly told herself she had to come clean with Mark. Soon. When he was not so tied up with Elaine.

It had taken her by surprise then when it was Mark who brought the matter to a head. Returning home from another weekend visit to England, he had seemed distracted and morose.

'I can't keep doing this,' he said.

Kathryn assumed he meant the regular trips away from home.

'Elaine will manage. I mean, she's settled in her new place now. It's been eight months, nearly nine, and she's doing much better.'

'I'm not talking about Elaine,' he had said wearily and it was then that she knew that he knew. Afterwards, she wondered how she could have imagined she had hidden it from him. She wondered if Elaine had said something. Possibly. But it was more likely he had seen, as clear as day, that she had changed, in the way that people who fall in love change.

'Are you going to leave me for him?'

She knew better than to lie.

And so the next phase of their lives began. Mark turned away from his marriage, unsalvageable as it was, and towards Elaine. Kathryn knew that for her friend, tired from holding everything together for years, Mark was the solid, dependable rock she needed most in the world.

Kathryn was left with an aching sadness. Because of Alice. And because Mark was one of the kindest people she had ever known. But his kindness – his goodness – hadn't been enough for her. Not when her heart had always been else-where.

And now, on this hillside with Ed next to her, his bare arm warm against hers, she gave thanks for what she had. With their marriage at an end, Mark and Kathryn had dismantled, piece by piece, the life they had built together. Decisions had to be made about who left and who stayed, who got to keep the dog, what to do with the years of possessions which filled each room. Ed had listened to her at length, as she had once listened to him. He had been the friend she needed when friends were suddenly thin on the ground, and for that she was grateful.

'Did you always know that this was ahead of us?'

'I had a fair idea,' he said.

She waited for him to elaborate.

'Meeting again the way we did, how we immediately fitted back into being what we'd been before when we were young, before I messed up. We'll never fully understand what happened. I mean, if you hadn't walked through the woods that evening, would we be here now? Would I even be here to tell the tale?'

Kathryn shuddered.

'Have you had one of those dreams since?'

'Nah, that all stopped when you came back into my life.

So, you know, cheers for that at least,' he joked. 'But straight up, I feel like the luckiest bloke in the world to have found you again.'

Kathryn grinned at the blue sky above.

'And Mark and Elaine?' she asked. 'Did you ever think they'd fall for each other?'

'Nah, I didn't see that coming. They're both so…'

'What?'

'I don't know, straight-laced? But it's better this way, isn't it?'

'You think it's better that my husband is now living with my best friend?' she said.

'Don't you? It just makes life easier for everyone.'

He was right. Again.

'After everything she's been through, she deserves to find happiness with Mark. Did I tell you that she texted earlier to ask if I can call in on Sunday afternoon on the way back to the airport?'

'Are you okay seeing them both so soon? I mean, it's not that long since Mark left.'

She was more than okay with it. She wanted Mark and Elaine to be in her life always. She was lucky to have people she loved and she wasn't going to throw those friendships away now.

'What did Paul say when you told him about us?' she said.

Ed launched into an imitation of Paul's strong Liverpudlian accent. 'Slumming it, ain't she? Getting back with our kid.'

Kathryn laughed. 'I'm looking forward to seeing him again. I bet he's just the same.'

'Yeah, unfortunately,' Ed said, pulling a face.

Out of the corner of her eye, she saw him pull himself up so that he was propped up on one elbow, watching her.

'I tell you something though. Sometimes I feel that this isn't the first time,' he murmured, suddenly serious.

She felt the blaze of the sun on her face but also from within her as he stroked her hair. His touch had always done that to her, made her insides feel like liquid light.

'First time for what?'

'Us. I know it sounds daft but I just think we've done this before.'

It made sense to Kathryn. That feeling she had when she was with him, that she was ignited with an energy that had travelled across lifetimes.

She held his gaze.

'Do you believe in past lives? Is that what you're saying?'

'Well, yeah, maybe. It's mad, I know. But it's the way I feel when I'm with you.' She watched him lift the water bottle to his lips and take a mouthful before turning back to her, as if giving himself time to consider what he was going to say next

'Remember that fortune teller I went to on Brighton Pier that time?'

'The one who couldn't tell you much about your mum?'

'Yeah, I thought she was the lamest psychic on the south coast. Except she did actually get something right. I mean, I thought it was rubbish at the time but now I'm not so sure. She told me that she saw this huge tapestry made from all these threads, woven together. She said the threads were all the lives we had. I mean, I thought she was just having me on. You know, like she had to say something because she'd drawn a blank about my mum. But anyway, she said that in my tapestry, she kept seeing these two threads, one red, one green, that kept meeting, crossing again and again.'

It felt like too much to take in, too different from what

she had always believed life – and love – to be. But it also felt like the truth. How else could she explain the intensity of her desire for him?

'Again and again,' Kathryn said, closing her eyes. 'I like the sound of that.'

Acknowledgements

Within You, Without You has taken me on a magical journey, in which a door opened and through it stepped someone who left this world too young. In doing so, he gifted me a sense of a world beyond this one. I couldn't have written it without him.

I would like to thank Jamie McGarry and the wonderful team at Valley Press who saw something in the book. They were such a joy to work with. I'm so grateful to editor Jo Haywood for her vision, insight and humour, picking the ideal title and shaping the book into its final version. I had no idea that the editing process could be such fun. Thanks to Peter Barnfather for a cover which captures the essence of the book so perfectly.

I would also like to thank my daughter Annie McCarthy, Grace O'Mahony and Mary Stanley for reading and giving their invaluable opinion on what worked – and what didn't; Vanessa Fox O'Loughlin for being so enthusiastic, supportive and generous with her time and advice; Lara Darby for so much guidance and for helping me to keep the faith that the right publisher would appear at the right time – which it did; Stuart Coughlan for his advice and for years of encouragement; Connie Gorry for encouraging my ten year old self to keep writing and for typing up that first manuscript; my mum Ruth O'Donovan for filling my childhood with books; and my dad Dan O'Donovan for his support.

To be able to spend time in my favourite places, both physically and in my imagination, was a treat. For my heart-felt connection with the Yorkshire Dales and Liverpool, I'm very grateful.

And finally, Damien, Annie and Tom for their constant belief in me and for putting up with the hours I was buried away bringing the story to life. Without them, it wouldn't have happened.